Eyes of the Seer

ALSO BY ASHLEY YORK

Eyes of the Seer

Ashley York

DEDICATION

To Nicole
My soul...
you'll always be
my little monkey

AUTHOR'S NOTE

The Warrior Kings Series takes place a thousand years ago when every tribe elected their own *ri*, or king, from among themselves. This was the way of the Gaels of both ancient *Éire* and *Alba* (modern day Ireland and Scotland).

The first requirement for kingship was to come from the direct line of previous kings: son, grandson, great-grandson. The second was to have proven your ability to provide for and defend their *túath* or land. A king needed to be a great warrior. He also needed to be trusted as a leader as that was the only way he'd have his own warband. There was no distinction made between a gentleman and a nobleman as in other countries. Here a king was inaugurated and revered.

A glossary of the levels of kingship, explanation of certain words, and a pronunciation key for the names can be found at the back of this book.

My special thanks to Sheila Currie for sharing her love of the Gaels and her willingness to answer my seemingly endless questions.

Chapter One

The low ceiling of the Meic Murchadha longhouse was stained with the smoke of a hundred years' worth of fires. Too many of the men gathered around the open flame looked like they could easily have been present at the very first one. Their leering eyes darting toward Astrid as if she were a sweet to be tasted, challenging her desire to appear aloof. She'd much prefer to stick her tongue out at them. And cover herself. And rub her ankle. She'd fallen earlier and the throbbing pain was near unbearable.

Instead, Astrid kept her shoulders back, ignoring their roving eyes. Despite the ache in her foot, she was happy to remain where the handsome Pádraig

1

Meic Murchadha had deposited her after the repast. So gallant of him to have carried her in his arms after her injury! With a wink and smile, he had assured her it was "the best view" of the entertainment, which, naturally, included him. That his attention had just as quickly been drawn to the others in the overcrowded room full of warriors and lovely women was a little disconcerting. Especially so after the way his hand had touched her own in an overlong caress before he'd turned away. There were at least two other clans present for the feast, and they were all packed in very tightly.

Brushing her hair over her shoulder, Astrid glanced at Pádraig's petite sister, Daimhin, standing in front of her brother and beguiling all present with her lively story of Brian Boru, the last *árd rí*, High King. It was not long before her gaze darted to the storyteller's handsome brother—settled on the cushioned seat and leaning back against the wall, a dark fur hanging from his broad shoulders. She'd been hoping Pádraig would shift his interest from the mead in his wooden mug to *her*, but instead he was listening intently to his sister. Astrid sighed and smiled. She didn't mind one bit that Daimhin had chosen to stand and act out the story rather than sit. It made it easier for Astrid to watch the object of her attention. She only wished to catch his eye again.

The sudden burst of laughter made her jump, but she quickly recovered, smiling along with those around her, nodding in enthusiasm. She cared nothing for these boring stories, but she did so like the look of Pádraig. The thick bearded face and bright blue eyes mesmerized her, which was the only reason she remained in the visiting hall. Her mother had long since retired for the evening. The two of them were visitors for only the one night, and Astrid was determined to do anything she could—well, almost anything—to finally win the handsome warrior's interest.

"Are ye satisfied?" Astrid frowned at the low, quiet voice interrupting her thoughts before she realized it was only Marcán speaking to her.

It took a moment for her to understand his meaning. Glancing down, she realized she'd barely touched the jeweled goblet of wine he'd procured for her. "'Tis fine, Marcán. Many thanks."

"And many thanks to ye." Marcán's tone seemed odd, but when she glanced into his eyes, one blue and one green, she saw no sign of irritation. She shrugged and turned her attention back to Pádraig.

The Meic Murchadha *túath* was close to her own, only a quick ride away, yet it was so different here, almost like another world. The warriors seemed bigger than life, but their stories failed to hold her attention. They all lacked Marcán's ability to make the words create pictures in her mind, though she'd never admit as much to him. Astrid held back a yawn as she scanned the faces of the men and a few women, whose eyes were wide with excitement as Daimhin started on yet another long-winded *árd rí* story.

"Ye look tired, Astrid. I can see ye to yer mother."

She turned her gaze toward her brother's closest friend, surprised he was still beside her. "If ye wish to leave, I am certain I can find another to escort me."

His eyes held hers for the smallest moment before he glanced toward Pádraig. "I've no doubt the man ye've been admiring all night would be glad to see ye to her. I am only wondering the state ye'd be in when ye finally made it there."

Astrid's jaw dropped. "What are ye saying?"

"I know ye understand me fine."

Shooting daggers at the man with her expression apparently had no effect. He held her gaze, the dark shadow of a beard hiding his strong chin. His thick brows were raised in irritation—an expression that put her in mind of her brother—the only indication he knew exactly what she was about. Both he and Diarmuid were constantly thwarting her attempts at finding a suitable husband, as if their only goal in life was to have her remain unmarried, untouched, and at her mother's side.

Of the two, Marcán was by far the worst. She could rile her brother into anger and get him to back off. Not so with Marcán. He was solid as a rock and just as immoveable. He'd proven that just hours earlier. Pádraig had quite rightly offered her a ride to his home, and her and her mother an invitation to the evening feast, upon learning of her injury. After all, she'd been injured on *his* land, trying to retrieve sheep *he* had stolen from her clan. The Meic Murchadha were forever stealing her brother's sheep. True, the sheep were the offspring of one of *their* ewes, but Diarmuid had only taken the animal from them because they'd first stolen a cow.

Astrid's mother had her own mount, and for one glorious minute, Astrid had thought she'd be able to ride with Pádraig. Marcán had insisted on taking her onto his own mount, of course, and Diarmuid had used that kingly tone of his, saying, "So be it!" Her brother had not even seen fit to join them, but Marcán could not be dissuaded.

A more miserable ride Astrid could not remember. She should have been happily ensconced in Pádraig's arms, enthralling him with her wit and beauty, but she was instead pressed against Marcán's rock-hard chest. His musky scent had lingered on her even after she'd limped away from him to follow Pádraig. Instead of taking the hint and allowing her a graceful retreat, the odious man had scooped her into his arms as if she were a child and asked to see the healer.

The healer's ranting and raving about God's wrath had been even more unbearable with Marcán looking on and hearing it all, his arms about his chest, leaning against the closed door. A closed door! If she needed privacy from outside eyes, she wanted to ask why *he* had remained. But such an argument would not have moved him. His expression had been tight and stubborn, much as it was now, and it was obvious he lacked any desire to do her bidding.

"I'll be here when ye say the word, Astrid," he said now, his eyebrows still furrowed.

As if she'd ever *say the word*.

Marcán drifted back to the bench alongside the door, where he'd been sitting all night. This seat kept him quite aware of the many sordid liaisons taking place just outside the visiting hall, under the cover of night. It also ensured he knew exactly where Astrid was.

His head ached and the smoke from the fire was burning his eyes. If not for guarding her, he'd have taken a respite outside long ago. The stars were no doubt twinkling overhead and the warm breeze off the ocean would smell of sea salt. It had been a long

5

day, and he would not have minded sleeping under those stars.

He sighed and looked again toward the blonde beauty. If she sat up any straighter, she'd break her back. But admittedly, those bountiful breasts were one of her best assets. The fact that she was using that knowledge to catch the leering eye of that weakling Pádraig was what was keeping Marcán at full alert.

Between that and her lovely, round arse, the woman was setting off a fire in most of the men in the room. And she was oblivious. If Pádraig ever caught sight of the longing in her eyes when she stared after him, Astrid would be beneath him in no time and in no particular place. The man had no consideration for the women he took. His entire clan shared that trait, even following the old custom of taking several wives. It was as if they all frowned on the notion of restraint as practiced by Christ himself. If Marcán let his guard down, Astrid would no doubt realize her mistake—but only after the damage had been done.

He could not allow that to happen.

"What about yer clan, Marcán?" It was Daimhin, trying yet again to lure him into the circle. Between her flirting and blatant overtures, which had even included straddling his lap while the trestles were being set up for the meal, Marcán was having a hell of a time staying clear of her advances. He wouldn't mind taking what was offered, but she was the daughter of their king, and he did not want to be beholden to any members of the Meic Murchadha clan.

Now all eyes were on Marcán. He held back a sigh of resignation. Daimhin had worded her request in such a way that he could not refuse without a stain against his clan. His leader, Diarmuid, had returned home to finally bed his new wife, and the pride of the entire clan now rested on Marcán's ability to tell a good story. It was a challenge he would normally savor, but he'd prefer to see to his main duty.

One glance at Astrid, whose head was the only one not turned toward him, no doubt because she knew what he looked like, Marcán stood. There was no help for it.

"We've just opened a new cask," Daimhin said, extending a gilded cup to him. "Only the best for ye."

There were at least two smaller clans present this eve. Marcán suspected his unplanned arrival, demanding the release of Astrid and her mother along with the missing sheep, had disrupted whatever Pádraig and his father had been planning. Doran had been in such a hurry to see Marcán gone, they'd returned the sheep and even helped find the missing women, who, it turned out, had suffered a mishap on their way to retrieve the sheep.

Marcán accepted the vessel. Daimhin quirked a brow and went toward the seat her brother was just leaving. Though small in stature, she was solidly packed with large, heavy breasts and an arse to match. She behaved like a lass who knew how to please a man, but Marcán seriously doubted she was not a virgin. After all, she was daughter to their king and valuable as a prize for the right alliance. If she did not prove chaste, any such alliance would be broken and bring shame to Doran. Her flirtatiousness only increased her value, for it could deaden the good sense of a lustful *ri túaithe*. The message from those

7

swaying hips was as well received as if she'd cupped his balls in her hot little hand. But while he was admittedly a man with strong needs, Marcán alone decided with who and when. *This* one was never.

Marcán took a full swallow to soothe his suddenly parched throat before walking to the far center of the circle. A hush fell over the room. Even the voices of the lasses who had been in a quiet, ceaseless conversation since just after the meal finally went silent. It wasn't anything he wasn't used to. The women liked to watch him, assess him, consider if the stories they'd heard about him were true. Nothing he couldn't handle, but definitely something he would put an end to if only he could tempt the lass he desired above all others to become his wife. He also knew it was never going to happen. Astrid refused to see him as a man.

His mug was quickly refilled by a lass with dark eyes and fine black hair. She'd met him at the door, her eyes passing over him with far too much interest. Even now, when he took the spot still covered by Pádraig's fur, she snuggled closer to him while Daimhin sat on his left, at a discreet distance.

"What of the caves?" It was Pádraig's younger brother. "Tell us about *árd rí* in our caves!"

Ian was a charming lad and very smart. Smarter and more circumspect than the rest of his siblings and quick witted, too. Oftentimes his humor was overlooked by others in the clan because it was beyond their grasp. Marcán found that most amusing.

He set all other concerns aside to smile at the lad. "Ye like the stories of the caves?"

The boy, nearly a man now but still awkward, nodded eagerly.

"The caves it is, then."

Marcán's eyes scanned the quiet room, looking at all the faces turned up to him with expectant expressions. For the smallest second, he felt a fit of fear down in his gut. His panic. But he'd overpowered that when he was much younger with the help of his *Da*—God rest his soul—even though it still liked to poke at him every now and then. Marcán smiled, and all the women, save one, immediately returned the gesture.

"The caves are as dark as they are long, heading deep inside the ground, but ye can still hear the ocean crashing against the hills. The relentless waves from a thousand years past, coming finally to our shores, pounding here just as they did in that faraway place. But the sound is over ye, and around ye, and ye can feel the heaviness of the water pushing down on ye…"

Little concentration was required to keep the story going as Marcán had told this tale, or some variation on it, more times than he could count. Still, the eager faces of those around him, enraptured by the legends of Brian Boru, held his interest. The pride in their expressions was the same as his own, and truth be told, he loved to tell the stories.

As High King, Brian Boru had united the clans. A strong force, they had moved across the island, subduing any who thought to resist. And all these warriors had that same fighting blood in them. It was why they kept the old legends alive. The stories of the way things had been and could be again. The stories of their past.

The small, eager hand sliding up the underside of Marcán's bare leg demanded his attention. A

9

glance at the black-haired lass beside him showed her wetting her lips with a long, slow tongue. An effective gesture, and she'd find more than a handful if she continued her journey up his thigh. But Marcán shifted his legs away from her, offering his best look of disapproval without missing a single detail of his story. Her pout was for his eyes only, as was the seductive smile she flashed him as she shifted, the action disguised as an attempt to get more comfortable, and dropped her hand alongside his hip, waiting for a second try.

Again his mead was refilled, and as the story came to an end, Marcán glanced at the empty spot where Astrid had been not a second earlier, ignoring him completely. Thanks to the determined lass at his side, standing would be an issue. She smiled at him. A knowing smile. A smile that promised much.

He finished the story and then tipped a hand to his head in thanks. The applause was louder than usual, and he chose that moment to turn to the comely lass. "Choose yer ministrations for a better time if ye're wanting anything to come of it."

Marcán grabbed Pádraig's fur to wrap around him and stood. He moved toward the door, which was now open.

"Another, Marcán!" a man's voice called out, but Marcán ignored him. Astrid was nowhere in the room, a realization that put him in a near panic.

Daimhin came up beside him, watching as he turned this way and that, searching for Astrid. She put a small hand on his arm. "That is my favorite story. My thanks."

"My pleasure."

Daimhin smiled up at him. "Is it Diarmuid's sister

10

ye search for?"

Marcán's eyes fell to her. "Did ye see where she went?"

"I believe she followed my brother outside."

His chest tightened, and in five long strides he was through the door and outside, the air surprisingly cool against his face and other parts that had become heated.

"Astrid?" he called into the darkness. There were several groups gathered about. Some glanced at him, but he saw no sign of her light hair.

Approaching the first group of men to his left, he yanked back on the shoulder of a red-haired man.

"Hey!" The young man's protest was quickly cut off when he caught sight of Marcán. Instead, he raised his hands up before smiling. "D'ye wish to join us?"

It was Eric, one of their young warriors. A pup! But smart enough to know not to mess with Marcán. Beside him a tall, dark-haired woman was undulating against Eric's twin brother. Their mouths were locked together, and Eoghan's hands were making free with her body. Two other men were watching, mesmerized and no doubt aroused.

Marcán glanced back at Eric with disgust. "Have ye no care how ye treat yer women?"

Eric merely shrugged, turning back to his brother, and smiled. "Is she even one of ours?"

The man's hands slid down to grab her arse, his hips assuring all that his tarse pushed against her. The other two moved in closer, not keeping their hands off. The lass did not appear to protest, but Marcán had to be certain. He pulled on her bare arm to break her from the embrace.

11

Her mouth fell open, her hooded eyes flying open, too, and an angry expression stole across her face. "Hey!"

"Ye're wanting this attention?"

She wiped at her mouth, eyed him up and down with interest, and then smiled. "Aye, and I would be pleased to have ye join us."

He shook his head, more in disgust than in answer, and turned toward the next group. They were tall warriors, older than the other four, discussing Brian Boru in what sounded like a heated debate. No women among them.

"Marcán?" Eric called to him, pointing as he spoke. "If 'tis Astrid ye're looking for, ye best follow the path back up through the woods."

Eoghan again had his hands on the lass, making free with her along with the others, but she broke free to speak. "Do not fash yerself," she said with a laugh. "Pádraig was with them."

Them? With a clenched jaw and fisted hands, Marcán pushed his way through the brush to follow the path, no bigger than a deer trail. Astrid wouldn't even be marriageable if Pádraig got his hands on her. Diarmuid cared for his sister, but he was tempting fate by leaving her unmarried so long. The lass was ripe to experience being with a man. She'd be in trouble if left on her own.

Her lilting laughter carried to him and he followed the sound.

"Oh, Pádraig." Astrid's voice.

The lower voices didn't carry as well, but as he approached them, he saw there were four men in total with her.

Marcán's blood rushed through his body like a

river ready to flood its banks, his heart pumping as fast as if he were preparing for battle. And in truth he was, a battle for her innocence. He paused and watched, forcing himself to regain control of his emotions before he went charging in.

Sitting in the small circle, Astrid leaned nearer to Pádraig and laughed again, her head tipping up and her shoulders dipping forward, giving them all an eyeful of her assets. Again she was offering herself up to any man with eyes in his head, and the men encircling her leaned in closer. Pádraig was the closest, touching her hair and then her shoulder, but no doubt all were stiff in anticipation of accepting her blatant invitation. Removing the fur from his shoulders and draping it across his arms, Marcán approached.

"Astrid?" Marcán kept his tone low and controlled. "What d'ye here?"

The men stood, appearing surprised, ripped out of their lustful thoughts. That confusion swiftly changed to discomfort when they caught sight of Marcán's expression. They moved away from her, opening the circle and allowing him a direct view of her, still seated beside Pádraig.

Her hair was tousled and her eyes were widely innocent. She dipped her head, eyeing the men from beneath her lashes.

"Nothing." Her voice held a husky tone. "We are… talking."

The men turned back to him and waited. Could they actually have any expectation of his consent? Mayhap in the Meic Murchadha clan. Marcán slowly gazed at each man in turn, looking him right in the eye, before finally settling his gaze again on Astrid.

"Do they all know ye are Diarmuid's little sister?"

Each man took a step back. All but Pádraig, whose face maintained a look of superiority, his hand still on her shoulder like he owned her.

Marcán moved closer to Astrid, and the other men continued to yield, stepping even farther away. "Pádraig."

"I thought ye were telling yer stories, Marcán," Pádraig said.

Marcán looked at his hand on Astrid's shoulder. And waited. Time slipped by. One of the other men coughed, and Pádraig finally removed his hand. Heaving a deep sigh, he moved to stand with the others. Marcán refused to acknowledge Astrid's crestfallen expression when he extended his hand to her.

"And I thought ye would keep to yer own women rather than taking advantage of an innocent lass." Marcán handed the man his fur.

"This lovely lass asked me to show her the hot springs."

When Marcán looked again at Astrid, he had hoped for some show of guilt. Instead, he was met with a defiant glare.

"Oh did she?" Marcán asked as he shifted his gaze to the other men. "Were ye afraid ye'd lose yer way on yer own?"

Pádraig offered a small smile. "If the lass wishes for the men to join us, they are more than willing, and I do not object."

The man was speaking of accepting the offer he'd believed she was making. Marcán tasted blood where he'd bitten his cheek to hold back his angry words. Rather than speak to Pádraig, whom he was

14

tempted to strike, he turned to Astrid. "Did ye wish for more from these men than seeing the hot springs?"

Her eyes were angry, and her shoulders had rounded to their natural bend. Relieved to see her drop the flirtatious facade, he smiled. Just in time, he noticed the flash of anger and realized his smile had been misinterpreted. She thought he was laughing at her. He caught her hand just before it made contact with his cheek.

"How dare ye!" Astrid said, letting loose her tirade.

Though striking another was a punishable offense, Marcán was more than willing to stand there and let her have at him. She did not care for him, but her behavior—willfulness… stubbornness… whatever Diarmuid wanted to label her rants—was merely an indication of the great depth of her passion. Marcán recognized it because he was the same way. Mayhap that was what drew him to her. That he would not be the one to guide her to that knowledge was like a knife to his gut.

His tone hardened. "I dare because I am here to protect ye."

She ripped her hand out of his grasp and stopped just short of stomping her injured foot. Her voice shrill, she said, "I do not want ye to protect me! I want nothing of ye!"

Marcán debated the wisdom of continuing this discussion in front of the men shifting uncomfortably around them. The right thing for him to do would be to allow them to leave, but he did not feel so inclined. Better the men wait to learn what he planned to do to them for leading the innocent sister of a powerful, neighboring *ri túaithe* off to have their way with her.

"I'll not allow any man to take advantage of ye."

She fisted her hands to her waist, bending toward him. "They were not taking advantage of me."

"No?"

Marcán spread his arms, his palms facing upward, indicating the men around her with his gaze. In turn, each man looked anywhere but at her. Or him. She looked at only one man. Pádraig. And when her eyes started to fill with tears, Marcán took a step closer. It was a response he couldn't have stopped if his life depended on it. She looked so small and helpless, he wanted to pull her into his arms, stroke her hair, and reassure her she was safe and protected. That was not what she wanted, so he moved no closer.

Astrid turned on him, her mouth tight and her nostrils flaring. "Ye have no right to interfere, Marcán."

When she would have stomped past him, she winced at the pain in her damaged ankle. He grabbed her arm before she fell. "We are not done here."

She huffed, turning her back to all of them, but remained silent. Marcán's palm twitched to spank that bottom, so sweetly presented. She deserved that and much, much more. Battles had been started over less than this. It gave Marcán no small relief that Astrid was showing off her worst side in front of the great Pádraig Meic Murchadha. The thought was enough to make him lightheaded. Surely now the man would keep clear.

"Well?" Marcán said to the others, widening his stance when the lightheadedness increased. Music drifted to them from the longhouse. The dancing had begun. The men exchanged uneasy glances, but it was Pádraig who finally spoke up.

"We've not touched her, Marcán."

"Aye. Not even a kiss," one of the other men said.

Astrid snorted loudly.

"Can ye see clear to allow us our leave?"

Marcán wanted to punch the man right in the face, but the sincerity he saw there soothed his ire. It was Astrid's behavior that had led to this situation, and he knew she had no notion of what she had done.

Marcán blew out a breath. "Ye're not to touch this one, do ye understand me?"

The men nodded while Astrid shifted, her head turned away from them.

One of the men thought to speak, a true mistake. "Ye *do* know how she—"

Marcán held up a hand to halt the words. "Ye'll not touch her."

"We'll not," the man said, shifting from one foot to another. "Ye have our word."

Each man passed by, one by one, nodding at Marcán and glancing back toward Astrid. Only Pádraig hesitated. Marcán wondered if the man was actually considering trying to take her with him. Let him try! To Marcán's great disappointment, Pádraig continued on, disappearing with the rest of the men toward the music.

Alone with Astrid, Marcán felt the weight of her dismissal of the situation. She still had no idea what they had expected—she'd only wanted the attention. Again he cursed Diarmuid for believing he should continue to wait to marry her off. That Marcán wanted her for himself was irrelevant. He was the same as Diarmuid in *her* mind and wanted nothing to do with him. It was not meant to be.

Watching her stiff back, Marcán knew things had to be said that she didn't want to hear—things *he* didn't want to say. It was her behavior that had gotten her into this predicament, and if Marcán hadn't arrived so quickly, she might have been ruined.

Marcán pulled at his neck, finally feeling a wash of heat from the nearby pools.

"Astrid. Look at me."

She lifted a hand to her face, wiping her cheek. "I do not want to see ye… ever again."

"Now, Astrid."

"Do not talk to me as if ye have a right to order me around."

"I'll not ask again."

Astrid whirled around, her mouth squeezed tight with anger, her face awash in tears. Marcán struggled against the sight of her frailty and innocence and his duty as the one protecting her.

"Ye have no idea what ye've done," Marcán said.

"What *I've* done? How dare ye…"

Marcán closed his eyes and stopped listening. Diarmuid was a thousand times a fool. His sister was going to get herself with child, and nothing Marcán could say would make a difference. She wanted to be taken! She begged to be taken! Not out of the carnal need for sex, but for the thrill of being desired.

He opened his eyes, and she slammed her mouth shut.

"Let us sit." He was suddenly done in, and it was a relief to settle onto the ground. Astrid obeyed but kept her distance. "These men would have taken yer maidenhead and given ye no further thought."

Her eyes widened at his bawdy words.

"Not Pádraig!" She all but spat the words at him, her faith in the sly fox that strong.

Marcán scoffed. "Pádraig would have been first betwixt yer legs."

Her quiet gasp surprised him, and he swallowed hard before continuing.

"Ye're a lovely lass, but yer need is for a man to love ye." He didn't dare touch her, despite the heat pouring off her. She kept her eyes on him as he spoke. "I wish only to protect ye from those who would take what is meant for yer husband alone."

Her eyes were unusually bright, as if he held her full attention. "Yer husband is the man who should take ye to his bed and show ye what it is to be loved in *all* ways until ye are moaning his name in yer release."

Marcán's words were shattering him inside. Little though she knew it, he was revealing his deepest desires, sharing what he wanted with her but would never have.

"I was not taking something away from ye. Never that. I want something more *for* ye. Ye'd not have known passion with these men. Men don't need passion for release, just a willing lass, and ye send out a sign that ye are willing with every flip of yer hair."

Her expression flashed with anger, but he had to finish, to tell her what she needed to hear. Then he would never say these words to her again, because it was ripping his heart out to imagine her with another.

"Ye need to save yer maidenhead for the man who'll protect ye, even from yerself. The man who will unselfishly put yer needs above his own and come to ye alone for his release. The man who will stay by yer side no matter what. That is the way of our clan, Astrid. Mayhap not all clans care so strongly for their women, but *we* do."

She continued to watch him a bit longer, the anger slipping from her expression. When she glanced back toward the sound of the music, Marcán's eyes closed ever so slightly, and he finally released the breath he'd been holding.

"I do not see how I can go back in there." She turned a sideways glance at him. "I've been out here alone with *ye*."

She said the last with such displeasure, he squared his shoulders and stiffened his expression.

"What will they think?" she asked.

"I'll be happy to redden yer bottom as ye deserve." His flat tone left little room for argument. In truth, he'd not be able to punish her, not now. Not when the reality that he must give her up to whoever would become her husband felt like a cold blade piercing the depths of his heart. But she didn't need to know that. Let her wonder if he would carry out the punishment. When her expression turned dubious, he added, "Or I can bring ye to where yer mother is sleeping. Ye could curl up beside her and rest for the night. We're headed back at daybreak."

She smiled up at him, and his breath caught at her loveliness. "With the sheep, I hope?"

He offered a wide grin. "Indeed!"

"Then I will accept yer suggestion. Ye may bring me to my mother."

Chapter Two

Astrid remained motionless in the small thatched building she and her mother had been given the use of for the night. An old pallet had been thrown together for them on the floor with barely enough straw to protect them from the cold, dirt floor. Her mother snored an arm's length from her, and the opening to the outside revealed the dark-haired warrior as he walked away in the moonlight. Marcán. He was being ridiculously overprotective of her.

Marcán stopped at the road, roughed up his hair, then looked skyward with open arms. Astrid frowned. She heard something that sounded like yelling, but he was too far away for her to hear the words. She moved nearer the doorway. Was he screaming up at the heavens?

When he turned back toward the hut, Astrid dropped out of sight. She dared not even breathe, expecting him to appear at the door at any moment. Marcán had seemed a bit out of control just now. A shiver of something she couldn't name traveled over her skin. Was it fear? But she would never fear Marcán, no matter how he acted.

She glanced at her mother's sleeping form, a dark bump covered with heavy wool. Her back to the door, the woman slept like the dead. Oblivious to all around her now, but she had encouraged Astrid to stay for the feast and entertainment. She'd even told her to enjoy herself, which was very odd for the woman to say. Astrid's pleasure was not something Beibhinn ever gave much thought to.

Pádraig had lied to Marcán. She had never asked to see any hot springs. She'd asked only if they could speak alone.

It would be best if Astrid just did as Marcán had told her she should. She was here, so why venture out again? She scratched at her head, surprised to find her hair such a mess, then suppressed a yawn.

Pádraig's earlier interest in the redhead with the curly hair and bright green eyes came to mind. The woman was beautiful, and she'd definitely returned his gazes, even kissing him!

That was the way of the Meic Murchadha. Pádraig's sister had straddled Marcán's lap earlier, and the man had barely flinched. Astrid had expected some kind of reaction, but instead he'd just held Daimhin's gaze, his hands at his sides. Astrid had half expected her to kiss Marcán. That would have gotten a reaction, for certain. He probably would have dumped her right off his lap. Instead, Daimhin had moved in

22

closer, said something to him, then climbed back off. Very strange.

Astrid couldn't be certain who had initiated the kissing between Pádraig and the redhead, but he appeared to be quite good at it. Remaining just inside the open door, she'd watched them, imagining it was *her* Pádraig was kissing. It would have been a very enjoyable kiss indeed.

She sighed.

Astrid touched her lips. She'd never been kissed by a man before. Well, she'd had to kiss Marcán once in a game of Pull the Ribbon, but that didn't count. He'd looked so irritated... When he'd leaned in close to her, she'd almost been afraid to let their lips touch, his eyes had been so dark. He hadn't wanted to play— in fact, he'd tried to talk Diarmuid out of it. This was back before Diarmuid had become *ri túaithe,* when their father was still alive. Astrid assumed the whole game had only been started because her brother had wanted to kiss one of the lasses. *That* kiss had lasted quite a while.

It had been so irritating to sit and watch that she'd rolled her eyes and looked toward Marcán, expecting to see the same reaction. She'd found him watching her instead, that darkness still in his eyes. Diarmuid should not have insisted that he play. Marcán had not been happy about any of it. She hoped Pádraig would be much more agreeable to both the idea of kissing her and their union.

What she needed was to have a forthright conversation with him tonight—a discussion of how their match would bind the two clans together. Certainly he *should* agree with her. She smiled. And then she would be the one receiving his attention and his kisses.

That was the reason she'd approached him. It was why she had agreed to take a walk with him when he'd offered. Despite what he'd told Marcán, he had not asked her if the other three could come. She'd been trying to think of a way to speak with Pádraig privately and then Marcán had shown up.

When her mother flipped onto her back, Astrid gasped. Offering a prayer, Astrid slowly rose and stood beside the opening. There was no sign of Marcán, so she grabbed her mantle, ready to head back to the main house.

"Well?" Her mother's tired voice startled her. "Were ye successful?"

Astrid let out a slow breath to calm her racing heart. "I did not know ye were awake."

Beibhinn would not speak again until Astrid answered her. That was the way of it with her mother.

"Pádraig did notice me and I spoke to him."

Beibhinn did not sit up, and her chuckle had a strange, throaty sound. "I am duly impressed then. Ye have done something right, daughter."

With slow, controlled movements, the woman rolled over to lean on an elbow. Astrid's breath caught at the cruel lines on her mother's face. "Then why are ye here instead of with him?"

Explanations and excuses spun in her head. None would be acceptable to her mother. "I tried to speak to him alone, but the other men—"

"*Other* men?"

"Pádraig invited others to join us. Some men. I did not know them."

"Men from the other clans, no doubt." Beibhinn sat up, blowing out an exasperated breath. "We may be too late. If ye had explained yerself—or used what

24

little bit of attraction ye have—we might have stood a chance."

"But I thought ye said—"

Her mother halted her words with a raised hand. "Do not make excuses now. Ye had the perfect chance to win over the man, and ye failed. I need to think."

Astrid stood there, afraid to even sit beside her mother when Beibhinn was this irritated. With a small voice, she voiced her defense. "I approached him. Boldly! I even asked him if we could speak."

The memory of the sudden interest in the man's eyes came to mind. It was as if he'd seen her for the first time. He'd studied her body for a long moment, and his smile of approval had given her a heady sense of power. Her mother had been correct. A man could easily be led if a woman went on the offensive, using any weapon she had.

"Then what went wrong?"

"Well, he insisted we should take a walk and grabbed my hand."

A slow smile started on her mother's face.

"He led us to a small path in the woods." A very *dark* path. "When he called other men to join us, I tried to explain we needed to speak alone, but he said we would talk later."

He'd actually told the men to come "for some entertainment," which had shaken her confidence a bit, though surely Marcán had been mistaken about their intentions.

"We'd settled on the ground. Pádraig placed a protective arm around me."

Astrid knew she had very little with which to attract attention from someone as handsome and powerful as Pádraig. If she wanted to get herself married, she needed to continue to take bold steps, so she had tapped down her trepidation.

"I thought that Pádraig may have needed to speak to these men, so I laughed at their jokes while they passed around a wineskin." Their jokes had nearly burned her ears with their bawdiness. "And I kept his attention. I did!"

Her mother was still smiling as she nodded, encouraging the story.

"The other men, too, so I'd hoped they would leave—"

The smile dropped. "Do not tell me ye insulted the man by saying as much!"

"Of course I said no such thing. I was very pleasant. Very interested in all they said." She'd even encouraged their interest in her. It had made her feel powerful again. Wanted. "I had just hoped the others would leave."

"Astrid!" Her mother's scolding tone continued. "Do I need to remind ye how important this is to me? To us? I cannot stay another winter with yer father's people."

Astrid sighed. She'd heard the story enough times to recite it by heart. There was only one man her mother had ever loved. Only one man she had been willing to leave her own clan to marry, and that man was not Astrid's father. The man Beibhinn had loved had been bewitched by a heathen woman.

"No, *mamaídh*. I am satisfied to accept him as my husband, but he does not ask!"

It made Astrid sad to think of her father being so despised by his wife. According to Beibhinn, he was the reason for all her unhappiness—and one needed only to spend a few moments with her to know she was a very unhappy woman. Astrid remembered her father differently. He had been a good man. A loving man. She had missed him desperately when his trips away from home had started to stretch out longer and longer. No doubt he had felt the loss of her little brother, Fergus, just as she still did. The only time she'd ever seen her father cry had been after Fergus's death.

After that, when her father did come home, he never stayed long—until he finally stopped coming back at all. The occasional missive had done little to fill the hole in her heart from not seeing him. The day they received news of his death had been the saddest one of her life. He'd died in battle, his best friend and *tánaiste* beside him.

"Have I not explained to ye how this is done?"

Astrid nodded, but she did not like the idea of being sneaky. It went against her grain. She would prefer to be forthright. Approach him with the idea. Show him the merits of the two clans joining.

The furrow between her mother's eyes deepened. "Ye had an opportunity with the man and... Oh well. Ye did yer best, I suppose."

Desperation clawed at her gut. She would not be so easily defeated! Marrying Pádraig might be the only chance she'd have for a family, and with her mother helping her, it seemed like a real possibility.

"I was doing very well, but then Marcán—"

"Marcán?" Her mother spoke the man's name as if it were poisonous. "What does *he* have to do with this?"

"He was afeared for my innocence and he brought me back—"

Beibhinn was on her feet in an instant, pacing the

small space, a hand on her forehead and a fist at her hip. "That one! He is like a thorn in my side."

Astrid's lips parted. "What are ye saying? He is Diarmuid's dearest friend."

The woman turned her sharp gaze back to Astrid before pasting a smile on her face. "Ye have it right. Forgive me, Astrid. I fear I am overwrought. Marcán was no doubt looking out for ye."

Settling down on the flat pallet, Beibhinn patted the spot beside her and Astrid took the seat. They sat in silence.

Astrid hesitated before sharing her idea. "I'd had a thought... to mayhap return? Seek Pádraig out again?"

"Could ye do that?"

Astrid shrugged. "The feasting is ongoing. I could slip in and see if I can get him alone again."

She hated how conniving she sounded, but her mother enjoyed such things. If Astrid actually saw Pádraig and found an occasion to speak to him, her approach would be more direct.

"A fine idea." Beibhinn stood beside her, smoothing her hair down. "Remember the importance of this."

Astrid saw the opportunity for what it was. Surely she would be successful this time, at the very least in expressing her interest in the man. If he rejected her? Well, she would deal with that if it happened. Straightening her *léine*, she headed out the door.

The lively music called to her, but the path she traveled was very empty. The groups that had been scattered about earlier were gone. She hobbled faster, holding the wool tight around her. Marcán's warning about all the men being after her was making her more nervous. Although she would never admit it, the way he'd mentioned Pádraig being the first betwixt her legs had sent a slight thrill to her innards.

Astrid stopped in her tracks, realizing something that shocked her. When Marcán had said those words, she'd imagined *his* face over her—not Pádraig's. She licked her lips, more moved by the image than she would like to admit.

"Are ye still looking for trouble?"

Astrid turned, half expecting to see Marcán, but it was Pádraig who stood behind her. The redhead was nowhere in sight. Astrid beamed, pulling her shoulders back like her mother always advised her to. "I did not mean to cause trouble."

Pádraig's expression had lost some of its earlier cheerfulness.

"Sorry I am that we were interrupted," Astrid said, feeling more nervous now that she was finally alone with him.

He crossed his arms, staring at her with a stern expression. His long fur was once again draped over his shoulders. "Are ye?"

The depth of his anger at the situation brought a lump to her throat. "Pádraig, I am—"

He held his hand up. "I am certain we should not be standing here. In the dark. Alone. Talking."

She understood his sarcastic tone and nodded.

"Or has yer guard finally gone off to bed?" he asked.

His expression shifted ever so slightly, and she was filled with intense relief. He was still interested in her. She shrugged. "I do not know for certain where he is, only that he is not here."

Pádraig came closer, pushing her hair behind her ear.

"Good." His voice was low. Enticing. Astrid wetted

her lips. "Because I've been wanting to do this all night."

His lips were soft against hers, his tongue flicking across her tightly sealed mouth just before he pulled away.

Struggling to suppress her sigh, Astrid merely smiled, unable to look any higher than his lips. "Ye have?"

With a finger to her chin, he pulled her lips to his again, his mouth firmer this time, more insistent. He wrapped his arms around her in a tight embrace, giving her a lot of things to pay attention to. His prodding tongue slid against her closed mouth again, and when she thought to protest, it darted inside. Her breath caught in her throat. And yet… it was a surprisingly pleasant sensation. She relaxed her lips and he groaned, kissing her more deeply.

The hands around her waist glided up along the curve of her hips, over her lower back, and all the way up to her arms before moving back down again—caressing her in an ever-widening arc. Each time his hands moved up, they were closer to her breasts, and they kept dipping lower until he was grabbing her arse. Alarm bells were going off in her head. Her tongue stopped trying to spar with his, but he didn't seem to notice.

He made strange little sounds in his throat, as if he was quite enjoying the feel of her. Even though that pleased her, she knew she had to stop him, especially when he cupped her buttocks in his hands to hold her still, then rubbed his stiff prick against her.

"Umm, Pádraig?" She spoke against his insistent lips.

Pádraig broke the kiss, turned his head, dropped

his arms, and stepped away with a disgusted sigh. When he looked back, his eyebrows arched over his wide eyes. "I'm listening."

Astrid wasn't sure how to respond. She had wanted him to kiss her but not to feel his… his need. "I wanted us to talk."

The man stood perfectly still, as if his thoughts were requiring all of his concentration. He placed his hands on his hips and lowered his head.

With a sideways glance, he said, "And what would ye like us to talk of?"

Despite his tone, which was pleasant enough, she sensed he was not happy with her. She turned away slightly, nibbling on her bottom lip. "I had an idea for us."

"Oh?" He reached toward her and moved in closer, his voice low. "As do I. D'ye believe it could be the same idea?"

His lips against her ear sent an unexpected shiver of repulsion through her. She backed away from him. "Please do not."

His expression screamed ye-cannot-be-saying-no-to-me. Astrid gave him her back, frowning in confusion. She had not expected this from him. In her mind, he had listened to her suggestion and considered the merit of her words.

This was a side of him she was not sure she liked.

"Forgiveness, please, Astrid." Pádraig's voice carried clear concern, and she searched his face for his sincerity without success. "There are many here this night, and I admit it tires me. I am not myself."

Something told her his words did not match his thoughts. She swallowed again, unsure of herself, but they were finally alone. It was now or never.

"My thought was of our joining." Her lips parted at the sheer lust now visible on his face and the wide grin that followed.

"As was mine!"

Holding up a hand to ward him off, she paused before continuing, no longer convinced herself that the idea was a good one. But if she went back to the hut now, Beibhinn would never let her hear the last of it…

"I was referring to ye taking me to wife, with the blessing of God and our families." Regret bloomed in her chest at his crestfallen expression, but she couldn't lose her courage now. She spoke even faster. "Surely 'twould be a good bond between our clans. My mother is from yer clan as well. She would like the idea, I am certain." Especially since it had been her idea to begin with.

Pádraig's face tightened, but she remained hopeful as she waited for him to respond. His gaze dropped to her bosom, caressing each breast with his gaze before continuing lower. Finally, he looked back up to her face. "I could imagine us wed."

Astrid had imagined this moment dozens of times, but she felt none of the relief she'd expected. Instead, there was a surprising sensation of trepidation. What terrible thing was she getting herself into? He watched her now, his eyes narrowing.

"Is that not the answer ye wished to hear, Astrid?" He took a step closer. "I agree with ye. A good bond between my clan and yers."

Whereas his closeness had set off sparks of excitement earlier in the evening, before their first kiss, she was feeling nothing but… stifled the closer he got. She swallowed and looked up at him. He stood that close.

"My mother is here now, and we could approach her with the idea... and yer father?" She hoped talk of the arrangement would keep him from touching her again.

Pádraig tipped his head. "Ah, my father is not well enough to hear of this. What of yer brother?"

"He has returned home, but we can speak of it to him on the morrow."

The man puckered his lips in a thoughtful way, his brows lowering. "I do not know if that is the best idea."

"Why ever not?"

He glanced back toward the longhouse. "One of the clans here tonight has a lovely young lass my father would like me to take to wife. I believe ye may have seen her? Curly red hair?"

"I thought ye said yer father was not well?"

"This is something he put his seal to before he took to his bed. If I am to approach him with another offer, I would need to have knowledge that only yer brother as clan leader could offer."

Pádraig's expression seemed pleasant enough, but she sensed his tension. Mayhap he was truly interested in a joining of the clans. Mayhap he was so eager for their clans to join together he did not wish to miss the opportunity.

"D'ye not agree?" he asked.

"With what?"

"That we should see yer brother now. Approach him with yer idea and see if he would consider it."

Astrid glanced back toward the longhouse, the music and laughter spilling out.

"But we would need to leave at this very moment," Pádraig pressed. "My father will make the announcement on the morrow."

She whipped back to face him.

His brows raised in expectation. "D'ye not agree?"

Well, at least he wanted to know her thoughts.

She sighed. "Mayhap ye are correct. We should see Diarmuid before yer father commits ye to another."

"Come." Pádraig's arm was a bit too tight around her shoulders. A strong sense of foreboding flooded Astrid. Damn Marcán for sharing his lurid thoughts.

Pádraig led her toward the stable, his pace fast and sure. He paused outside and offered an unexpected peck to her cheek.

"My horse is very fast. We will be there by daybreak."

Pádraig disappeared inside and Astrid stared up at the night sky full of stars. This was a good idea. If they approached Diarmuid, certainly he would see the wisdom of the joining of the two clans and agree to the match. She took the weight off her injured foot. Suddenly overcome with the chill, she rubbed her arms. Pádraig reappeared, mounted, and reached down to her.

This was the ride she had hoped for earlier. Now she would learn just how it felt to be ensconced in his bonny, strong arms. She took his hand and he settled her in front of him.

"Are ye comfortable?"

"A bit chilled."

Pádraig leaned forward, enveloping her with his heat, and wrapping her up in his fur. Very romantic. Some of her earlier excitement returned.

"That will ward off the chill." Wrapping his arm around her hips, he yanked her closer to fit between his spread legs. His tarse poked against her thigh, and her excitement made a quick exit. She stilled, not sure what she should do. When she looked up at him, he merely smiled. "Ye're a bonny lass, Astrid. I'd be lying if I did not admit taking ye would give me great pleasure."

Yanking the horse's head to the left, he jabbed the beast into a gallop, and they headed back toward Clonascra, moving away from the others.

Chapter Three

Marcán could think of no way to leave this procession without causing offense. Pádraig's brother, Ian, had been asking him for more details about the caves, then several others had joined in, and now here they were making the long trek to the caves from the story.

"We are close?" Ian's eyes were wide. He stood head and shoulders above the other men, his limbs long and lanky.

"Not long now." Exhausted, Marcán could barely discern the path before him.

The mead had flowed freely in the hall, but he should not be this sotted. The others looked the same. It was as if they'd been drinking all day.

"And the blood is still on the wall?"

Legend had it that Brian Boru's blood was still on the wall of one of the nearby caves. Marcán suspected that was what had compelled Ian to ask for that particular story.

"Ye tell me when ye see it," Marcán said.

Admittedly, Marcán enjoyed the lad's enthusiasm, although at the moment he wanted nothing more than to be off to his bed. It would be a long enough trip home on the morrow. With Astrid and her mother, it would be even longer. Truth be told, it was Beibhinn's mouth that would make the trip unbearable but he wanted more time with Astrid.

When she was wed, Marcán would have no more opportunities to spend time with her. He dreaded that day, and yet being with her was also difficult. The woman thwarted him at every turn, almost as if she realized he just wanted to be around her. That could not be true though, because she seemed oblivious to his feelings, let alone the fact that he was a man capable of emotion. Of desire. If she wasn't angry at something he said, she was angry with Diarmuid and taking it out on him.

"There it is! The cave!" Ian ran forward, tripped, and got back up. "I found it."

The group of twenty men tramped into the cave with heavy feet. Ian yawned, a hand to the wall as if for support. "Where exactly is the blood?"

The others settled on the ground, some stretching out. Marcán struggled to fight the disorientation overtaking him.

"Toward the back." He yawned. "See if ye can find it, Ian. I'll wait here for ye."

Like a bag of bones, Marcán plopped onto the ground. The distant sound of snoring carried to him, and he realized his eyes were closed.

He couldn't remember why they shouldn't be.

The uncomfortable trip in Pádraig's arms seemed never-ending. He smelled of sweat and something she couldn't name. His breath was even worse, no matter how many times he drank from his skin.

Astrid had accepted the first offer of a drink, but the moment she tipped back her head to drink from the vessel, Pádraig latched on to her flesh, sucking the skin at her neck into his mouth. His hand against the other side of her head, holding her in place, so she had no choice but to submit to him until he was finished. After that she decided to go thirsty.

"D'ye not like me anymore?" Pádraig spoke close to her ear, his hips quirking against her, pressing his unrelenting arousal against her.

"I do like ye. Ye're a fine man, Pádraig. A good warrior. I have heard my brother say as much many times."

Pádraig slowed the horse and watched her for so long she became uncomfortable. Did he realize she was lying? She had never actually heard Diarmuid speak of Pádraig in any meaningful way. The next thing she knew, he was pulling back on the reins and dropping from the horse.

"I need to take a piss."

He disappeared into the woods. When he came out a short time later, he stretched, scratching at his belly. Turning a smile on her, he moved toward her with up stretched arms.

"I've been remiss. Ye need to stretch as well."

She'd prefer they keep going. "No. I am fine."

He did not lower his arms at her refusal and his fingers beckoned to her. "Come."

Astrid could practically hear her mother's voice in her head: *Do not insult the man!* She leaned into his arms and allowed him to help her dismount. Then she brushed down her gown, bending her shoulders, which ached from being up against him. He was not as comfortable as she'd thought he would be. Overall, the entire ride was a disappointment.

"Share with me yer thoughts," he said.

"I have none to share."

Pádraig tipped his head, a telling smirk on his face. "I know ye well enough to know that is a lie, Astrid."

"A lie? How so?"

"Ye are always thinking. Thinking about this. Thinking about that." He came up alongside her, standing far too close. "Making yer plans."

His thoughts were the ones to be concerned about. Chill bumps spread across her arms and she glanced around at the secluded clearing.

"Ye know me not at all. Who told ye such a thing as that?"

"Yer mother."

Astrid's chest tightened at the betrayal. "I do not know what she was talking about. Ye know how mothers are."

"I do." He crossed his arms about his chest. And waited.

He had a stern expression and she felt the weight of his judgment. "What is it ye wish to know?"

"Have ye changed yer feelings toward me?"

She glanced around, wary about sharing what she

was actually thinking. "Ye have been a bit more forward than I expected ye to be."

"Have I?" He moved in closer, his eyes rounded with concern. "Forgiveness, please."

His expression did not waver as he slid a finger along the curve of her face, his eyes holding her gaze. "I did not mean to offend."

"No offense—"

He placed a finger to her lips, silencing her.

"Never offend." The tip of his finger traced her lips, and he dropped his gaze to follow the movement. "Never offend. Not luscious Astrid."

Luscious? Not an endearment she would have chosen for herself. A shiver shook her when he licked his lips. She would have spoken, but he again held a single finger to her lips.

Pádraig moved in to kiss her, and she closed her eyes, her breath trapped in her chest. She was petrified of what he was about to do. Surely whatever Marcán had seen her do to indicate her willingness earlier, she had not done it again. She couldn't have. She had only sat upon a horse, her hands on her lap, facing front, while he rubbed himself against her and she pretended not to notice.

Near panicked, she tried to turn her head away, but his mouth kept following her.

"Please." Her voice reflected her fear.

"Yes." He murmured against her lips.

"Umm."

He slipped his tongue in again, and his hands were suddenly at her breasts. She tried to grab the fingers groping her, working the neck of her gown lower. She should have been measuring each word, watching his expression, listening for the quickening of his breath.

Speaking with his lips still against hers, he said, "Yer breasts are as sweet as overripe peaches. They beg for me to pluck them."

One strong arm snaked around her when she tried to pull away, yanking her up against his body, his tarse most prominent.

He groaned low in his throat. "Let me feast on ye."

When he finally released her lips, she gasped as his mouth latched onto her suddenly exposed breast. His other hand grabbed lower, where no one had ever touched her.

"Stop, Pádraig!"

Her voice was loud and shrill. He rubbed between her legs, ignoring her. When he put his teeth to her breast, she cuffed him.

"Ow!" Pádraig pulled back, his mouth gaping open and a hand to his ear. "What did ye do that for?"

Astrid was beside herself, shifting her clothes back into place, including the neckline of her gown, which refused to be returned to its higher position.

"Ye are nothing but a tease, ye little bitch!" Both his tone and his words were insulting.

She gasped, her eyes widening with her hurt and fear. He was breathing heavy, and the bulging of his knee-length *léine* left little doubt of his intent.

"Marcán protected ye once, but ye have no protection now." Pádraig crushed her flush against him, his mouth chasing hers when she twisted to avoid his kisses.

"Stop!" Her voice echoed back from the trees around them.

He shoved her away. She fell into a heap on the cold, hard ground, her face covered with tears and her stomach ready to be violently sick.

"Enough!" Pádraig stood over her, his hand rubbing his rod, his chest heaving. "I know ye want it."

She shook her head, scooting away from him. He kept on her, closing the distance between them. When he yanked up his *léine* to grab his hardened length, she couldn't look away. It was like a snake ready to strike at her.

"D'ye fear so for the loss of yer maidenhead, Astrid?" With a firm grip, he fisted himself. "Ye can still pleasure me."

She shook her head.

"Open yer mouth."

He moved in closer and she covered her mouth, her throat tight.

"Then let me help ye," Pádraig said.

"H-hello?" a voice called out from the distance.

Pádraig turned away, a look of exasperation on his face, and covered himself.

"Is au-aught amiss?"

Astrid recognized the voice—Faolán, a warrior from her own clan. He had to be securing their boundaries. She'd believed they were close to home, and this confirmed it. When he broke through the trees on his mount, she was just standing. Unassisted. Pádraig stood a few feet from her—a hand on his jutting hip, annoyance radiating off him.

"A-Astrid?" Faolán jumped off his horse, his concern apparent. He hurried toward her, but Pádraig interceded.

Faolán shoved the man away, paying him no heed in his hurry to get to Astrid. "Wha-what has ha-happened here?" His gentle hand wiped at her tears.

Pádraig jerked him about. "Naught ye need to

concern yerself with."

Faolán's punch landed squarely in Pádraig's face and the man dropped to the ground.

Astrid gasped. "Oh, no, Faolán. Do not—"

Pádraig growled as he stood, driving into Faolán's middle with enough force to take him down.

"No!" Astrid yelled, but there was no indication either man heard her.

Sitting atop Faolán, Pádraig hit him with solid fists to the face and then the stomach. But it was not long before Faolán once again got the upper hand, flipping Pádraig off him.

Faolán stood, blood dripping from his nose, and yanked his opponent up by his *léine*, hitting him in the stomach hard enough that he doubled over. Pádraig's moan of pain did nothing to stop his assault.

Finally, Faolán withdrew his sword, stepping far enough away that the point touched Pádraig's chest, remaining there even as the winded man slowly righted himself, his arm still wrapped around his middle.

"Let. Me. Hear. It. From. The. Lass!" Faolán said.

Astrid's jaw dropped. She had never heard the man speak without a stutter before. Faolán remained still. Unyielding. Unmoving. Waiting. When Pádraig gave a curt nod, Faolán glanced at her.

"Wh-what is amiss here, Astrid?"

Pádraig opened his mouth, but Faolán was quick to press the tip of the blade in, piercing his skin. Blood trickled through his *léine*. Pádraig's fierce anger was frightening to behold and Astrid feared for Faolán.

"Faolán. Ye know this man is the son of the *ri túaithe*."

"He i-is the son. That d-does not give him the sa-

same rights as the father."

Leadership was not decided by birth. That would never protect the clans. The *tánaiste*, the next in line, was always named at the time of the anointing of a new king. Someone who was able and ready to take over should the king die. Pádraig had been far too young at the time of his father's anointing to have this position.

"Please." Astrid was not sure what to say to get Faolán to back down. Running Pádraig through would cause even more bloodshed. It would be the start of a war between their clans. "I… He was bringing me home."

Faolán's eyes narrowed, remaining on Pádraig. "Wh-why did I he-hear ye c-call out 'stop'?"

"I… I needed… needed him to… stop."

"And wh-what was he d-doing that ye wa-wanted him to stop?" His voice was menacingly quiet.

If Astrid spoke the truth, she had no doubt Faolán would run his sword right through the man's chest. Then there would be hell to pay.

She clenched her teeth. "I needed to relieve myself."

Pádraig and Faolán turned to her as one, their shock obvious.

"He thought I could… wait, but I could not." It was impossible for her to say any more. Not when the scream she wanted to let loose was stuck in her throat. When she saw Pádraig's smug smile, she forced herself to look away. It was either that or she would throw herself against the man, beating him with her fists, ordering Faolán to finish him off.

Faolán lowered his sword with great reluctance, and Pádraig had him in a throat clutch in a flash. "Ye impudent dog! Ye'll regret this with yer last breath!"

Before Astrid could fully react, Pádraig had shoved him to the ground. Faolán's sword clanged harmlessly beside him.

"Enough, Pádraig."

Turning to her, the anger disappeared from his face. He smiled at her. A beaming smile. His eyes bright.

"As ye wish." He extended his arm to her, as if he were escorting her to a celebration in their honor. "Come, let me see ye home."

Faolán stood slowly, his gaze upon her. Watching her. Boring into her. He had not believed her story at all. He knew better. He was a warrior. And he was of her clan.

Mayhap not all clans care so strongly for their women, but we do.

She wanted so badly to cringe from his touch, but if she refused Pádraig's hand now, Faolán would have confirmation that she had lied. He would come to her defense, even if it meant his doom. He would fight Pádraig, and regardless of who won, what she had feared would happen a moment earlier would indeed come to pass. Her entire body stiffened with revulsion. She had trouble getting her arm to rise to meet Pádraig's, her hand to touch his hand, but somehow she managed. When Pádraig lifted her onto the horse, she turned her face away.

"Well done." Pádraig's softly spoken words were for her ears alone.

Chapter Four

Marcán could not remember ever having pain as bad as this. His head throbbed. He was barely able to sit before the vomit spewed out. Moans carried to his ears from all around him, but his eyes remained tightly shut.

"Father?" It was Ian's voice. "Pádraig? I fear I am dying."

Sympathy for the lad gave Marcán strength. Forcing down the bile flooding his mouth, he said, "No. Ye're not dying, but do not try to sit up. 'Twill only make it worse."

"Marcán? What is amiss?" Ian asked.

Moving carefully, Marcán sat up and opened his eyes. He scanned the cave—the others were in a similar state. Marcán forced a smile for Ian, but it felt more like a grimace.

"Mayhap we will not drink so much next time?"

"Oh, Marcán, I'd nothing but one horn of the mead. Something else ails me."

Marcán gritted his teeth and stood, waiting for the nausea to pass. "We need some water, Ian. Try to sit up now. Slowly."

The lad moaned with his first few attempts, both hands holding his head, but was finally able to get into a hunched-over standing position.

His movements slower than an old man's, Marcán made his way to the cave entrance, followed by Ian. The bright sunlight nearly knocked him on his arse again. He held up his hand to shield his eyes as he stumbled toward the nearby spring, fighting disorientation.

The cool water was refreshing, and they were soon joined by more of the men who'd come with them last night in search of Brian Boru's blood.

"I have never been this sick," one of the men said, his eyes intent on Marcán. "D'ye believe the Meic Murchadha is trying to kill us all?"

This man was from a clan farther south. Marcán's foggy brain refused to come up with his name.

"Why?" Ian asked the obvious question, his tone revealing his hurt. The two men had been friendly, even joking, on the way to the cave last night.

"Ah, ye do not know the ways of the warrior, lad."

Marcán wasn't surprised by the flash of resentment from Ian.

"Those are casks we had only just acquired from a merchant."

"Intentional or not, I agree we have been poisoned," Marcán said. He wiped his face on his sleeve, resting his forehead on his bent arm.

"D'ye think the hour is still early?" the visitor asked. "Our clan had plans to return this day."

Marcán's eyes flew open and he jumped up. Astrid had been left unprotected. He glanced around the group of groaning warriors. Pádraig was not among them.

"Ian, d'ye know if yer brother had a hunt planned for this day?"

It wasn't unusual to take visiting clans out to show them the bounty of yer land, especially if ye were hoping for a treaty with them.

Ian scratched his scalp and shrugged.

Marcán's annoyance reared its head. His worry about Astrid cut short any sympathy he felt for the lad. "I will head back. D'ye know the way?"

A few heads nodded, enough that Marcán was comfortable relinquishing his position as guide. Despite the pounding that flooded his head with every step, he hurried back to the Meic Murchadha camp.

Much to his dislike, Beibhinn was the first person he saw. But she didn't see him, which suited him fine. She was too busy smiling and talking to the men who were still hanging on her every word. The old woman basked in the attention of those who waited on her. That they'd clearly been ordered to do her bidding mattered not in the least to her. They had not yet been shredded to pieces by her fierce tongue.

At least the Meic Murchadha had the decency to feel guilty about the timing they'd chosen for their raid to steal the sheep. It was no coincidence they'd come *after* Diarmuid and most of his warriors had ridden off to join a gathering of the clans at the order of their overking, Sean. The Meic Murchadha might have felt slighted because Sean was also their overking and they had not been invited.

They certainly could not have guessed Astrid and her mother would try to retrieve the sheep alone. No one would have guessed the two would attempt such a ridiculous feat. Only Astrid would come up with such an idea.

Even in his current condition, Marcán's face eased into a smile at the thought of her. The ideas she came up with could leave a man exhausted trying to protect her. He blew a breath and decided to avoid Beibhinn altogether. It was Astrid he wanted to find. He was certain he could locate her without her mother's assistance. She paid her daughter so little attention, he doubted she even knew where she was.

"Oh, Marcán!" Beibhinn's voice grated on his nerves. "Glad I am that I have found ye."

He swallowed and planted a pleasant look on his face before turning around. "Beibhinn."

The woman had no use for him, and despite her sickly sweet tone, her face was tight with dislike. Marcán had heard the Legend of the Seer many times, mostly from her. It was said that anyone with two different-colored eyes could see into the future. Both the legends and the church agreed that Seers were to be avoided. But having two different-colored eyes, while certainly unusual, did not make a person a Seer. Those around him could keep watch all they liked, full of suspicion and talk.

Beibhinn believed every legend—she'd even gone so far as to tell Diarmuid to stay away from Marcán, claiming he worshipped the devil. Marcán had yet to discover where her hatred of him came from. Thankfully, Diarmuid had been old enough to discern

Marcán's belief in the true faith and discount his mother's stories.

"Ye need not concern yerself with bringing us back," Beibhinn nearly purred the words, and Marcán was instantly on guard.

"Us?"

"Me and Astrid."

Marcán glanced around the busy village, searching out Astrid's light hair, but he spoke in an even tone. "Why would that be?"

"Well…" Beibhinn smiled like a cat just coming out of the milking shed. "*I* am going back with Eric and his brother."

Nodding politely, Marcán felt his breath slow as he prepared himself for whatever she was about to drop on him. Beibhinn said no more, but that smile remained, her eyes closing slightly in pleasure at whatever she was keeping from him.

The realization hit Marcán like a sharp slap to his face. Beibhinn knew of his feelings for Astrid! But how could she, when he'd never spoken of them to a soul, not even Diarmuid? The last thing she would ever condone was a match between the two of them. She would fight it tooth and nail, which was of no consequence, since Astrid seemed to be of the same mind. So why the pleased look?

Marcán refused to give in to her dramatic ploy. "Is that all ye needed to tell me, lady?"

"No!" Her face screwed up in confusion.

He allowed himself to savor her irritation with him for not playing along. Until she spoke again.

"I want to be certain ye know that Astrid has returned with Pádraig."

All sound around him seemed to stop, but he held

back his questions, his demands for how that had come about, his dislike for the woman in general. Forcing a steady breath, he wetted his lips before speaking. "Are *ye* the one who gave her leave to do so?"

"Well"—she tilted her head and shrugged before continuing—"Astrid knows what she wants and she wanted to be home. Pádraig took care of her."

Pádraig took care of her.

"Lady, yer disregard for my authority is at an end." Marcán ground his teeth and scanned the area. "Philip!"

He motioned the warrior closer, glad to find one of his own men. "Philip, I give ye leave to see to Beibhinn in whatever manner is necessary to return her home *now*—"

"Hey!" Beibhinn said, dropping all pretense of pleasure.

Philip immediately took hold of her arm. He would obey his orders no matter what wiles Beibhinn tried to use on him.

"Ye cannot do this to me!" Her face reddened.

"—and ye will receive no punishment whatsoever for the means ye must use to see this done."

"How dare ye, Seer!" She shouted the word at him.

Seer!

Many halted what they were doing, turning to look at them, their eyes narrowing. The word got the expected response and Marcán's nostrils flared at the insult even as he struggled to maintain a calm facade.

"If gagging is required, Philip, so be it."

Marcán strode toward the *ráth* where the horses were kept, ignoring the commotion behind him. The commotion Beibhinn had started with that single word. Seers were considered akin to witches, practicing the dark arts, and they were not allowed to live within the villages. If there was even a hint that someone was a Seer, a council was called and a priest was asked to consider the charges.

Stopping at the rain barrel, Marcán dowsed his head up to his neck. This day was just getting better and better. At least the cold water helped numb the unrelenting throbbing. When he pulled his head out, he whipped his hair back.

"Marcán?"

Turning to face Ian, Marcán wasn't prepared for the look of disappointment and betrayal he saw there.

"Ian."

"Is there truth to what Beibhinn said? Are ye a Seer?"

The others had drifted toward Marcán, standing idly by as if not listening. But they did listen. Intently. Tension was obvious in their closed mouths and stiff bodies. They were the same people who had so enjoyed his storytelling the night before. Just like that! It baffled him how quickly one word had changed their smiles and applause into suspicion and distrust.

Exhaling slowly, Marcán offered a tight smile to Ian. "And if I were a Seer, lad? Would I truly have indulged so in the poisoned mead?"

Ian frowned, considering his words, before offering a relaxed smile. "True! Not a Seer then." He patted Marcán awkwardly on the shoulder and nodded.

The people around them seemed to relax as well, for they all went about their duties. He didn't miss the few sidelong glances that continued to come his way. Suspicions had been ignited. Damn Beibhinn and her manipulative ways.

"My thanks, Ian. I hope to see ye again before too long," Marcán said.

"I am not hopeful," the lad said darkly. "My father is very ill. I am going to him now."

"I will pray for his quick recovery this very night. Please give him my regards. I must return. I have… duties."

Ian smiled, a knowing smile. "Aye. Astrid. Daimhin tells me she snuck off with Pádraig in the middle of the night."

Without another word, Marcán raced into the *ráth*, grabbing the first available mount.

By the time Pádraig got Astrid home, the sun had still not broken the horizon. At least in that instance, he had been true to his word. The more she pondered the events of the night, the more certain she became that he had always planned on having his way with her. And she had made it far too easy for him.

Her back ached from the effort of sitting as far from him as possible while on the same mount, but at least Faolán had insisted on accompanying them. Pádraig dared not appear openly disrespectful of her in the other man's presence. He'd kept himself apart and allowed her to do the same. The yard was quiet—not even the animals were awake yet.

Faolán dismounted with them and moved to help her down. The look he received from Pádraig would have shriveled a lesser man. With both men ready to assist her, she clenched her jaw and leaned toward

Pádraig. It was the only way to avert conflict. Once the man was gone, she'd never have to endure his touch again, and that could not be soon enough.

"I thank ye, Pádraig, for—"

"Faolán! Refreshments would be much appreciated." Pádraig sounded as if he were at an inn, ordering drinks for all.

Faolán tipped his chin and walked to the roundhouse.

Stopping in front of the large wooden door without opening it, Faolán turned to Pádraig, who had followed him.

"Y-ye'll have to w-wait there"—Faolán indicated a bench more than a stone's throw away—"a-as the others are not yet awake."

"I do not wait outside!" Pádraig's voice was louder than it needed to be. He was clearly insulted.

"Hard working men and w-women require their rest. I-I will not have ye startling them from their sleep. Y-yer arrival in the middle of the night does not give y-ye license to w-wake everyone."

"*Ye'll* not have… are ye certain ye wish to continue in this manner?" Pádraig jutted out his chin, an intimidating gesture to be sure.

Faolán simply crossed his arms, revealing nothing on his face. Astrid wanted to cheer him on. Pat him on the back. Give him a big smile.

Pádraig turned his exasperated face toward her, his eyes wide in disbelief. She offered no response, and after another moment, he simply shook his head and walked toward the bench.

"My thanks," she said to Faolán in a quiet voice.

Too late, she realized her mistake. She tried to push past him to go inside, but he was not having it.

"A-A-Astrid, d-do not let him get away w-with

whatever he has done to ye. He is o-only one m-man."

His sincerity melted her heart, but she couldn't allow herself tears. She smiled. "'Tis fine. Ye're imagining things again."

She looked down at his hand on the latch, pressing her lips together to stop them quivering, waiting for him to open the door. She could not look at him. Not if she was to continue her lie.

"I-I a-am here for ye. Yer b-brother is here. Marcán i-is here."

Startled, she glanced at him. "Marcán is here?"

He swallowed. "No. I-I d-did not m-mean now. He has yet to r-return."

Ignoring the disappointment she felt, she went inside and was met with the smell of fresh bread. "Who is making bread so early?"

Faolán smiled and led the way to the food, both of them moving as quietly as they could manage with no more talking.

She'd hoped Pádraig would leave during the time it took to prepare the repast. Instead, he was up and pacing, irritation evident in every step.

"Glad I am to have ye rejoin me." Pádraig's clipped tone was directed at Faolán.

He moved close to Astrid, acting as if he had that right, but Faolán pushed between them to set down the wooden platter on the bench. Aside from his willingness to come to blows over Faolán taking the only other seat—beside her—Pádraig seemed oblivious to the deferential treatment the other warrior showed her. Faolán even went so far as to fill her cup before his own and cut off some bread for her with his dagger, offering her some cheese to accompany it.

Pádraig took a deep breath, ignoring both the bread

and the drink. "Astrid! I wish to speak to Diarmuid at once."

She blanched, her mouth going dry, making it difficult to swallow the bread. "Why?"

"As we've discussed." He turned wide eyes on her. "The joining of our two clans."

Faolán turned to her as well. She swore she saw betrayal on his face, but she refused to be distracted. This needed to be stopped. She would never marry a man who would force himself on her or treat her so disrespectfully.

"I do not believe—"

"*I* will speak with Diarmuid, Astrid. I will not be set aside."

The conviction of his words caught her unaware. He actually thought they should be married? Never!

"Pádraig, 'tis not time for visits. Return later, when she's rested." Faolán's commanding tone brooked no discussion, and he stood, arms about his chest, ready to do whatever was necessary to ensure his words were followed.

Astrid lifted the cup to her mouth to hide any sign of the absolute bliss she felt at Faolán's dismissal of the man. She lowered her gaze in case Pádraig looked to her for assistance. When she could no longer take the suspense—or the silence—she glanced at Pádraig. His eyes were narrowed, and he stared at Faolán as if considering how best to take him down. Pádraig finally clenched his jaw, dropped his arms, and nodded.

"Ye have the right of it, Faolán. I need to return to my father." His eyes darted to her before he continued. "There are many things we need to see to, but rest assured, I will be back."

When the man bent down to kiss her on the cheek, she gasped so hard her head jerked away. He was not deterred—he merely leaned in closer. He might as well announce her as his betrothed. She was trapped! The smug smile he offered her screamed that he'd done it intentionally. Astrid nearly stumbled in her haste to stand and move away from him.

Faolán was alongside her in a moment, ready to ward off any more demonstrations, but Pádraig had made his statement. He mounted his horse and rode off without a backward glance. Filled with a mix of relief and alarm, Astrid turned to Faolán, unsure of what to say, and found him watching her. He said nothing.

Then he picked up the heavy tray of items to be brought within and walked to the door of the roundhouse. Relief washed over her until he stopped. He paused. He was considering what to say to her. She swallowed and struggled to calm her expression, ready for him to turn toward her. When he finally did, his words shocked her.

"Y-ye need to come i-in with me so that I-I know y-ye are unmolested."

He definitely knew!

And he didn't understand why she was not saying anything.

Astrid wished she could scream out how thankful she was that he had come along when he had. If he hadn't…

She couldn't allow that thought to continue. Scanning his face, she realized he might feel hurt that she wasn't confiding in him. They were the same age and had played together as children. Diarmuid disliked the man, but Faolán had always looked out for her.

How could she confirm his suspicions? He would then have to tell Diarmuid. Such an act would require retribution against Pádraig. Against his entire clan.

Faolán was as diligent as any man in their clan. If she said nothing, there would be no recourse but also no bloodshed because of her ignorance. She would have to find another way to avoid a match with Pádraig.

"My thanks, Faolán. I am very tired."

Astrid went within, moving toward the others who slept peacefully. Dreaming. Unbothered by guilt or shame. She doubted she would get much rest, but it didn't matter. Now she was safely home and this entire terrible night could be put behind her.

Chapter Five

"What were ye thinking, Astrid?" Diarmuid's anger at Astrid for allowing Pádraig to bring her home was inflamed by the fact that Marcán had still not returned. She was the one who'd brought him the news—calling him out of his marriage bed to do it— something that had only heaped more ashes upon her head.

"I do not understand how he could be so unkind to me. And in front of others." Tears trickled down her cheeks. Tears of regret. She would choose Marcán's rudeness over Pádraig's behavior in a heartbeat.

"I'll not speak a word against the man, Astrid. Ye should think on what ye were doing for Marcán to behave in such a way."

Astrid wanted to scream. She said nothing.

"Marcán would never belittle ye. He is a good man, but he will protect ye even from yerself. If any of the lads there thought to make free with ye and he believed 'twas yer behavior encouraging them? He'd not just stand by and watch."

His words could not have been truer, but she could not tell him that. He'd know something was wrong.

"Of course ye take his side."

"But I cannot understand why he allowed ye to go off with Pádraig alone."

"*I* was not so obvious as that! *I* snuck off with him." And more the fool for her disobedience. It was a mistake she'd never repeat if given another chance.

"And that confession will get ye a sore backside upon my return."

Her brother had questioned her about the ride by now, and Astrid had been satisfied to let him believe Pádraig had merely kissed her, though she'd made the honest admission that she had not liked it. If Pádraig had somehow done something to Marcán, she would never forgive herself for not condemning him further.

Her brother tossed her over his shoulder like she was a child, even slapping her bottom to still her objections, and headed back to the stone house he called home.

"Ye'll return to my wife, and I will go to the Meic Murchadha. If all ye've said is true, something is still amiss, as Marcán has not yet returned with the others. Ye best pray no offense has been taken and no blood has been spilled on account of ye."

She stilled. He had voiced her greatest fear.

When he set her down in front of the closed door, she spoke to him from her heart. "Oh, Diarmuid, I would be beside myself if any blood was shed on account of me." The tears flooding her eyes dripped down her cheeks. "Please! Go bring Marcán back."

He stroked her cheek, an unexpected display of comfort from her brother. "No doubt I will find them all passed out from overindulgence, and I will bring them home myself. The men, our mother, and the sheep. Ye will see my wife, the healer, and she will help lessen yer pain."

"She is a healer?" They both knew the scorn their mother bore for healers, but she held her tongue.

When they entered, the woman she'd only gotten a peek of earlier stood there, now fully covered. Mayhap a few years older than herself. She had long, brown hair and wide eyes. She was lovely.

"Astrid? Meet my wife, Aednat."

Astrid could barely contain her surprise and shock at this turn of events. Her brother had sworn off taking a wife. This woman must have charmed him powerfully to change his mind.

"For *now* ye may see to my sister's ankle while I retrieve the sheep and locate the men. Both of ye stay within!"

When he shut the door behind him, Astrid had to bite her cheeks to keep from smiling. She crossed her arms, not sure what to say. Ultimately, she decided it would be best to start with the truth. "I am very glad ye have wed my brother."

"Oh?"

Aednat's eyes spoke of a mischievous side and Astrid could not help but tease. "I thought he would never find a woman who could overlook his many faults."

"Has he so many?"

Astrid fought against the smile that threatened to

stretch across her face. "Ahh! Too many to speak of, but ye will learn about them all yerself, I am certain."

It became obvious that Aednat was holding back a grin as well. "I am certain."

Astrid finally let loose her laughter and Aednat joined in. What an unexpected pleasure!

"I must tease him even if he is not here to witness it." Astrid wiped the tears from her eyes, happy they were now tears of joy. A sister! Someone to talk to and share things with. How wonderful. Having a sister was something she'd always wanted but had never believed she'd have. "Ye are very beautiful. He must have been pleased to take ye to wife."

"I do not know. In truth, he did not have much of a choice."

Astrid gasped, her encounter with Pádraig swiftly coming to mind. "Tell me he was chivalrous with ye."

"He was! He just did not have a chance to say no. 'Twas for my protection. Sean—"

"Sean of Drogheda?" She spoke of the overking, whom Diarmuid had ridden out to meet these many days past.

"He *was* of Drogheda."

"Ah, I forget. I have not seen him much of late. He has always spent more time with my brother. How fares he? Is Thomasina big with child?"

"She is not. Lorccán is their last, and he is nigh on six years now."

The throbbing in Astrid's ankle was near unbearable, and she settled on the bench before she spoke. "When I was very young, our clans would gather for celebrations. That was when my father was still alive."

The memory of her father started her tears anew.

She had loved him very deeply. A handsome man and a great warrior with grand ideas of virtue and honor, he'd held every man in their clan to the same ideals. *His* father had been at the Battle of Clontarf, and that was something that was never forgotten. Though Brian Boru died that day, the unity of the people and the line of kings that followed continued still. They would not give up who they were and what they believed. And her father would never have allowed any of his men to treat a woman as Pádraig had treated her.

"But I am not allowed far from here now. My mother keeps me close to her side. I also think Diarmuid does not trust me to not make a fuss. He leaves me behind for his own peace."

Astrid lifted her gown to check her foot. It had grown quite large from her injury.

Aednat gasped. "Who has done this to ye?" She turned the leg just the slightest, inspecting the bindings. "This is not the way to help it mend."

"Meic Murchadha's healer covered it up." Astrid flushed at the memory of Marcán leaning against the door with his dark, brooding expression, looking on as the woman insisted it was Astrid's behavior that had brought God's wrath down on her.

"May I see it?" Aednat asked.

Astrid nodded. Aednat carefully unwrapped it.

"Does it hurt?"

The ankle looked terrible, all purple and black, and Astrid was overwhelmed with sadness. She had been in such a hurry to get to the Meic Murchadha, that was why she had gotten hurt. Foolish to a fault, she'd convinced herself all of her problems would disappear if she spent time with Pádraig and spoke to him of their joining. Instead, her problems were just starting.

"Astrid?"

Aednat's gently inquiring tone threatened to unleash the torrent of sadness in her, but Astrid cleared her throat and said, "I am often hurting myself. My mother says I am clumsy."

Everyone knew if her mother said it, then it was so. No discussion. No questions. No thoughts of yer own unless ye cared to listen to all the ways in which ye were wrong.

Lost in her thoughts, Astrid didn't realize Aednat had finished caring for her injury until she said, "That should ease the aching."

Astrid rubbed the clean, tight covering and smiled. "A much better job than the Meic Murchadha's healer."

"Did she put anything on it?"

Astrid shook her head. "She was more interested in speaking of God's curse on me, saying it was my behavior alone that caused me to have so many accidents."

Again, Marcán's expression came to her mind. Not exactly condemning, but he'd said nothing to silence the women either. Seeing Aednat's frown, Astrid wished she'd not been so honest in her answer. She did not want her new sister to think badly of her.

"Mayhap ye need to be more careful," Aednat said.

"According to her, 'tis irrelevant whether I am careful or not." Astrid decided to take a chance with Aednat. She could use an ally. "D'ye believe it as well? That God is angry with me?"

"I do not know how God feels, but were ye walking at a steady pace? Was the ground sound beneath yer feet?"

"Oh, no. I was hurrying along the sheep trail that connects our land with the Meic Murchadha."

"Rutted? And well worn?"

Astrid nodded.

"Then it would seem ye put yerself in harm's way by not giving the path the diligence it required."

Astrid wrapped her arms around Aednat, holding her tight. Astrid had done so many things wrong, she was beginning to feel cursed. She needed reassurance of God's love. "My thanks! I do not like to believe God is angry with me whenever something bad happens."

Aednat squeezed her back and asked, her voice muffled against her shoulder, "Is yer behavior so terrible that ye deserve God's wrath?"

Astrid pulled away. This was a question she didn't know the answer to. Marcán said she did things, but was it intentional?

"No! It's just that—" She wiped her tears before continuing. "I am of marriageable age… and… well, I wish to be married! Why would my brother not see to it? Am I never to be a wife?"

That was the real reason she had decided to find a match for herself rather than waiting for her brother. Pádraig had seemed like an ideal husband—pleasing to look upon, from a clan close to home, and a good warrior.

Only it had been the wrong thing to do. She knew that now.

"D'ye seek out men on yer own then?"

Had the woman read her mind? It seemed the answer would be yes, but Astrid could not confess to her what she didn't understand herself, so she answered as honestly as she could. "I enjoy their attention when they talk to me, but they seldom do."

And that was the problem. How was she to find a husband? If her brother was not looking out for her, she had no one looking out for her. Her mother wanted her to marry Pádraig, but that was mostly because Beibhinn wished to return to the Meic Murchadha.

Marcán protected ye once, but ye have no protection now.

Pádraig's words came back to her. Despite her belief that Marcán was a good man, she'd treated him like he was no better than a fly buzzing about her head. He had indeed looked out for her. More than she'd wanted him to at the time. She was wiser now. And with that wisdom came the realization she had not given Marcán, or his words, their due respect.

"And all ye do is talk?"

Astrid's face heated with shame. No matter what the men believed, she did not seek to be bedded before marriage. "I remain untouched!"

Her words sounded a bit harsher than need be, but Aednat did not seem to notice.

"For good measure, go to the priest with yer confession and be sure Diarmuid is aware of it." Aednat grinned. "And be more careful of yerself. That starts with being mindful not to walk on yer injured leg overmuch. It needs to rest to be healed."

"My thanks."

Astrid needed time to think, but she didn't want to rush off from Aednat. Listening to Aednat speak of *ri túath* Sean's decision that she and Diarmuid would be wed, Astrid longed for someone to make that decision for her. A husband was someone ye could talk to and share things with. Have children with.

66

Diarmuid would not accept that she was ready for marriage, but he was wrong. She was more than ready. His wish was for her to stay and care for their mother so he did not have to. It was not a kind thought, but sometimes it seemed to be the truth.

Chapter Six

Aednat had gone to fetch some eggs and Astrid, tired after a long night, had fallen asleep. Neither of them had thought of the danger.

Astrid awakened to a nightmare. Her new sister had been stolen by the men whose pursuit of Aednat had led to her marriage to Diarmuid. Astrid was flooded with guilt as she stood beside her brother and the men preparing to hunt down whomever had stolen his wife.

"And what of Marcán?" Astrid asked.

"It was as I said. They had passed out in a cave, though he swears they were not drunk. They will be here anon. Our mother as well. Marcán especially desires to speak with *ye*." Diarmuid mounted his horse and signaled the others to fall in line with him. "Have them follow me. I will track her down."

Astrid shivered, afraid to think of what Marcán wanted to say to her. "I did not know I needed to watch out for her, brother."

"Wheesht now, Astrid! I will find her. Do as I said!"

By the time she made it to the roundhouse, the horses coming from the west could be heard. Her chest squeezed the louder they got. When she caught sight of Marcán and the few men with him, relief soared within her. The feeling caught her unguarded, and she was struck by how much she had feared for him.

If he knew Pádraig had taken her home, he also knew she'd only pretended to retire for the night. That she had left the hut behind his back. He might have even confronted Pádraig for not seeking his permission as he should have. Marcán had clearly shown she was under his protection.

Dark and foreboding, Marcán sat high in his saddle, scanning the people who'd gathered around them until his gaze came to rest on her. The force of his attention made it hard for her to take a breath. He was menacing in the extreme and he had her in his sights—jumping from the horse before the beast had come to a complete stop, striding toward her.

His face lined with concern, he studied her. His hand came up and she thought he might touch her, but then it dropped back to his side. "What is amiss?"

Astrid swallowed the lump in her throat. "Aednat has been taken."

Stepping back as if he'd been struck, he quickly became livid. "When?"

His sharp tone made her jump. Her vision blurring

with tears, she confessed her guilt. "While I slept on their bed!"

His expression softened, but he was frowning. "I do not understand."

"Diarmuid left to find out what was amiss with ye when I told him ye'd not returned. He said nothing to me about keeping her hidden or protecting her. She went for eggs and never came back."

"And now the fresh casks of mead being poisoned makes sense." He spoke as if to himself before focusing again on her. "Black Oengus and his men had hoped to knock us all on our arses so taking Aednat would be that much easier."

"Diarmuid has gone to track down those who took her. He wants ye to follow him."

Marcán shouted orders over his shoulder, sending each of the men in a different direction to see to gathering enough supplies and horses, but he did not walk away. Instead, he stepped closer, leaning in, his eyes searching her.

Some inner turmoil twisted inside her that she couldn't name. His musky scent surrounded her and her pulse quickened. Not fear exactly. She would never fear Marcán. Excitement?

Then he closed down his expression and moved back. "Now will ye tell me what has happened to *ye*?"

Shocked that he could read her so well, she took a moment to respond. Hoping to distract him from whatever else he thought he knew, she said, "I am concerned for Diarmuid's wife! 'Tis my fault she was taken."

"If Diarmuid did not tell ye, ye could not have known." Marcán shook his head, his gaze still assessing her. "'Tis something else. Ye tell me. Now!"

How could he know? He couldn't. And she couldn't tell him. She still feared what Faolán would do, but Marcán was sure to hunt Pádraig down if he knew the truth. "Nothing, Marcán."

"Is it Pádraig?" His eyes narrowed even as the words came out. The man was far too perceptive. Mayhap he was a Seer after all, just as her mother always said.

"Pádraig?" She scoffed, attempting a nonchalance she did not feel.

His expression changed as soon as she said the man's name. It hardened into fierce anger, different from how he'd reacted to the news about Aednat. His men came toward him, mounted on fresh horses, and one on a lead for him.

"I am not finished with ye, Astrid. Ye *will* tell me."

When he turned toward the field, she was certain he was not seeing the animals. He swallowed, almost as if attempting to get himself under control.

Then he mounted but turned his horse back to her. "Which way did Diarmuid go?"

With a heavy sigh of relief, she pointed them in the right direction.

He spoke to his men, his voice low and commanding. "Go on. I will catch up."

Astrid gulped, shocked by his order. Marcán never sent his men ahead. He always led them. He stepped aside for no one but Diarmuid.

When he turned back to her, his expression was black.

"Ye *will* tell me what that ravening wolf has done to ye." His words were laced with unbending resolve. "And if ye hope to protect him by not telling me? Rest assured, I'll happily rip him apart piece by piece until I

71

hear the truth from *his* mouth."

His horse was racing toward the trees before her jaw fell all the way open. Astrid covered her mouth, her gaze dropping. She'd said nothing to indicate Pádraig had mistreated her.

How could he know?

What if he truly was a Seer? But Astrid could not believe that. He would never practice the dark arts.

She looked up to see Faolán emerging from the roundhouse.

"W-was that Marcán?" he asked, coming straight toward her.

She nodded.

He scratched his cheek before narrowing his gaze on her. "A-and ye?"

His words were packed with meaning, but she gave him a sad smile and met him halfway. "I am fine. Just concerned for Diarmuid's wife."

Faolán glanced off the way the men had gone. "But w-we have our o-own p-problems, ye a-and I."

His level gaze was unrelenting and heat rose in her face. She needed to stop this. When she began to push past him, Faolán grabbed her arm. While not a harsh action, it was not at all like Faolán.

"Y-ye lied to m-me about Pádraig."

"I did not! And ye've no reason to believe that."

He pointed a finger at the crook of her neck. "I-I do not know of a-any other way a w-woman can get a m-mark like that e-except by a man's mouth, suckling her hard. U-usually w-while he takes his fill of her."

Astrid immediately covered the place where he'd been looking. She met his gaze while her mind worked frantically to come up with a reasonable explanation. Damn her for not checking herself. Then again, she wouldn't even know what such a mark would look like, but Marcán would. He must have seen it as well.

The door to the roundhouse slammed open and her mother came out, a beaming smile on her face. "Astrid!"

Faolán stood his ground, lowering his voice. "If the man returns while I am in charge, Astrid, there will be blood."

Her eyes rounded.

"Astrid! Come hither!"

Astrid yanked her arm from him and hurried toward the roundhouse, turning the marked side of her neck away. Faolán followed close behind.

"Well? How was yer ride with the handsome warrior?" Her mother's eyes were bright with anticipation.

"Handsome w-warrior? Pádraig?" Faolán frowned.

"The most handsome," Beibhinn gushed. "A wonderful match."

He searched Beibhinn's face, and Astrid could almost feel the wind changing around them. "Y-ye would have a m-match with the man?"

The woman held up her hand, glancing around in a secretive way before speaking. "Ye must not say a word! Diarmuid has much on his mind, so I will see to my daughter."

Faolán nodded, his face an unreadable mask. "Y-ye w-would want this for yer daughter?"

Beibhinn's brows slashed down. "Are ye daft, man? I have said as much. Go! Go... see to the fence."

Now in a huff, she gave him her back. Faolán wandered toward the *ráth*. Placing an arm around Astrid's shoulder, Beibhinn turned her toward the roundhouse.

"How was yer ride?"

"Not as I had expected."

Beibhinn's expression was immediately filled with an emotion with which Astrid had become achingly familiar. Disappointment. "Oh, Astrid! Ye did not offend him, did ye?"

Astrid nearly choked on the very idea. "I did not offend him."

Pádraig's angry expression flashed through her mind. He had not liked being refused.

"Good. We do not want to do that. Pádraig has *always* been good to me, and that's all I can go by."

"I do not see Diarmuid working on any special alliances with them. Surely there is nothing that clan has that we would need."

Beibhinn gave her a bland smile. Her mother's belief that Astrid knew nothing was quite apparent. "Diarmuid is a warrior. He thinks like a warrior. He does not have civility and foresight—"

"Foresight?" Astrid's shocked tone had her mother studying her. "That sounds very much like a Seer."

Beibhinn's mouth dropped open before twisting into a tight smile. "And ye know I do not abide by such things. 'Tis merely the difference between men and women." She gazed off in the distance. "A man sees only a pretty face and a handsome figure, while a woman will see the children to come of the union. I can see the union will be a blessing for our clan."

Astrid could not be certain to which clan her mother referred—she'd made no secret of her preference for the Meic Murchadha—but the determined set of her jaw was troublesome.

"Their clan is very different from ours," Astrid said.

Beibhinn turned a sharp eye on her. "Of what do ye speak?"

"They are very… free with… their women. Not protective like us."

"I do not understand."

"The fathers of our children are always known because of the protection given us. Women."

"What are ye saying?"

"They are not as protective of their women as our men try to be."

"Ah, our men!" She laughed, a quiet, belittling sound. "Ye refer to Faolán?"

Astrid swallowed.

"Faolán mentioned to me that he helped ye with Pádraig."

"He did?"

"No doubt Pádraig was exhausted from the demanding ride. I believe Faolán only wanted me to know that the man had seen ye safely to our border."

Astrid scoffed.

"I am well pleased by that." Beibhinn heaved a great sigh. "Ye may not be able to understand this, but I have felt very much alone since I came to this clan. With yer father gone, I wish to return to my home. It would give me great pleasure to have my daughter by my side when I did that."

"Certainly I can understand that." And she did. But it was not reason enough for her to marry a man who would treat her badly.

Her mother tipped her head as if she were not convinced. "No matter. I will do what I can for ye."

"But—"

Her mother's piercing gaze halted her words. "Ye were not going to speak ill of Pádraig, were ye? He is of great stock. Ye will have healthy babies as often as ye can stand him coming to ye."

The heat rose in Astrid's cheeks. Her mother had never before spoken so blatantly about the intimacy of the marriage bed. Beibhinn had borne only three children—Diarmuid, Astrid, and Fergus—which might mean her husband had not come to her often.

With that, Beibhinn went back inside.

The kind gray eyes of Astrid's father came to her mind. She could again see her mother stepping away from his embrace, a common sight. Astrid had never shrunk away from her father. He'd always known how to make her feel special. He'd always thought she was good enough. He used to smile down at her and smooth her hair. "Ye are a sweet thing, my Astrid," he'd say.

Astrid became overwhelmed with sadness. She needed time to think. Rounding the main house, she continued on toward the small buildings behind it. She ducked into the first one. A small room. Her refuge. She slid to the floor, tucking herself between the new barrels stacked two high, and lowered her head into her hands and sobbed.

Chapter Seven

Astrid had stayed clear of her mother for the rest of the day. Thankfully the woman had found a place to rest from her excitement at the Meic Murchadha. Astrid had tried to rest, but the sounds of others nearby had invaded her refuge and constantly put her on alert.

Working on the evening meal with the other women gave Astrid a sense of purpose and calm. It made everything seem normal. No secrets to hide. No lies to keep straight. No one to take advantage of her.

She slammed the bread dough on the table again.

"Ye best hurry with that one, Astrid!"

Joan was gray-haired and stout, with three dark hairs adorning her chin. She was also the cook, although most of the women pitched in unless they had other duties. Joan was the one who decided who would be doing what. If she liked ye, she gave ye the job ye wanted. If she didn't like ye, it was best to watch out.

Being the daughter, and now sister, of the chieftain had many benefits. Astrid received first helpings of food, the others deferred to her for decisions over Joan, and she was given first choice whenever new provisions were acquired. Some through battle and some through merchants that traveled from town to town. Items from faraway places like fine silks, exotic lotions, and herbs. Though their visitors were few, she made the most of those purchases and even more of the spoils of war.

"What ails ye that ye're so droopy with yer work?" Joan adjusted Astrid's neckline, their eyes locking for the smallest second, before she spoke again. "Ye're usually such a fine help to me."

Astrid nibbled at her lower lip, not sure what to say. She was usually talkative with Joan. The older woman was genuinely interested in her and what she had to say. Unlike her mother, who just wanted someone to listen to *her* talk. But if Astrid suddenly became quiet around Joan, the woman would certainly notice it. Maybe she would even mention it to Diarmuid when he returned.

"I have my menses." Astrid looked away.

"And that usually makes ye even more talkative." The woman knew everything, so of course she knew about *that*, too. Joan stopped her chopping to put a hand to her hip. "That bread has done nothing to ye as far as I can see."

Glancing down, Astrid realized she'd been taking out her irritation on the overworked ball of dough. She laughed and scooped it into the waiting pan. Joan grinned as she added the pan to the overloaded hearth.

"Faolán seems quite concerned for ye as well."

Astrid scanned the area. With the rains outside, there were far more people within than was usual at this time of day. "What has he said?"

The little woman snorted. "That one talks constantly. Who can listen to him?"

She knew without looking that the woman's eyes were still on her. It was only because Joan was concerned for her, which Astrid appreciated most times. Not this time, though. Astrid need only convince Joan she was fine, and she'd stop worrying.

"Joan, I am—"

"Astrid!" Beibhinn's sharp voice rang through the hall so loudly that all present ceased talking and turned to look between her and Astrid.

Astrid's face heated.

"God in heaven, what have ye done now, darling?" Joan's words were intended for Astrid's ears alone.

"She does not like my helping with chores."

Joan winked to her and then crossed to meet Beibhinn, intercepting her before she could reach her obvious target.

"Beibhinn, are ye not feeling well?" Joan asked.

Her mother's gaze shifted to Joan, her eyes rounding, and she halted. "Of what d'ye speak?"

"Ye look a bit… mottled."

"I do?" Beibhinn reached up to feel along her cheeks and then her throat.

"Is it yer throat that's bothering ye then?"

Beibhinn put a hand to her throat as if deciding if she had difficulty swallowing. When Joan's eyes flashed to Astrid then darted toward the door, Astrid did not hesitate to accept the gift.

"I… I did feel a bit lightheaded this morning."

The voices faded behind her as Astrid made her way into the yard. She blew out a breath, hands at her hips, and wondered what her mother could be going on about now. But Astrid could certainly guess. She wanted to question her about the ride home with Pádraig. Astrid was thankful Faolán had sent him on his way and her mother had not had a chance to interrogate him herself.

Her mind is too busy.

That's how Marcán had described Beibhinn to Diarmuid. Was that two summers past? They hadn't realized Astrid was nearby. It had been extremely hot and the sun relentless, beating down on everyone and everything. Too hot even to cook or to eat. The older men had gone off to hunt in the forest, hoping to find a cool respite. The younger men had been delegated to stay behind for protection. Marcán and Diarmuid were just coming into their own as warriors at the time. Both quite impressive.

Forgotten as usual, Astrid had been lying between the rowan trees and the honeysuckle bush. The bush close enough to surround her with the flowers' sweet aroma. She had learned to lie perfectly still to keep the bees from her. The scent was intoxicating and the leaves of the bush and the trees offered plenty of shade.

Diarmuid and Marcán had taken off their *léines*, clothed only in their short *braies*, and stretched out resting—Marcán on the wooden bench, Diarmuid on the ground.

"I know she's a foolish woman. Who could believe *ye* were a Seer?" It was Diarmuid who'd voiced the question, of course. Astrid had often wondered at it herself.

"Her mind is too busy," Marcán answered. "She needs something to keep herself occupied. Something to keep her out of trouble."

"Ah, that one is never out of trouble. *She* is the reason my father always found a reason to be somewhere else."

His voice got quieter. "Kane told ye that?"

"I believe it is how he felt. He told me to either take a caring woman to wife or never marry at all."

"D'ye think of him often?"

The silence had Astrid looking toward them, waiting to see how her brother would respond. His arm was draped over his face, shading it from the sun.

"I wonder how he would have advised me in certain situations. Like when the Meic Murchadha came to offer his daughter to me. Would he have had me accept?"

Astrid had no notion of when such a visit had taken place, but she was usually sent off on some wild goose chase when anyone came.

Marcán nodded, a smile in his voice. "Daimhin? Comely. With breasts that hang like heavy fruit. More than a handful."

Astrid cupped her own breasts, which were more than her palm could hold, but surely he meant *his* hands. Marcán's hands were huge. She was of an age that all those changes were well underway, but Daimhin was not that much older than her. How was she so well-endowed by this time that men spoke of her thus?

"Ho ho! *More* than a handful, is it?" Diarmuid laughed. "And she did not mind me noticing them either."

"And what else did ye notice?"

Diarmuid turned to Marcán, a huge grin on his face. "Everything she wanted to show me. I did not refuse her."

"Ah, a true gentleman."

"I am that."

Astrid was on the verge of sleep when they finally spoke again.

"I do not wish to take a wife. Kane was so unhappy in his marriage. Why should I believe mine would be any better?" Diarmuid's words surprised her. The *derb fine* had to decide on their *ri túaithe* within the next few weeks since the death of their *tánaiste*. Kane's successor had survived long enough to bring word of their father's death, but the wounds he'd received were mortal. A slow, long-suffering death. Everyone assumed Diarmuid would be chosen as the next king, and it would be unusual for a *ri* to remain unmarried for long.

"Do not despair. Ye have not found the one who sparks yer attention *and* pleases ye in bed. Although ye've done yer best with the bedding."

Astrid covered her mouth. She knew some of the women were regularly taking the men into their beds, but it shocked her to realize her own brother was one of them.

"The ones I bed have bedded many before me."

Marcán said nothing.

Diarmuid shrugged. "They believe their experience will please me. What would please me more is if Daimhin would speak to me as if she were even half witted." There was a pause before he continued. "And what of ye, Marcán? The women are more than pleased with ye, but I do not see ye feeling

82

the same toward them."

The sigh Astrid heard brought a lump to her throat, it was that sad. She watched Marcán when he answered. "The one woman I want is as elusive as smoke."

Setting her mind to the puzzle of which woman he might fancy, she forgot to be quiet when she rolled over. She could still see Diarmuid's scowl when he turned toward her. He bolted upright at the waist, ready to yell at her, but Marcán put out a hand to halt his angry advance.

"Astrid?" Marcán's voice was calm. "Come."

He sat up more slowly than her brother, his eyes on her while she scooted out from beneath the bush to stand. Her gown was drenched with sweat, flat against her. For a moment she wished she were young again so she could take off her gown as they had doffed their *léines*. Then she noticed Marcán's eyes, watching her. Noticing everything. The sweat puddling between her breasts and molding the coarse fabric against her, scratching her tender skin.

"Come closer, Astrid." His eyes finally came back to her face and she did as he told her.

"Ye've been told not to sneak around!" Diarmuid all but barked the words at her.

But Marcán patted Diarmuid's arm to quiet him, his eyes staying on her. One blue. One green. He watched her as she pulled the damp gown away from her chest.

"Were ye sneaking?" His voice was low and quiet, his eyes bright.

She swiped at a drip of sweat slipping down her face and then another slipping between her breasts. "No."

Marcán continued to watch her hand. "Did ye hear what we spoke of?"

"Let it be, Marcán! She's like a little rat sneaking in where she doesn't belong."

"Ye underestimate yer sister." Patting the empty bench beside him, he said. "Sit!"

"Enough, Marcán." Diarmuid directed his anger at his friend, but his friend never flinched. That intrigued Astrid. She couldn't remember Marcán ever losing his control.

Marcán's eyes did not leave hers, not even when he spoke to Diarmuid. "Ye make me even hotter with yer growing irritation. Calm yerself."

"I am for the shade of the *ráth*," Diarmuid said.

"The animals are hot, so the stable is hot!" Astrid spat the words at her brother, who just shook his head.

That got her a chiding expression from Marcán, and her face heated. He had included her and even stood up for her. Then she had immediately acted like the child her brother thought her to be. Mayhap Diarmuid was correct about her. When she turned away, Marcán put a finger to her chin and gently turned her face back to his.

"When the men are returned, I am going to the lough, Marcán. Mayhap when ye are done here ye will join me." Diarmuid delivered the words like an ultimatum before he huffed off.

Astrid scrunched up her face and stuck her tongue out at his retreating back.

Grinning, Marcán said. "Is that a show of proper respect ye give yer brother?"

"He does not deserve my respect."

He held her gaze. "Every warrior deserves respect from ye."

Astrid stopped just short of rolling her eyes, and he smiled as if he knew that. She remembered the warm feeling that had bloomed in her chest. She'd liked that he knew her so well he could guess what she was going to do.

"Can I come to swim at the lough with ye?" The words tumbled out before she'd given them enough thought, but she wiped at the sweat dripping from her chin. And waited for his answer.

He dropped his head, the first time he'd stopped watching her. His wide expanse of chest grew even wider, and when he looked up again, he had a hard expression. Tight. As if he were flinching. Uncomfortable. He must have realized Diarmuid would not be happy with him if he said yes to her.

"Ye best not, Astrid. Not this time."

So she did roll her eyes and didn't care what he thought about it, but he surprised her by reaching out to caress her cheek. His eyes intent on her.

Now, all these years later, Astrid put light fingers against her cheek, imagining his caress again. Suddenly overly aware of everything around her and at the same time nothing at all, she saw again that intent gaze on Marcán's face, the way he'd glanced at her lips. The way he'd looked at her that day…

Her jaw dropped.

Reality slapped her in the face.

When he'd glanced at her lips, she'd assumed it was because he saw crumbs. She'd wiped her mouth with the back of her hand.

Astrid had a hard time catching her breath.

She was truly an idiot. And Marcán?

"Oh." She groaned, standing alone in the yard

while everyone else went about their duties.

Marcán had wanted to kiss her. *She* was the girl he'd mentioned—the one he fancied. The thought sent heat rippling through her innards.

Only she had badly misunderstood him at the time. Diarmuid treated her as a nuisance more often than not, and she'd assumed his best friend felt the same way—at once fond and annoyed.

She had been too young to understand his feelings.

Her mother told her often enough how demanding husbands could be. Her advice was that it was best to marry a warrior since he would spend much of his time away.

And yet… if Astrid had a husband like Marcán, certainly his attention would be welcome. He was intelligent, respected, an exceptional storyteller. The tales *he* told never bored her. She hugged herself, swamped with emotions.

Astrid pressed her lips together and moved away from the roundhouse, heading down the road to Diarmuid's little home. No one would look for her there, and she needed time to think, to consider Marcán's words and actions in this new light.

It wasn't until the cock crowed that Astrid finally stirred. She'd fallen asleep in Diarmuid's bed, exhausted in both body and soul. No daylight showed around the door. It must still be raining, and the damn rooster didn't even know whether it was morning.

Poking around the fire, she hoped for a spark but found none. She shivered from cold. She'd missed the evening repast to avoid Beibhinn, something she could not regret, but her stomach was growling now. That she'd slept like the dead should have been a reprieve from her troubled thoughts, but she hadn't stopped dreaming. And all her dreams had been of Marcán.

She now saw every past encounter in a new light, including the game of Pull the Ribbon, in which he'd given Astrid her first kiss. He had wanted desperately to kiss her, and that was why he'd tried to convince Diarmuid to back down. He hadn't wanted their kiss to be so contrived, so public. And Astrid had believed he was angry!

Did a more naive woman even exist? But what to do now? She'd clearly seen his interest in her, but she had no way of knowing if those feelings persisted. Astrid went back to the bed, pulling the red squirrel covering atop her. At the Meic Murchadha, he'd *carried* her to the healer in his strong arms, seen to all her needs, and kept her in his sights the entire time. Had he merely been acting the part of her leader and protector, or was there something more?

Her heart soared at the very idea of having a man like Marcán care for her. She would be treated like a special treasure. Never yelled at in anger. Never pushed around. He would hold her in his heart. Except it might be too late…

Years had passed since that day near the honeysuckle bush. She had been so mean to him, snapping at him, even fighting him when he sought to protect her from Pádraig. The tears slid down her cheeks to disappear in her hair.

And she might be forced to marry someone cruel like Pádraig. No! Never him! But to remain alone?

That was no life. Happy couples smiled and laughed. They touched each other in love. And if she had children, they would laugh with her and hug her and love her. Her mother never hugged anyone, not even little Fergus, but her father had. He'd hugged all of them, even taking Fergus up on his shoulders to march around the village. Certainly Marcán would be that type of father. And whenever Astrid's mother had been cruel to her, her father had stroked Astrid's hair as if to say, "Take none of this to heart, *a ghráidh*."

"The loss of something I didn't even know I had would be the cruelest of all fates." She whispered the words aloud, giving them the solemnity they deserved.

A loud knock on the door startled her into sitting up. No one knew she was here. Who would they be looking for? Not her. She decided to remain quiet. The knock came again, even more insistent.

"A-A-Astrid?" It was Faolán.

She snuggled under the covers, turning away from the room, feigning sleep. The door opened. Faolán walked in, but he wasn't alone. Quieter footsteps came closer, but someone was waiting at the door.

"Astrid?" She was so surprised to hear a woman's voice, one she didn't recognize, that she sat up. The lovely Daimhin stood there—a dark mantle covering her, her long, shiny hair glistening with rain. She really was quite attractive, even with a slight darkening on her jaw. "Did I awaken ye?"

Astrid pushed down her hair, trying to sit up despite the softness of the bed. "I have overslept."

Daimhin smiled. A genuine smile. "I understand. This rain…"

Faolán stood at the door, hand still on the latch, and Astrid seethed inside. God help him if he thought to leave her here with this woman. She sought solitude, and both of them were interrupting that. Astrid slid her legs to the side of the bed, preparing to stand, but Daimhin put her hand out.

"Ye need not rise for me." Again she smiled. "My father wished to extend a personal invitation to ye to attend a feast in three days' time."

Astrid tucked her legs back under the covers. A quick glance toward Faolán showed no sign he was going to come to her rescue. "To what purpose?"

"My father has been very ill, and he was not able to properly greet ye the last time ye were with us. My brother has... shown an interest in ye, so my father wishes to meet ye."

Swallowing was difficult. Faolán crossed his arms, his eyes squinting as if he were observing a hare gripped in the claws of a hawk, waiting to see if the hawk would be successful.

"Me? And my mother?"

Beibhinn had told Astrid she'd been to visit Doran, the *ri* of the Meic Murchadha and Pádraig's father, while Astrid was with the healer.

"Oh, she could come, but 'tis ye he wishes to meet."

They had met several times. There was more that Daimhin wasn't saying. "Please give yer father my regards, but I am not able to come at this time."

It would not be seemly to disclose any personal situation to a rival clan, even if they were peaceful at the moment. She did not expect Daimhin to question her further.

"Unable for what reason?"

Astrid flattened her lips. "'Tis best not to discuss these things now, but do extend to him my appreciation for the invitation."

Laughing slightly, Daimhin glanced down before facing her again, her bottom lip between her teeth. "I would call it more of a summons, Astrid."

Faolán shifted, but Astrid did not even glance his way. He had left her here to ward off this woman alone, and she would do just that.

"I am not coming, Daimhin. Ye may call it whatever ye choose, but the decision is mine."

For a moment everything seemed to stop. Astrid could not be certain if it was shock or fear she saw in Daimhin's face, but when she spoke, she was once again the gracious daughter of the Meic Murchadha. "I will be sure to tell him what ye said."

Faolán opened the door for Daimhin, and she left without a backward glance. Astrid avoided eye contact with the man, even though she could feel his gaze on her. How had he known to find her here? Was he watching her?

Dropping her face into her hands, she struggled against tears. These games could not go on. Pádraig was going to act as if he had an interest in taking her to wife? His interest had been in ravaging her. Now what game was he playing at, talking to his father? She had been foolish not to see him for the brute he was.

She pushed off the bed and went to the washstand, sloshing cold water over her face. If Astrid did not stand up for herself, she could spend the rest of her life married to a lecher of the worst kind. What she had foolishly considered an option for herself was not. It was better to be alone.

Chapter Eight

Astrid was not able to avoid her mother once she had returned to her regular duties. The woman was unrelenting in her praise of Pádraig, and Astrid cringed every time she spoke of him, wondering yet again if she should confess what he had tried to do. Hoping to find peace and some time to think, she retreated to their garden.

Faolán found her there. He was relentless. "H-have ye told Beibhinn about Pádraig yet?"

"I heard *ye* have said something to her."

He frowned. "I-I gave no details."

"And I told ye. Nothing happened." Astrid usually enjoyed working in the garden, but there was no peace to be found here today, not with Faolán trailing her, insisting she talk of things she would rather forget.

"A-and I-I know ye l-lied. Someone should be told the truth, or h-he will get away with i-it a-again and again."

Astrid snapped the peas she sorted with a vengeance. They would be a nice addition to the evening meal. "How d'ye know 'tis not the case even now?"

Damn, he had done it again, getting her to make a near confession.

She looked up at him, but his expression was unchanged.

"What I meant to say is that if Pádraig is such a vile man, surely he will be vile to someone else as well." No, that wasn't exactly what she had meant to say to him either. "*Stop*, Faolán. Do not speak to me of this again."

"There's been word. D-Diarmuid has located A-Aednat."

Astrid's joy could not be contained. "Is she unharmed?"

"I-I do not know for certain, but I-I did not hear she w-was hurt."

"That is wonderful news." Astrid squeezed her hands together.

Faolán was more reserved, giving her a cursory glance. "D-Diarmuid will be r-returning, A-Astrid."

Tears flooded her throat, but she swallowed them down. "Ye need to let this go, Faolán. No good will come of it."

"Punishment that i-is due for a w-wrong done to u-us? O-or d'ye argue 'twas not w-wrong?" His eyes narrowed as he continued to watch her. "A-am I-I m-mistaken in a-all this? Y-yer mother speaks h-highly of the man. D-did I-I-I-interrupt what ye had a-agreed to?"

Damn tears. She swatted them away, gazing anywhere but at him. People were coming out of the roundhouse now, no doubt in expectation of Diarmuid's arrival. Some were glancing toward them with curiosity. Her shame was all encompassing. The only way to get Faolán to drop his inquiry forever would be to claim she'd sought the attentions that had been forced upon her, but she could not do it. She could not stand to see the look of disappointment in his eyes.

"Ye did not," she said softly. "I cannot speak to my mother's choice of whom she will praise. Suffice it to say, she is not always correct. Neither in those she condemns nor in those she praises." Her voice trembled. "I thank ye that ye came when ye did."

She opened her mouth, struggling for control, turning away from the crowd gathering behind her. Faolán's eyes never wavered from her.

Shouting started behind them. "'Tis Diarmuid!"

Cheers went up. Astrid wiped at the tears.

"D'ye see his wife?" someone asked.

"I believe I will always be alone." Astrid struggled to not sound quite so pathetic.

"Ah, and there is Marcán." Another said.

Her gaze turned toward the procession, and when she turned back, Faolán's eyes narrowed.

"Shall we?" Astrid asked.

"Let us w-welcome A-Aednat back."

Faolán put a hand to the small of her back and they moved to the front of the crowd. Marcán had dismounted to come up alongside Diarmuid, who was holding his wife in his arms, a stern look on his face. A hush fell over the crowd, the people no longer certain a celebration was in order.

Astrid willed her new sister to stir, anything to indicate she was still alive, but she did not. With the greatest gentleness, Marcán took Aednat from Diarmuid, holding her against his chest. The look in his eyes was hopeless.

Aednat teetered at death's door, but Marcán could find no injury to cause it. Black Oengus, the bastard who'd kidnapped her, had held her in a throat clutch, which could mean her neck was broken. Even now her head rolled against his shoulders.

"Bring the healer." Diarmuid gave the order as he dismounted.

Marcán's concern for his friend was great. His lovely bride had not yet awakened, her face pale. When Diarmuid moved to retrieve her, Marcán said, "Allow me to relieve ye, Diarmuid. Ye've held her the entire way, surely ye can take a rest."

"I cannot." The pain in Diarmuid's face pulled at Marcán, and he relinquished her without further comment.

Astrid's light hair caught his attention. She stepped closer, and he sighed. The mere sight of her was as refreshing as sunshine on a rainy day.

"I will bring the healer to ye," Astrid said.

That her eyes did not glance his way was not a surprise, but still he watched her until she disappeared into the roundhouse.

Some of the men in the procession were still bleeding from wounds they'd received in the battle against Aednat's kidnappers. That bastard Black

Oengus was dead, but his men had escaped. That and Aednat's injury made the whole battle seem like a loss, but they had indeed been the victors, without a single loss of life among their own warriors.

At the back of the procession were the spoils. Women and children who had been left behind by the defeated warriors. The children were wide-eyed with fear, but most of the women knew the way of it. Some of Marcán's own clansmen had slaked themselves on the women by this time. That was the way of battle. Diarmuid had been beside himself with concern for his wife, so Marcán had protected the women who were not willing. Most were willing, which made it go easier for them.

Black Oengus's clan had been without a home, running from capture most of the time, but the man had nonetheless possessed powerful ambitions, envisioning himself as the next High King of Éire. He had enlisted the help of a witch, and it was the old hag who had told him of the legend regarding the Great Healer. The man hadn't known for certain if Aednat was the one, but the uncertainty hadn't deterred him from stealing her away. He would have used her in front of the entire clan in an attempt to steal her power. He and Diarmuid had witnessed his rough treatment of Aednat as they were preparing to attack the camp.

"Philip, can ye see that the hostages are fed?" Marcán asked the warrior who came up behind them.

"Hostages or slaves?"

Marcán glanced toward the sorry group, barely clothed, and scrawny from a lack of food. "They have nothing and no one, or they would not have been with the likes of Black Oengus. Treat them as slaves and distribute them accordingly."

"I will question them about relatives and have word sent."

"And ye will see to their care. I will attend Diarmuid." Marcán had chosen Philip for this duty because he had a kind heart. He knew Philip would not allow them to be abused.

Philip ushered the women and children inside the roundhouse, but Marcán paused to take a deep breath to settle himself. He was exhausted. Blood and mud spattered his clothes, the scent wafting up to him. His mail, removed by this time, was in an even worse condition.

The horses were being seen to. He couldn't even remember the last time he had eaten. The battle had been tough against surprisingly well-trained warriors. They had fought like men with nothing to lose. Worthy opponents.

Not long after, Marcán finally settled himself on the garden bench. He nodded to the men who wandered past. Their arms around their smiling wives, who were no doubt relieved their husbands had survived another battle. Children skipped alongside them, laughing. Their loved ones had been there to greet them.

The thought made him feel more alone than he had in a long while.

"Mead?" It was one of the women from Oengus's clan. She had long, auburn hair and bright green eyes. A pretty lass with a brazen look. Marcán glanced around, searching for Philip, but saw no one with her. He frowned.

"Philip told me to bring this to ye," she explained

before he could question her.

"My thanks." He drank it down without ceremony, he was that parched. Closing his eyes, he struggled to stay awake.

"I can bring ye more." The lass stood before him still. "Ye look to be done in."

Marcán was not about to get into a discussion with a slave. He preferred to stay away from them in general. "I do not believe Philip wanted ye to tarry here."

With a nod, she turned about just as the door to the roundhouse swung open. Like a cool breath of refreshing air, Astrid came toward him. She noticed the other woman, surprise evident, and seemed to assess her as they crossed paths.

Marcán dropped his head in his hands.

"Thank ye for bringing Diarmuid and Aednat back to us." Astrid settled beside him, leaving a discreet distance between them. "Ye look done in."

He smirked. "I have heard as much."

"Is there anything I can get for ye?"

Somewhere in his mind, he struggled to determine if her behavior was as unusual as it seemed.

"I need to see to Diarmuid," he said.

"Surely he can wait until ye've at least rested?"

He must look near death to elicit that type of concern from her. He tried to rally, but found he could not even lift his head.

So he simply sighed, a heavy sigh. "Unfortunately, I am not convinced his lady will survive."

Astrid stood. "Oh no!"

His eyes flew open, rounding. She clutched her arms to her chest, her face a mask of dread.

"Oh, Astrid." He gripped his hands to keep from

reaching for her. "Forgive my heartless words. Ye do not need to hear such things." He was babbling like a damn fool and shook his head. "Please do not feel ye must stay here with me. I am fine, but I am not fit company."

The auburn-haired lass returned. Closing the door behind her, she waited until Marcán's eyes found her. Then, a fresh horn in her hand, she approached him with determined steps. Looking into her eyes, he knew her willingness. Suddenly, it seemed to matter very little that she was a slave. He needed to be close to someone now, if only to convince himself he was still alive after seeing so many dead.

"My thanks." He sipped from the horn, his gaze never wavering from the lass.

Astrid coughed beside them. "Well… I will return inside. Maeve is with Aednat now. Ah"—she turned to the lass—"Merewyn? Is it?"

"I am called Merewyn."

Marcán was not surprised that Merewyn's smile was so fetching. In fact, there was nothing about her he did not care for. This may be a slave he took for himself.

"Ye've been given to me," Astrid said.

Astrid would own her? Then she would definitely be off limits and his disappointment was acute.

Something stirred at Astrid's tone. It had sharpened. Marcán looked on, intrigued by this unexpected turn of events. So much so he felt a second wind, his tiredness leaving.

He sipped at his mead, the lass's eyes on Astrid alone now, her backside to him. A fine arse, but when he glanced at Astrid, he found his gaze returned. His chest tightened. *That* was the face he wanted to see looking up at him as he sought his release. Those were the eyes he wanted to see closing in passion as he rode her. That was where he'd prefer to see his needs met. Raw desire slammed into him. Desperation. It wasn't possible to take a full breath.

"Ye can sit with the others and eat," Astrid said to Merewyn, "but remain there until I come for ye. Do not venture out again."

Marcán could not be certain Merewyn did not glance his way before she obeyed her mistress. His attention was elsewhere.

Astrid swallowed, her neck exposed now, the bruise he'd seen earlier barely visible. It was enough to remind him that he had things to settle with her. A good reason to keep her in his company.

"Sit." He indicated the spot beside him.

"Let me see to yer bath, Marcán."

Dumbfounded, he simply stared at her retreating back. It was usually Joan who saw to such things for Marcán. He was shown this deference as a sign of his value to the clan. An unmarried warrior was usually seen to by the king's wife, but until now Diarmuid had had no wife, and the late king's wife, Beibhinn, chose to ignore him.

The thought of Astrid helping him in his bath stiffened his prick in an instant. Followed by the realization that it would not be a good idea to allow her to touch him. The simple act of assisting in his bath could be his undoing; he wanted her that much.

The mere thought of the scent of her hair, the feel of her hands, her bosom innocently pressing against him was enough to banish his exhaustion. He was painfully hard with need for her. Standing, he turned away from the opening door. He needed to get out of this, or she would finally learn just how besotted he was with her. And she would not be happy.

Chapter Nine

Watching as Marcán's eyes traveled the length of
the new slave, assessing her, had made Astrid feel like
she was being doused with cold water. The man was
considering taking the slave to his bed! He wanted her.
She was a pretty thing, obviously intrigued by
Marcán—what woman wouldn't be?—and as far as
Astrid could tell, she'd given every indication she was
more than willing.

A sick feeling had unfurled inside Astrid.
Certainly Marcán had taken plenty of women to his
bed, or mayhap he went to theirs as Diarmuid had.
Astrid was not ignorant, but she had never actually
thought of Marcán in that way—until now. She
struggled to contain the emotions that threatened to
overwhelm her.

If only she'd trusted Marcán instead of Pádraig, the disaster in the woods could have been averted. Pádraig would have forced her. Forced her to do anything he wanted, and she would not have been able to stop him. Marcán had warned her, he'd tried to protect her, but she'd fought him every step of the way. She had been determined to speak to Pádraig. Alone and in the dark had been fine with her.

Shame washed over her at her own ignorance, her stubbornness, her inability to see what was right in front of her.

Ye need to save yer maidenhead for the man who'll protect ye, even from yerself.

A never-ending job!

When she stepped back out in the darkening night, eager to show Marcán how much she respected and valued him, he was nowhere in sight. Panic fluttered in her chest. She went back inside and grabbed her mantle, her eyes scanning the room. Merewyn sat with the other women, eating quietly by herself. Another look around assured her Marcán had not come inside while she was making arrangements with Joan.

The woman looked at her now, a question in her eyes. Astrid smiled and Joan went back to seeing to the bath water she'd ordered. It would be brought to the little building in the back since space in the roundhouse was at such a premium. Wives were happier to welcome back their men from battle after all the blood and sweat had been washed away.

Back outside, Astrid pulled the covering tight around her and headed toward the trees.

"Marcán?"

An owl answered her. Trying for a lightheartedness

102

she did not truly feel, she said, "I know my Marcán and ye are not him."

"*Yer* Marcán?"

The low voice vibrated through her and nervous excitement danced along her skin. She turned toward the shadows where the voice had come from just as he stepped toward her. He stopped.

"I am beyond exhausted. Forgiveness, please." He roughed up his hair. "My ears are playing tricks on me."

Although his face was in shadow, she knew exactly the expression he wore. A quiet smile. His eyes bright and clear. And intent on her. Astrid took a step closer.

"I am readying a bath for ye." She swallowed right before she reached a hand out to him. "Come."

She couldn't be sure, but she sensed there was some inner struggle.

Don't give up on me now!

When she moved closer, he finally closed the distance to her and accepted her hand. Heat shot up her arm, warming her innards. His palm was rough and she realized she'd never actually touched his hand before. It was quite large, making her hand seem as small as a child's.

"I need to get ye something to eat as well."

She started to move away, but he stood fast. "What are ye about, Astrid?"

Closing her eyes, she basked in the sound of her name on his lips. How could she have been so blind? When she opened her eyes, he had moved into the light. That same light revealed her expression to him, and he searched her face as if looking for answers.

"Are ye trying to talk me out of telling Diarmuid about Pádraig? Ye needn't bother. I have done so."

His tone was even. Steady. And his words meant far less to her than the sound of his voice. That was like a caress and she struggled to keep her eyes open and focused on him. He frowned.

"Ye can go back in, Astrid. I can see to my own needs."

Merewyn's willing expression flashed through her mind, but something in his eyes told her the regard he had once borne for her had not faded. He was protective of her, attentive, and not at all like her brother. He tilted his head now, his eyes squinting as if trying to read an unclear sign. And there was a good chance he *could*. He knew her very well. Better than she knew herself.

"This has nothing to do with my punishment."

"'Tis not up to me to say what that punishment may be. I hold no sway over yer *ri túaithe*."

She wetted her lips. "That I know. And I also know ye have every right to see to any punishment yerself… as 'twas *ye* I disrespected with my disobedience."

"I will not discipline ye."

Astrid could feel a scorching heat, but she wasn't sure if it was from her or from him. "No. Ye never have."

"And I will not."

Astrid wasn't sure what to say to convince him that she was sincere in her desire to see to his needs. His chest rose and fell and she noticed his breathing getting faster. Looking from blue eye to green eye, she said, "Allow me to assist ye. I have wronged ye, and I know that. Believe me, I do. I ask ye to allow me to show ye the respect due every warrior. Respect I have been sorely lacking."

Marcán would admit to being taken aback at the confession. This was so unlike the Astrid he knew. The moon shining on her face revealed her dampened lips with their soft pink hue, slightly parted, calling to him. Urging him to move in closer. Marcán struggled with the crazy idea of kissing her. Then she smiled at him, and he'd swear it was a smile of encouragement.

He was more exhausted than he had believed.

She was asking for his forgiveness. That was all. Her sincerity was obvious, and he knew he was damned. This might be the hardest trial he had ever faced. He could not refuse her, but he tried one last time to avoid the inevitable.

"I believe ye, and I offer ye my forgiveness with nothing more required of ye."

Her eyes rounded. "Please."

That simple request was his undoing. "Then let us see to this bath."

She turned, his hand still in hers, and led the way. The sight of her nicely rounded bottom was much more appealing than any slave's. He looked heavenward and blew out a breath.

God, help me keep my mind on anything other than what's about to happen.

The stars twinkled back, and he had the strange feeling he'd received an answer to his prayer. It wasn't the answer he'd expected.

The wooden tub sat in the middle of the small space. Baskets and new oaken barrels were stacked alongside the walls, making it an even tighter fit for the two of them. Marcán turned toward Astrid, and she lifted his *léine* over his head with no hesitation. His tired imagination heard a gasp of pleasure from her.

With nerves of iron, he willed himself to remain unmoved by the gesture. His tight *braies* might go unnoticed if he quickly submerged himself. But the water was hotter than he'd anticipated, and he had to wait to sit all the way in the tub.

Astrid had turned away to drape the blood and mud caked garment over the barrels. When she turned back to him, he took a deep breath and sank into the water.

"Is it not overly hot?" she asked, a cloth in one hand and soap in the other.

"I am fine." Marcán gritted his teeth, the steam rising around him, lapping against his chest. He felt like he was cooking, being prepared for a meal. With his knees bent up in front of him, he leaned forward to offer his back to her. Better to get this done quickly.

She hesitated but a moment before dipping the cloth into the water and lathering it. Surrounded by her scent, he closed his eyes in agony. "Yer own soap, Astrid?"

More sweet torture—and it would be clinging to him for many days.

"It is the best we have."

Her hand against his skin was gentle, the swiping motion precise as she traced from shoulder to shoulder, working her way lower. He leaned his forehead against his knees.

God, don't let her be gentle.

"Ye needn't be too gentle. I am a warrior after all." His laugh sounded stilted, but Astrid showed no sign of noticing.

She increased the pressure, her hand moving more quickly as she made her way down his back.

"I have helped Diarmuid with his bath, Marcán."

Her matter-of-fact tone helped settle him—it sounded more like what he would expect from her.

"I do not know why I never offered ye the same."

Because he usually made sure to stay clear of her after a battle, just as he had tried to do this night. Her insistence, however, had pushed him too far. The need to ease her guilt was the only reason he had agreed to the arrangement.

When she reached his bottom, he pushed back against the wood. She had no choice but to remove her hand from the water.

"That is fine. I can do the rest myself."

She frowned at him, the single torch casting strange shadows on her face before he turned away.

"Ye need help. I will help ye."

He tightened his jaw, watching with horror as she soaped the cloth again. He was going to burst into flames at any moment. When she slapped the cloth against his chest, her eyes met his, an intimacy that pleased him for a moment—until he remembered that this was not to be. He looked away.

With a slower motion, she swiped the cloth across his chest. Her scent rising to him, he resisted the need to close his eyes in pleasure.

"I can do this myself." He struggled to hide the arousal from his voice, trying for a firm tone. He refused to look at her, even when her hand slowed to a crawl. Even when her hand moved across his chest for the third time. Rubbing. Caressing.

He fought the need to look at her—and lost. Her

eyes were fixed on the movement of the cloth across his chest. She appeared mesmerized at the sight of him. The soap made the motion a gentle slide. A thousand sensations prickled across his skin. And then, without planning it, he took his arm out of the water and wrapped his fingers around her neck, bringing her lips to his.

He was ready for her to slap him, but he couldn't stop himself. Overcome with exhaustion and need, he hardly knew what he was doing. As if moving in a dream, the kiss he'd waited so long for happened with such slowness, every detail burned into his memory. Her eyes meeting his. Widening, but with pleasure rather than surprise. He definitely saw pleasure, just before they fluttered shut.

Her lips were as he'd imagined, rubbing across his in gentle exploration. He would have groaned, but feared the moment would be broken and she'd yank away from him. When the tip of her tongue slid against his lips, they parted and his moan finally escaped. His eyes flew open, but she did not pull back. Instead, she pressed herself against the tub, moving her tongue more fully into his mouth, its sweetness flooding his senses.

He forced himself to move slowly despite the pain in his groin, the unrelenting need for release. She was kissing him back! His Astrid was returning his kisses with sweet abandon! And things would never be the same.

The pleasure of Marcán's lips on hers exploded inside her. It could not be more different from Pádraig's kiss. This was a man holding back, in control, allowing her to move in whatever way she desired. This was a man who cared about her, and that knowledge gave her courage. When her tongue moved against his, he met her stroke for stroke, sucking her into his mouth to experience their joining more fully. His moan had set off not alarms but a deep well of need. A need that seemed right. A need that she knew he could see to when she was ready. It would be safe to open herself up. To open herself to *him*.

A sudden chill caught her attention and she shivered, the drastic difference between the air in the hut and the heat rising up from her core, no doubt.

But Marcán broke the kiss, concern on his face. "Are ye cold?"

She smiled, her breath easing out between her parted lips. Pulling away from the tub, she stood. Her gown was soaked. She might as well be standing there naked, and Marcán's hooded eyes were taking in every bit of her. She shivered again, not from the dampness, but from the look of longing on his face.

How easy it would have been for Pádraig to force himself on her. She could not have stopped him on her own. Her innocence would be gone now, ripped from her. Was it not better that she give herself willingly to a man who would treat her gently? One who cared for her?

Reaching for her hem, she doffed the gown.

His eyes locked onto hers and she could actually feel his desperation. Clothed in only her sleeveless undertunic, she urged him out of the water. The touch of his lips was tentative now, but she wrapped her arms around him, pulling him against her. He was hard for her and she canted her hips to feel him more fully against her.

Marcán yanked back, his breath heaving with his

struggle for self-control. "Astrid, ye do not—"

"I do. Stop being my protector. Ye are the one I need no protection from."

"Aye, ye do!" His eyes were wide as he stepped out of the tub. "I am a man in great need."

Her eyes drifted close at his words. A wistful expression. When she opened them again, he was hit by the intense power of her gaze. She wanted him. "Please, Marcán."

He had never been in such need. And here the love of his life was offering herself to him. Her eyes assured him she knew what she was doing. A hiss escaped him as he struggled with himself. Her lovely body before him, all but naked, the material clinging to the breasts he'd only dreamed of until now, and the surprisingly dark patch of hair between her legs beckoning to him through the thin cloth. That was his undoing. He lowered his head as he gripped the underside of her breast, raising it to his watering mouth.

She gasped and he was lost. Both hands slid under the dampened garment until her chilled skin was pressed against his palms. His tongue flicked against her nipple as he raised the material higher. His hands came to a sudden stop on her soft thigh. One hand came up to grip her other breast for his desperate mouth, but realized he couldn't move the other. He was unable to cover the short distance to touch her most intimate spot. It had been so long that he'd wanted her. He had never thought to be here. What if her need was not as great as his own? If Astrid did not want him, he had nothing.

With the smallest movement, he finally touched

her. He was not disappointed. Near overwhelmed, he reluctantly released her breast to snuggle into her neck.

"Are ye giving yerself to me, Astrid?" His words sounded as desperate as he felt.

That her breath was as labored as his was a boon. Surely he could stop now and be satisfied until they were wed. When she widened her stance, his hand slid more fully between her legs. Pulling back, he gazed into her eyes, seeing only her passion. He stroked her, his fingers damp with her sweetness, and pressed his lips together as he entered her. And again. Her hips rocking with each motion. He tried to convince himself he could stop if she said the word. But she said nothing, so he asked her again.

"D'ye wish me to take yer maidenhead, knowing all that it would mean to me? Knowing all that it should mean to ye?"

She leveled her gaze at him, passion hooding her eyes. "No one else but ye."

Sweeping her into his arms, Marcán turned left and then right, frustrated by the lack of proper space. She giggled slightly and he gazed at her with his most formidable expression. "Ye'll pay a high price for that show of disrespect at my frustration."

A deep frown covered her face as she no doubt considered what he could mean. She would know soon enough. The thought of tasting her gave him such a heady sensation he had to close his eyes and take a steadying breath.

"Not the best place for a seduction," he said.

"It suited me fine."

He paused as he considered her words, searching her face. "So this was *yer* seduction?"

"This was *my* seduction."

Overcome, he let her find her footing and then he was pressing her against the wall with his kisses. She responded just as fiercely, her arms wrapping tight around his waist to flatten him against her. As she undulated against his length, he was struck by how adept she was at this. How passionate.

"I believe ye still need to remove something," Astrid said. Her words were wrapped in need.

He yanked at the bottom of her undergarment, where it was still hiked to her thighs.

Slipping his hands beneath the rough material to slide along her silken curves, he got only as far as her exposed breasts before he was feasting again on her, his fingers continuing their assault. Kissing her belly, he glanced up to see her watching him as he knelt before her, his lips traveling lower and lower. With a hand wrapped around each thigh, he met her eyes and lightly nuzzled her thatch of dark hair. And again. When he stroked her with the tip of his tongue, she sunk her teeth into her bottom lip.

And he licked her wetness, unable to stop his eyes from closing in ecstasy. Her scent called to him and he tasted her again, more fully, watching her again. Her concern quickly shifting to pleasure, she threw her head back, her hands drifting to his head. He parted her thighs, giving himself better access.

When she moaned, he nuzzled her more and then added a finger. Then another. Until her moans sounded from deep inside her throat. In one motion, he raised her leg, catching her knee in his arm and stood to press into her, yanking down the last bit of protection keeping him from her.

"There is not a chance ye'll be another's now. I've tasted ye," he slid his ready tarse along her wetness,

112

"and ye'll be mine in truth as ye've always been."

Opening her eyes, she took a deep breath and searched his face.

Awe-struck at this turn of events, he said, "I'd never thought to have ye myself."

"Marcán, I have always been yers. I was just too blind to see it."

With a solid thrust, he entered her, then stilled. Her hands squeezed his shoulders and her beautiful face had the look of betrayal.

"That will be the only time there is pain. Yer maidenhead is breeched. Ye've given yerself to me." He let out a slow breath as the words sunk in. He would have her forever now. The delight of that thought was cut short by the look on her face. He had to show her how good it would be between them.

"I was enjoying yer touch, but now…"

With the most controlled motions of his life, he pressed deeper into her. Her eyes narrowed as if in expectation of more pain, but that tight look soon fell away. He was overcome by her exquisite tautness, eager to be fully sheathed. His focus on her, he slowly entered her, deeper and deeper, until she had accepted his entire length. He fit perfectly inside her and he stilled, his eyes closing, enjoying the feel of her around him. Panting slightly from the exertion of self-restraint, he was determined to wait until she was ready for more. He was where he'd never thought to be.

"I knew ye would feel like this." He couldn't stop from sharing with her.

When she squeezed around him, his gaze flew to her and she smiled, a sly smile. "I can feel the length of ye filling me." Her words were breathy.

"Let me show ye more." He started with a steady rhythm, her legs wrapped around him for support. She canted her hips, a pleasant surprise that brought a groan from him.

"That's it." He entered her more insistently. "I knew ye would feel this good."

Moaning was her only answer, and he picked up his pace, prolonging her pleasure as she pulsed around him. He wanted her to know without a doubt they were meant to be joined together like this. The two of them. Always.

Her eyes opened and she looked toward the door. "What was that?"

Marcán stilled to listen. "I heard nothing." He took a deep, steadying breath. "Shhh, now. D'ye still feel me inside ye?"

Her eyes drifted shut and her head settled back against the wall. The tightening grip on his shoulders was her only answer. He entered her hard before pausing. "I've wanted ye like this forever."

And again, moving faster and giving in to his own need. He stilled, pressed into her, spilling his seed.

"Ah, Astrid." He sighed. "Never have I felt this complete in a woman's arms."

Marcán managed to move a few of the barrels to clear a spot for them to lie down. Astrid's mantle and his bathing cloth, slightly damp from where he'd gently cleansed away her virgin blood, served as their pallet. Resting her head on his solid chest, Astrid slept in his warm embrace. Her dreams were of sunny days beside clear loughs and children playing nearby.

Warm kisses across her shoulder awakened her.

"Mmm, that's it." Marcán's quiet voice was like a caress. "Open those beautiful eyes."

She did, impaling him with a look. "Ye believe my eyes are beautiful?"

"Ah, *grádh,* there is nothing about ye that is not beautiful." He continued with feather kisses along her shoulder before rising over her and taking her face in his hands. He followed a trail to her mouth. His lips were gentle but insistent, and she opened her mouth to him.

"Mmm, nothing."

His hands explored her body as if he couldn't get enough of touching her, and her eyes drifted shut in pleasure. When he clasped a breast and lowered his mouth to suckle her, she let out another moan.

"And that is a surprise." His words did not interrupt his ministrations.

She decided it wasn't actually necessary to open her eyes, not when she could *feel* so much more with them closed. "What is a surprise?"

"How much ye speak to me in yer passion."

That did require her to open her eyes. "Speak to ye?"

"Sighs too deep for words."

It was a familiar phrase. "Is that not referring to prayer?"

"Sighs of pleasure are still sighs too deep for words." Marcán smiled. "God created us for this pleasure."

It was strange to hear him speak of God. The priest put so much emphasis on abstinence or only joining for procreation.

"Then pleasure is not a sin?"

"I believe God created us to find pleasure in each other, just like this. Bone of my bone. Flesh of my flesh. And he said that it was good."

"As husband and wife."

Marcán gazed into her eyes. "Only a formality."

He gripped her hand, intertwining their fingers, then closed his eyes. "May God, who knows the heart of all His children, bestow His blessing on our union, that we shall never again seek another or cause dishonor to His name. Amen."

"Amen." Astrid was awed by his devotion to her. "Ye do still love me?"

"I have loved ye forever, wanting no one but ye for my wife."

"I was so blind."

Marcán kissed her lightly. "Ye are here now. Ye are where ye should be."

Astrid did like the sound of that. "Oh, but I did not call out yer name! Did I?"

"Ah, my love, ye will. This was only the first of many times when I will bring ye to yer release." He exhaled, dipping his head into the crook of her neck. "And I am wanting ye again."

Astrid hadn't missed the persistent length of him nudging her. She quirked a brow.

"But I am not heartless. Ye will be sore."

He put his head on her shoulder, looking down upon her nakedness, a hand following along.

"Ye are the most beautiful woman in the world."

"Ye said I did not compare to Daimhin." She remembered the moment well. It had happened the day she'd hidden in the honeysuckle. Marcán had told her that she couldn't swim with him and Diarmuid and then, like an idiot, she had blurted out, "Would ye say I was as comely as Daimhin?"

His eyes had darkened and he'd given her a quiet smile. "There is no comparison."

Her comment must have caught him off guard, for his hand stilled on her skin.

Astrid regretted the words as soon as she said them. It seemed very petty to bring it up after he had lavished such love on her.

"I have never believed that. Ye are more lovely to me than a sunrise on a clear day." He propped himself on an elbow and looked down at her. "There is no one that compares to ye."

Realizing she was an idiot, she rolled her eyes before facing him. "Ye had said there was no comparison."

He lightly traced her lips with the tip of a finger. "And there is not."

Bending closer, he took her mouth again. His hands sliding along her stomach to nudge her thighs apart and slip his fingers between them. With a gentle touch, he stroked her. "Is there soreness?"

He spoke the words against her lips and his exquisite touch mesmerized her.

"I do not care if there is."

Marcán broke the kiss, a frown creasing his brow. "That is not the answer I seek. I will never hurt ye. I do not want ye to associate anything with our joining but pleasure." He continued his movements. "And pleasure ye will get."

Astrid gasped as his fingers became more insistent.

"My size gives ye pain."

Her breathing started to match the steady pace of his fingers' movements.

Scooting down, he lowered his head, his tongue joining his fingers. And she couldn't hold back the moan.

"Mmm." Marcán's sound vibrated through her.

Astrid became overwhelmed with intensifying need. When he lifted his head and watched her, she wanted to be embarrassed, but she became lost to his touch. Like water pitching over the rapids, he sent her over the edge. She pressed against him and was met with wave after wave of pleasure.

"Ah, ye are beautiful to watch." His whispered words matched the awe on his face. She sighed as the pulsating of her body slowed down. Her eyes drifted shut and he snuggled close to her, pulling her into his arms. "I find it hard to trust that ye are here with me like this. I have loved ye for so very long."

His steady breathing lulled her into sleep. A peaceful sleep where she stayed with the man who loved her.

Chapter Ten

Astrid awoke to Marcán's arms wrapped around her. His face so close, his gentle breath teased at her hair. She sighed her contentment and snuggled closer.

"Mmm, I have been waiting on ye. An eternity now!" Marcán's low voice vibrated through her.

"An eternity? Oh my!"

He picked his head up, rising on an elbow to gaze down at her. A single finger traced along her face. "I wanted to see those beautiful eyes looking at me with love."

She smiled, barely able to contain her joy. "And d'ye see that? For that is how I feel about ye."

"I've loved *ye* forever while ye barely noticed me. I do not expect ye to return my love, Astrid. Not yet."

Astrid scoffed. "Then why is it I am here? Naked

in yer arms?"

His gaze dropped lower, a smile blooming. "I do not ask why when I have received a wonderful…" He kissed the tip of her nose. "…never expected…" He kissed her cheek. "…longed for gift."

With the gentlest motion, he caressed her lips with his own, gliding over them.

"I do love ye. *Mo chroí go deo thú*," he spoke the words between slow kisses. "Make no mistake on that. Ye are the fairest woman I've ever laid eyes on, with a spirit to match."

She opened her eyes, brimming with tears, when he looked down at her. "Ye believe I have spirit?"

"I *know* ye have spirit, lass."

Her lips quivered. "Having spirit would give me great pleasure."

"As it should."

"Diarmuid sees me as a nuisance more often than not. My mother always finds me lacking, never speaking any words of encouragement to me."

His eyes rounded. "This is a new beginning. Ye will no longer receive harsh words or belittling."

"I know ye would never speak to me thus."

Marcán tilted his head. "And *ye* will receive no harsh words or belittling from anyone."

When she took a breath to argue, he set a finger against her lips. "My wife will not be treated with less respect than she deserves. Not ever. Not by anyone."

"But I—"

"As yer husband…" A smile spread across his face, as bright as the sunshine. "I do so like the sound of that!" He kissed her, a deep, passionate kiss, before continuing. "I will not allow such treatment of ye."

She nodded, not quite sure how he would be able

to change the way people treated her, but it was beyond endearing that he wished to try. "How could I *not* love ye, Marcán?"

With a steady gaze, he searched her face.

"Everything I sought from any man, I received from ye. Ye always listened to me when I spoke, considering my words. Ye were always kind and thoughtful. That I did not believe ye would ever feel that way about me—"

He held up a hand. "So ye had set me aside as someone who would not be interested in ye?"

"Ye did always seem more interested in Diarmuid."

"Astrid, I am a bit older than ye. I did not wish to scare ye away with how much I wanted ye as my wife. I needed to wait until ye were ready to receive my attention."

She giggled. "It did please me when ye gave Diarmuid a talking to every time he belittled me."

"I was merely biding my time." His bright eyes clouded. "I did not expect ye to start showing interest in every other man save me. Even as a lass full grown, ye still didn't see me standing right beside ye. It near killed me."

She cupped his cheek. "And yer patience is commendable. Mayhap I lumped ye together with Diarmuid. I realize now ye were never the same."

"Never!"

"Ye always watched over me as if I was yers, protecting me."

"And ye fought me every step of the way until I knew—I *thought*," he corrected himself, "—ye would never be mine. And here ye are!"

"Where I belong."

"And I will never give ye up."

With delicious abandon, he took her mouth and her heart sang. The soreness nigh gone, they made love slowly. Enjoying each other. He worshipped every bit of her, as if to ensure her of the great worth she had in his eyes. And she loved him back in every way she could until they fell exhausted in each other's arms.

The cock crowed in the distance, and she became overcome with sadness.

"I have no desire to leave this place. I want to stay with ye."

"And I want ye to stay. I do not like the idea of going back to the way 'twas. We should approach Diarmuid this very day."

Her heart quickened.

"Ye do not agree? What would ye have us do?"

She hadn't realized she was so easy to read. She would need to work on that, but she did appreciate him seeking her input. "I know ye have duties to see to."

"That is true. No doubt, I have been missed."

She snorted. "And they'll assume ye are with some woman."

"Ah, they will not know I am with my betrothed!"

"But I am not under yer protection as of yet."

His hand stilled where it had been caressing her arm. "Ye have always been under my protection. Diarmuid expects it."

"I mean… if Pádraig comes back."

Marcán sat up to look at her, his heart hammering in his chest, but this time it was not from desire. "What is it he did to ye? I will see ye avenged."

"I did not heed ye, Marcán."

Marcán could not agree more, but when he took

her into his arms, she shuddered. "What has he done to ye, *grádh,* that ye tremble at the memory?"

The longer it took her to gather the courage to tell him, the more his trepidation grew. The harder it became to take a breath.

"He… he demanded I give him release, and he was angry when I refused."

His chest tightened with rage, but he continued to hold her, wanting her to finish her tale.

"I was sore afraid he would rape me. He… he said I was nothing but a tease."

She paused, still trembling in his arms. He stroked her hair.

"'Tis what a man says to put questions in a lass's mind when she tells him no," he said.

When she sat back, she averted her gaze.

"Pádraig assured me we would speak to Diarmuid about our joining—"

"What?" Marcán fought the urge to jump to his feet, to demand explanations. Instead, he sat perfectly still. "What joining?"

"I thought… I thought our clans joining, his and ours. I thought it would be agreeable. I… I wanted so badly to be married…"

Marcán remained silent, but he was unable to keep the anger from his expression. When she glanced at him, she immediately looked away.

"That was why I wanted to speak to him. When ye… interrupted us—"

"No, Astrid, I did not interrupt ye speaking to the man. I interrupted yer being raped by the four of them." Marcán blew a breath, hoping to calm his frustration at her innocence. Even now, her wide-eyed expression showed her lack of understanding. "Ye could have spoken to him in the visiting hall, where everyone could see ye."

"I know that now. I should have heeded yer warning." Her small voice spoke of her shame. "I did not believe he would behave so badly, that he would not listen to me, but he didn't hear anything I said. He just wanted to…"

"Have at ye." Marcán met her gaze when she finally looked at him again. "That was what the man wanted from ye."

"I know that now." She repeated herself in the same quiet voice. "And when he told me we would need to speak to Diarmuid to make plans, I realized he still intended…"

"To take ye!" Marcán struggled against the chords of betrayal her words struck in him. He had loved her for so very long, but she hadn't known. He must remember that. She was not betraying him or his love. "Did ye really want to marry such a man as that?"

Her inability to even voice the words reminded him again that she was innocent.

"I did not know him. He did not seem so bad until we were alone together."

Marcán wanted to remind her that she had been warned but held his tongue. She had not believed his warning. She'd thought he was being overprotective for Diarmuid's sake.

Astrid took a deep breath. "I am of an age to marry, but my father is dead and made no such agreements for me. I have a brother who still sees me as a child…"

He shook his head. Clearly she was no child.

"…and refused to make any moves toward that end."

His spirited lass had thought to see to her own betrothal! So she'd sought out Pádraig Meic Murchadha's attention? Not the choice he would have gone with. She deserved so much better. Of course, a better-behaved lass would not have wandered off in the middle of the night. She would have stayed with her mother. But a better-behaved lass was not what Marcán wanted. He wanted *this* lass.

He should have voiced his own desire to take her to wife long ago. Then this never would have happened.

"My mother said the Meic Murchadha—"

"Yer mother?" Marcán was instantly alert. "'Twas yer mother who put the idea of marrying Pádraig in yer head?"

And her mother knew of Marcán's feelings toward her. Everything seemed to fall into place.

"Well, she mentioned him a few times…"

And he knew his lovely lady. That would be all her active imagination needed before she started taking matters into her own hands.

"…and the advantages of an alliance with her clan."

"*Her* clan?"

"My mother is from the Meic Murchadha clan."

"Did she mention any of these 'advantages'?" He did not want to frighten her with his intent gaze, so he swiped an imaginary hair from her shoulder. And lovely shoulders they were. They could easily be her best asset now that he had seen her naked, but no, those lovely breasts called to him.

Glancing at her face, he licked his lips.

"Did ye hear me?" she asked.

"She mentioned nothing specific," he echoed her words.

Lowering his head, he sucked in one rosy peak and it tightened on his tongue. Met with her gentle sigh, he accepted her invitation. She pulled him closer to her, arching toward him.

"Ye have the loveliest breasts." Thoroughly aroused now, his voice was low. Seductive. He cupped both breasts, their bounty overflowing his hands, and nuzzled into her neck. "I would like to take ye again, but ye've yet to tell me what I asked ye."

"No. I... I believe I did."

"Did the man lay his hands on ye?" He licked her ear with a quick flick of his tongue over her lobe. "Tell me now, Astrid."

"He groped me... everywhere... and would have done more, but Faolán heard my call to stop."

Anger ripped through him at the thought of the man touching her. His gut tightened with the need to learn more. To get specifics. Her reluctance to discuss it told him it would not be an easy task.

No offense against a woman went unpunished.

It was her father's own code, one that Diarmuid also followed. The need for revenge cut deep, but he was determined not to show it. Not now.

Slowly pulling away, he offered her his sweetest smile. "Now that was not so difficult, was it?" He kept his tone steady, wanting to soothe her, but his need to avenge her had cooled his ardor. Slightly. Her eyes rounded suddenly, and he was overcome by the intensity of her gaze.

"Being with ye now. Here. I had no thought that this is what it could be like." She palmed his face, her hand warm against his cheek. "To be with someone so caring. I did not know..."

"Shh," Marcán said, pulling her face to his bare

shoulder, only to feel her tears sliding down his naked chest. "Now is all that matters."

Astrid nodded against him.

"*I* care for ye now just as I have wanted to care for ye for so long." He withdrew to watch her expression when he spoke the next words. "No one will take ye from me. No one! Ye are mine, and I will see to ye in all ways. Ye have nothing to worry about from *him*." He could not bear to say the man's name.

She kissed him.

"Ye are well worth the wait, *a ghráidh*."

"Astrid!" someone called outside.

Astrid gasped, a look of fear washing over her face, and started to jump up as if she'd been caught doing something wrong. He stilled her, waiting for her gaze to focus again on him. Then he took her hand and they slowly rose together, his eyes never leaving her face.

"We have done nothing wrong, Astrid. If someone comes? So be it. This was a private moment for us, but our love was never intended to be a secret."

Visibly strengthened by his words, she took a deep, cleansing breath. He looked for their clothing, helping her to dress first.

"Remember my words." He pulled her silky hair out from beneath the material. "No matter what happens."

He smoothed the long tresses down her back, then stood before her. "D'ye wish to go with me when I approach Diarmuid?"

"Now?"

"Of course now."

Astrid nibbled at her lip, glancing away, a deep furrow on her lovely face. "He has much to see to now… with Aednat not well."

He turned her face back to his, smiled, and said, "Ye will allow me to decide when? I cannot promise I will set aside our own pleasure for another's despair. I have wanted ye as my wife for a very long time."

Her eyes rounded, the hint of a smile on her lips. "Well, ye must be kind, Marcán. Diarmuid is overwrought now."

"So ye would have me wait? And I must sleep without ye by my side?"

She nodded. "Out of consideration for them and what they are going through."

He kissed her then. The sweetness of her lips and the passion with which she kissed him back were a boon that he hoped would see him through until she was less concerned for Aednat and Diarmuid.

"Astrid!" It sounded like Astrid's new slave.

Astrid tensed in his arms.

"Remember what I said," he told her.

Stepping away from him, she again nodded. He was filled with an overwhelming urge to pull her back. To keep her at his side always. To protect her from others. To not allow anyone to touch what they had shared. He shoved the feeling down, this sense of dread, and stayed his hands.

"I will go first," she said.

Her hand went to the latch, but he stilled the movement. He did not speak until she raised her gaze to him.

"We do not need to go out separately!"

Right before his eyes, the lovely flower he'd seen blossoming into its full beauty seemed to close up.

"My mother…"

Resentment swelled inside him—that woman would be the death of him—but he stepped away

128

from the door. "I love ye, Astrid."

Opening the door, she smiled back at him and was gone. He closed the door and stood there, his forehead pressed against the rough wood, feeling like all the light had just gone out of his life.

"There ye are." It was Merewyn.

"I told ye to stay with Joan…"

The voices faded as they walked away. Marcán shook out his *léine* and drew it over his head. The urgency came back, even more powerful this time. It became so overwhelming, he jerked the door open. She disappeared beside the roundhouse, Merewyn close behind. Too far for him to call her back.

Turning back into the room, the memory of their lovemaking came back in full force. The sound of her voice confessing her love, and his own assurances of her worth. It would take a hundred more such affirmations to counter the damage her mother had done to her. That Beibhinn cared only for herself had never been more apparent. It had galled Marcán these many years. A dangerous woman. And the damage she'd done to her children was not limited to Fergus. Marcán decided to stay closer still, hoping to ward off her poor treatment of Astrid.

That the woman hated him was obvious. Beibhinn hated him with an unimaginable passion. Unable to keep Diarmuid away from him, she'd taunted him since he was very young, even putting a hex on him. Unheard of from someone who claimed herself to be such a God-fearing woman.

Her claim that all Seers were from the devil was something no one disputed. It was commonly believed they were in the same league as witches. But did not God alone decide what color a person's eyes would be?

He must have been ten and five, just back from his first battle and feeling quite full of his own importance, when he'd first overheard her speaking of his eye color. It was right after Maeve had been accepted into the clan as their healer. Intrigued, he had stopped to listen, hiding behind the open door of the roundhouse. When Beibhinn had loudly proclaimed that anyone with two different-colored eyes was a Seer, Marcán had become so incensed he'd shoved the door shut and stepped into the room.

"Marcán." The woman had had the decency to look ashamed.

"And who is this handsome young man?" Maeve had smiled, showing no indication she'd noticed his eye coloring.

"I am called Marcán." Livid, he had kept his eyes on Beibhinn, nostrils flaring. "And this may be the wife of the *ri túaithe*, but she is wrong in what she is telling ye."

Beibhinn's face had turned beet red. The feeling of gratification had been heady. When he'd noticed the look of fear Maeve gave Beibhinn, he'd added. "As ye can see, I have two different-colored eyes and I am a warrior, not a Seer."

Maeve had shifted. "I have heard yer name mentioned, as well as yer ability in battle."

"And this woman should have something more to do than gossip," Marcán had said. "'Twas just this week the priest spoke against such devil's work as that."

Later that day, it had occurred to Marcán that his *ri túaithe* might not have appreciated such treatment of his wife. Much to his surprise, Diarmuid's father had actually laughed at the tale—but he had also issued a warning about his wife's vindictive nature. He had heard plenty of tales since, many of them from Diarmuid himself, that had proven the man right.

Now Marcán hoped to wed Beibhinn's daughter. She would fight him every step of the way, but it wasn't up to her. It would be up to Diarmuid to accept their union, and Marcán had no doubt his friend would. He stepped into the sunshine. Faolán and Philip passed him on their way to the roundhouse.

"Marcán." Faolán tipped his head but stopped a few feet away. "Go o-on, Philip. I-I will be there a-anon."

Faolán came over to him. The man who had stopped Pádraig's advances on Astrid. Apparently, he had perfect timing.

"Faolán."

Marcán wondered if Faolán knew what he had saved Astrid from. There was some discoloring on his jaw, a cut above his eyes, but there was no telling how he'd sustained the bruises.

"Were ye in a fight whilst we were away?"

"H-horseplay. No more."

Asking him flat out would indicate Marcán was in Astrid's confidence, which he was not yet ready to reveal.

"W-we missed ye a-at the celebration last night," Faolán said. "Though 'twas a quiet celebration out of respect for o-our king and his w-wife, w-we looked for ye to tell us o-of the battle."

Marcán sensed the accusation in his voice, so he countered it with his own. "I would prefer to wait until Aednat can also join us." He blocked the door when Faolán attempted to peer inside. It would be important to tread lightly with this. At least until his betrothal to

Astrid was announced.

"Did y-ye sleep in here l-last night? A-alone?"

Again, something in his tone did not sit well with Marcán.

"D'ye not have duties to see to, Faolán?"

The man narrowed his eyes. "I-I take my duties very seriously, a-as well ye know."

The duties he didn't mind doing. Diarmuid did not entirely trust this man, and while Marcán was grateful for Faolán's role in protecting Astrid, Marcán had to agree. "Then ye best see to them."

"O-one o-of those duties i-is protecting our w-women. That includes A-Astrid."

"Is there something ye wish to tell me?"

"Tell *ye?* No." Determination covered the man's face. "A-a special lass, that o-one."

Damn!

Marcán refused to flinch. "We all feel that way about the sister of our *ri túaithe*," he said.

Faolán's jaw visibly tightened, his animosity toward Marcán all but pouring out of him.

"I-is that the w-way ye feel a-about her, M-Marcán?"

Marcán gazed out toward the field, crossing his arms about his chest, ignoring Faolán's unrelenting gaze. While Marcán had no problem telling this man or any other how he truly felt about Astrid, she had asked him to wait. As difficult as it was, he wished to honor that.

"I feel just fine about her." Marcán pointed toward the far side of the field. The raised dirt wall protecting the animals was more prominent from this angle. Faolán's job was to secure the palisades atop the banks as needed. "And I see some damaged stakes that require repair. Come find me when ye're done with that."

Disappointment at the order was quickly replaced with anger. "But I-I a-am to relieve Diarmui—"

"Rest assured. *I* will see to Diarmuid. *Ye* do as I command."

Marcán went back within, shutting the door as the man huffed away. Back in the enclosed space, he breathed in the scent of Astrid that still lingered. Nothing about her should have surprised him after all these years of knowing her, of desiring her, but her passion was even more intense than he had guessed. It near overwhelmed him until he was struck with how well matched they were, how satisfying it was to be with a lass who always demanded more.

Taking the dry cloth from the side of the bath, he headed down the road to the stone longhouse, built in the style of the Norsemen, where Diarmuid sat with his wife. Marcán prayed he was wrong about Aednat's condition and that she would recover quickly. The man was smitten with her and the realization was hitting him hard. If the situation were less dire, Marcán would have laughed. Diarmuid finally understood how it felt, being helplessly in love with a woman who was his entire world.

Chapter Eleven

Merewyn's incessant chatter was trying Astrid's patience. At first, she'd believed the girl was interesting. She certainly had a great amount of knowledge. Walking into the roundhouse with Merewyn at her side—chatting away—had made Astrid feel less conspicuous about her long absence. Now, hours later, Astrid felt like a prisoner to the girl's mouth. She couldn't seem to get any distance from her. Her only choice was to send her somewhere else.

"Merewyn?"

The auburn-haired lass ceased her talking and turned to her with an expression of anticipation. "What d'ye need me to do for ye, Astrid?"

And just like that, Astrid felt like an unappreciative mistress. Merewyn was trying to please her. Earlier, the smaller children had been stomping all over her last nerves, and Merewyn had helped calm them, telling them in an even tone that their mistress preferred the sweet clover to the bitter dandelions. Settling beside the hearth, Astrid held the mending in her lap. That her fingers refused to stop shaking and her nether regions were more than tender was not Merewyn's fault.

When Merewyn settled on the ground beside her and took the *léine* with the torn elbow out of her hands, Astrid tried not to sigh in relief.

"Sometimes 'tis difficult to settle down to work." Merewyn paused, a great crease in her forehead as she pulled one thread and then another, trying to work out the mess Astrid had created. "And ye do seem to be having quite a bit of difficulty. D'ye not care for children?"

"I love children."

"Ah, then 'tis all the same feelings causing yer grouchiness."

The woman's perception was a bit too sharp, but her ability with the needle could not be denied.

"Glad I am that ye are well-trained in mending."

Astrid glanced toward the door again. She'd hoped Marcán would follow her in, but there had been no sign of him. All the men were missing. And though many worked the fields, it was more likely the warriors were preparing for another battle. There were men who had escaped Oengus's camp, men they would wish to find and imprison.

"He went to see Diarmuid." Merewyn's voice was so quiet, Astrid wasn't sure she'd heard her correctly.

"Who?"

Merewyn gave her a wide-eyed glance before returning to the mending. "Ye know."

Astrid swallowed. "I do not."

With a huff, Merewyn dropped the material in her lap, glanced around the empty room, and returned Astrid's gaze. "I am a good help to ye, am I not?"

"I have yet to decide—"

"When they tried to search ye out last night, I distracted them. Easy enough to do with yer mother, but Faolán was more difficult."

The confirmation that she had indeed been missed reminded Astrid of Marcán's assurances that they had done nothing wrong. "Ye learn names quickly."

"Out of need. Just as being here was not my choice, being in the clan of Black Oengus was not my choice. If I wish to survive, I must be accommodating, find a use for myself." Merewyn's eyes narrowed as if to see whether Astrid understood her meaning. She definitely did.

Merewyn continued, "And I must learn names quickly and serve my master or mistress well. That means paying attention when things are happening that no one else notices."

"Where I was is of no concern to ye."

"I am concerned only with my mistress and her pleasure." Astrid knew her face showed her surprise at Merewyn's words even though she tried to cover it. The smug smile she received in return increased her fear that this was some sort of threat. There was no question in Astrid's mind that Merewyn knew exactly where she had been and with whom.

"And ye may speak to no one without my bidding ye to do so."

"Of course." Merewyn glanced toward Joan. "Is Joan someone ye would have me speak to? Can *she* be trusted?"

"Aye, ye may speak with Joan and none other… and not about me."

Three children, winded and wide-eyed, came through the door. Merewyn immediately stopped talking and dropped her eyes to the material again.

"What d'ye here?" Astrid called to the tall boy, his face flushed from exertion.

"We have been sent for Maeve. Niall has been stung again. He cannot catch a breath."

Merewyn's hand halted its work before she resumed stitching.

"Look in the buttery. She's helping put up the foodstuff," Astrid answered.

After the lads left, Astrid sought Merewyn's gaze. "D'ye know something of bee stings?"

Merewyn shrugged and said, "A bit." She looked around but said no more.

Astrid had the distinct impression she was lying. "Now ye were telling me how ye were a good help to me? Aiding a man who may die from a bee sting would indeed be a great help."

She pierced her with a look. "If anyone finds out, they could burn me alive!"

Merewyn must have heard Beibhinn's ranting. And the poor girl had only just arrived! Beibhinn's favorite declaration was that all healers, Seers, and druids should be burned alive. It got just the reaction she sought. Fear and trembling.

Astrid blew a breath before answering. "I will not tell a soul. Ye give *me* the remedy."

Reaching inside her kirtle, Merewyn withdrew a small vial and handed it to Astrid. "He only needs a small amount mixed in water."

Moments later, Astrid had the cup filled and was

racing toward the field. The work on the fields had come to a complete stop and everyone was gathered around young Niall. His father had the lad's head propped on his lap as Niall struggled to breathe. Those standing around looked on with horror. It was a terrible sight to see a man so hearty struck down by such a condition. There was no sign of the old healer.

"Here." Astrid indicated the cup and the man tipped his son's head up.

She knelt beside them and brought the cup to his blue lips. Being careful not to spill any of the liquid, she held it to his mouth. The torturous wheezing caused her hand to shake.

"My thanks," the elder Niall said. "We appreciate ye coming yerself."

Astrid nodded, offering him a hopeful smile. "This will ease the pain."

And she prayed that it would. The liquid trickled in, slowly at first, then more quickly until the cup was empty.

Niall took one deep, shaky breath. He exhaled with a smile, nodding, and the crowd cheered. Niall sat up, his father's hand clasped on his shoulder.

"My thanks," Niall said.

"Mayhap ye need to be inside today?"

Niall stood, ducking his head in embarrassment at all the attention. "Oh, I'll be fine now. My thanks."

Astrid stood there, feeling in the way, as most of the farmers returned to their work. Niall and his father seemed ready to do the same, but they were clearly unsure of the wisdom of walking away from her.

She smiled. "Then best get on with it."

"My thanks." The elder Niall repeated. His son said the same and then they both headed toward the hefty plow sitting unattended. They must have been breaking up the soil, readying it for spring next.

Making her way to the edge of the field, Astrid was surprised to find Faolán standing there, leaning against a shovel and watching her. He was covered with dirt. A shiver passed over her, but she planted a smile on her lips.

"Good day, Faolán," she said, not pausing.

His grip on her arm made her stop.

"What is amiss?" Her heart leapt in her chest at his intent gaze. "Is it Aednat?"

"N-not A-Aednat."

Astrid sighed. "Ye gave me a scare."

He still had not released her arm.

"Then what has happened?"

"Y-ye tell me!"

She glanced around, trying to make sense of what he was asking, then shook her head. "Tell ye what?" She pulled on her arm until he released it. "What is wrong with ye?"

"What i-is it ye gave Niall?"

Astrid glanced across the field. Everyone had returned to their work.

"I gave him what his mother always gives him." Healing plants were of little interest to her. She actually didn't know any of the names, so she couldn't have hoped to answer him.

"They tried that b-before they sent the lads for Maeve." He shook his head, a determined movement. "I-It did not work this time."

She would not reveal where she had gotten the tincture, not after she'd given Merewyn her word. "I do not know what ye want."

"Did ye get i-it from A-Aednat?"

Faolán had spent some time with Aednat, enough to know she was a healer. Agreeing would protect Merewyn, and it certainly wouldn't hurt Aednat.

"She showed me some of her tinctures when she first arrived." Astrid's face heated. She was a terrible liar, something Faolán knew. His gaze never faltered.

"Yer mother will not like that she i-is a healer."

"My mother likes very little."

"She likes Pádraig."

Her jaw tightened, but she said nothing.

"But she doesn't like M-Marcán," he continued.

Astrid stilled, afraid to even breathe. His mentioning Marcán made no sense unless…

She snorted, feigning a lightheartedness to hide her fear. "And why are ye telling me what I know by now?"

"She w-wants w-what i-is best for her daughter."

"Ye believe she knows what is best for me?"

The sarcasm she felt came through in her tone and his expression shifted to one of surprise.

"So ye no longer plot w-with her?" he asked. "D-deciding h-how best to go a-about finding a man ye should m-marry?"

"Do ye listen at the door, Faolán?"

He tipped his chin. "The two of y-ye h-have never plotted in secret. I-I show an i-interest i-in ye because I-I care. Ye do remember that I-I cared for ye? P-protected ye? With Pádraig?"

"I thanked ye for yer assistance, did I not?"

Faolán heaved a heavy sigh, as if debating how best to proceed. "I-I would take ye a-as my o-own—"

She wasn't quick enough to hide her shocked expression from him, but he offered a small smile. An understanding smile.

"—but I-I do not believe I-I am what yer mother h-has planned for ye. She wants y-ye w-wed to Pádraig."

Astrid dropped her gaze. His words were far too unsettling in their truthfulness.

"What Beibhinn wants is to return to the home of her childhood, return to Meic Murchadha. And she will use her own daughter to do it," she said.

He was quiet for so long, she finally looked at him. Her pulse quickened as he studied her. "I-I w-wonder w-what w-*would* be best for ye."

"And why would ye do that? Why wonder such things about me?" Irritation was taking hold of her. She pressed her lips flat, not wanting to say anything she'd regret.

"Y-ye w-were missed last night."

Her gaze slammed into his.

"I-I was sent o-out to find ye. Y-yer mother wanted ye a-at her side a-as always. She seemed l-lost without ye."

"I am sorry. I did not know ye were looking for me."

"Oh, I-I found ye just fine."

The sound outside. It had been him at the door. Astrid struggled to take a breath, to stop her heart from racing and her palms from sweating. There was nothing she could say, so she waited. Her eyes on him.

"Y-ye are a good daughter, A-Astrid. Y-ye should remember that," Faolán said. Without another word or a backward look, he headed across the field, following the ring of the embankment topped with stakes. She watched him for a long time.

Astrid was in no hurry to return to Merewyn, who was too perceptive by half. Instead, she followed the trail that led to Diarmuid's stone longhouse. Mayhap this was where she would find Marcán. Excitement rippled across her skin.

The plan to wait until Aednat was recovered and Diarmuid had fewer worries was looking worse and worse. What if she never recovered? Were she and Marcán destined to sneak around forever, hiding their love for one another? Both Merewyn and Faolán had indicated they knew something was amiss. Who would be next?

The sight of the door opening at the stone longhouse caught Astrid's attention. When Diarmuid came out, she felt the acute disappointment all the way to her toes.

"Diarmuid?"

He stopped and waited for her.

"How is Aednat?"

Diarmuid scrubbed his face with both palms, and they began to walk together toward the roundhouse.

"I am beside myself, but Maeve assures me her neck is not broken."

Astrid gasped, and Diarmuid's regret was apparent but, unlike Marcán, who usually sought to comfort her, her brother only became irritated.

"Hold yer tongue. She will recover. I need to believe that," he said.

"As do I." That her own brother did not recognize her concern was no surprise. He often thought the worst of her, lumping her in with their mother, who truly did not care for others. "If ye need someone to sit with her, I am happy to do so."

"I do not. I wish to remain with her, but Marcán has insisted I leave. He is with her now."

Astrid's feet stopped dead and she turned toward the house. Marcán was inside. Her breathing became shallower and she took a step closer. Diarmuid continued on, pausing only when he realized she was no longer beside him.

"What are ye about?" he asked.

Excitement like she'd never experienced gripped her. It took a moment to respond, she was so overcome. "I... would... see her now?"

"No. I prefer she not be disturbed with more than one person at a time."

Deep frustration sliced through her heart. "But... I will be quiet, Diarmuid. I know she is not well."

Diarmuid searched her face, a hand at his hip. "Is aught amiss?"

Yes, Diarmuid. I am in love with Marcán. I want to be with him.

"No. There is naught," she said.

His eyes narrowed.

Mayhap it would be best for her to speak now. There was no guarantee of when Aednat would recover.

Before she could speak, Diarmuid nodded and continued. "Good. Come. Tell me of yer time with Pádraig Meic Murchadha. I need some entertainment."

Entertainment? Had she been the only one ignorant to the man's nature?

They strolled back, Diarmuid stretching his back and rounding his shoulders as he went.

"Pádraig's father took to his bed. 'Twas quite sudden, but the celebrations continued."

She debated how much to tell him, but she suddenly realized he was not taking in her words. Her brother was beyond exhaustion. "Have ye not even had a soak to ease yer battle-weary body? How can ye expect to keep going without taking care of yerself?"

Diarmuid roughed up his hair and laughed. The smell of roasting meat assailed them when they entered the roundhouse.

"Food for now. That will suffice."

Astrid signaled to Joan, who hurried to get him a plate. "I will get ye a bath."

"I am done in, Astrid, but yer attention to my welfare seems unlike ye."

A slap in the face would have hurt less, and the fact that it was true made it sting all the more. "I am concerned for ye, and mayhap I realize better now what ye take on as our leader."

"*Our* leader? I am not certain I have heard ye refer to me as such before."

She bit her lip, but when his gaze dropped to her lips and narrowed, again searching her face, she clamped her teeth tight. "I spoke with yer wife and I liked her very much. A very special woman. I want the two of ye to be happy. Ye deserve such happiness, brother. Do not begrudge me feeling this way."

"D'ye lie to me when ye say there is naught amiss? Ye do seem… different."

Her breath quickened. Could he actually tell she had been with Marcán?

Our love was never intended to be a secret.

Then why did she feel so guilty? She knew the reason. It was because Marcán was not beside her, reassuring her with his smile and that intent gaze, standing up for her and what they'd shared. It was because Faolán had seen them together. Abruptly she turned.

"I will get ye a bath. Aednat will not want ye stinking when she awakens."

Diarmuid tipped his head and then turned his full

attention to the well-soaked trencher Joan had placed before him. Astrid followed the older woman to the fire.

"Can ye get a bath for yer *ri?*"

"With pleasure." Joan wiped her hands on the ever-present towel at her waist. "Did he say how his bride was faring?"

Her lowered voice had Astrid leaning in closer and answering with the same restraint. "She is not recovered. Prayers would be good."

"Then prayers she shall have. Yer mother says the priest will be here by the new moon as long as there is not an early snow." Joan nodded, retrieving two of the large buckets stored beneath the wall shelf. "Do not look now, but she is coming this way and may be seeking ye out."

Astrid took the woman's advice. Ducking her head, she slipped out through the back door. She did not glance behind her and no one called after her. As she put distance between herself and the roundhouse, she found herself glancing back toward Diarmuid's house. An idea formed even as she made her way to the narrow trail she and her brother had just left. Excitement traipsed along her skin and her face heated.

The whistle of warning, low then high, filled the air. Astrid froze in her tracks and turned back. In the distance, a man jumped to the ground before his horse had come to a complete stop.

"Diarmuid!" she shouted.

Her brother came out of the house, followed by the others, all eager to see what was happening. Field hands and warriors alike converged on the exhausted man, bent over and out of breath.

Astrid approached at a slower pace, joining Merewyn and Joan, who stood together.

"Black Oengus's men," the man finally gasped out. Diarmuid's tension could be felt by all, but he remained silent. "We've found them!"

The man stood, wiping the moisture from his face, and smiled. "We've got them."

Excitement rippled across the throng, sharp like a sword, while Diarmuid gave orders for his warriors to prepare to ride out.

Relief flooded Astrid. Finding the men who had dared to steal the wife of their *rí túaithe* was a step in the right direction. Mayhap it would improve her brother's spirits enough that she and Marcán could consider approaching him with their betrothal. Ideally, Aednat would be fully recovered.

"Faolán!" Diarmuid grabbed the man's arm. "Go tell Marcán the news."

"I can tell him, Diarmuid." Astrid's eyes rounded with guilt when he shifted his narrowed gaze to her. She did not like keeping such a secret.

"Go then. And stay with her? Please, Astrid?" Diarmuid's desperate concern for his wife came through in his voice.

"Of course I will stay with her, brother." The tears that sprang to her eyes did not go unnoticed and he quickly gave her his back. He never could abide tears.

Heading down the narrow path, Astrid was irritated that she could not break into a full run. Her ankle, though healing, still required a slower gait.

"Marcán!" She called to him when she was close enough, and the sight of him filling the door made her catch her breath.

The look of appreciation on his face was quickly

146

replaced by one of alarm. "What has happened?"

He closed the distance, stopping just short of reaching out to her.

"Is aught amiss?" Marcán glanced around before putting his warm hand to her cheek. "Tell me what has happened." Thumbing a tear away, he added. "Why are ye crying?"

The relief she felt at his concern bolstered her confidence. "They've found the men. Black Oengus's men."

Marcán's expression shut down with the dropping of his hand. "Good. We'll see this finished."

As if forgetting she even existed, he disappeared inside, only to come out with his sword and heavy fur mantle.

"Stay with Aednat," he called over his shoulder without a backward glance.

She watched him silently as he headed down the path she'd just walked, full of excitement at seeing him, her disappointment so keen, it hurt. Astrid walked inside, assailed by the scent of him, and closed her eyes. It was hard to breathe.

"Oh, Astrid!"

Marcán was suddenly behind her, gathering her into a tight embrace before she could fully turn to face him.

"*A ghráidh*. Forgiveness, please." He spoke the words against her hair, and her heart soared. The sensation of his warm body pressed against her, so strong and comforting, sent all her disappointment from her.

"Always."

"It is new for me to be able to take ye in my arms." A warm hand cupped her face and then he was kissing her, passionately. All too quickly he set her aside. "I must see to my men. Please? Stay here with Aednat."

"I will." She smiled, reassured now, able to watch him go. But he stopped at the door and turned back to her.

"Shall I speak to Diarmuid of our joining when we have seen to these bastards?"

Marcán's expectant expression did not match his wary tone. She considered why that would be. Did he question her desire for him?

"My love, I do not wish to wait, but Diarmuid is so upset."

Aednat's still form was covered with the heavy red squirrel coverlet, tucked in as if to keep out any danger. So small in Diarmuid's big bed.

"And if ye are with child?"

The thought sent a ripple of anticipation through her body.

"We would have *some* time. I would prefer for our news to be an occasion for celebration."

Marcán's disappointment was obvious, but he nodded his consent and was gone.

The room was dark, a small fire casting long shadows along the roof and walls. She brushed a stray hair from Aednat's face. "Ye need to recover quickly, sister."

No response. Not even a change in her breathing. Astrid glanced to the door before speaking again. "I miss ye even now."

Chapter Twelve

The days passed at a very slow pace. Astrid had taken to spending her afternoons with Aednat, who showed no signs of improvement. It was exhausting. Beibhinn had come to visit Aednat a few minutes each day, blissfully ignorant about her being a healer, and more than impressed she was the cousin to their powerful *ri túath*, Sean.

Thankfully, there had been little opportunity to further discuss Astrid's encounter with Pádraig. Beibhinn assumed it had been wonderful, and Astrid did not feel inclined to argue that fact, especially since it would lead to a much more intense argument. Faolán had taken to watching her from the shadows but not approaching her. She could feel his censure. Probably because despite Marcán's assurances they'd done nothing wrong, the lack of a betrothal seemed to indicate otherwise.

Word of the men's return was a boon to Astrid's dark thoughts. Dressed in a floor-length dark-blue *léine* with red and green embroidery along the hem and sleeves, Astrid wanted to look her best for Marcán's return. Surely now all would move forward as it should.

Faolán stood when she entered Diarmuid's longhouse, but there was no smile for her.

"How is she today?" Astrid shrugged off his sober expression.

"She i-is the same." His eyes bore into her. "A-and ye, A-Astrid? H-how are ye to-today?"

"I am relieved that the men return today. Aednat will certainly take a turn for the better now that her husband will again be by her side."

But Aednat still had not stirred, so there would be very little in way of celebration. Astrid took Aednat's hand, small and cold, ignoring the fact that Faolán continued to watch her.

"Ye can go now. I will remain here with her."

He didn't respond. Pointedly ignoring him, she held a small drinking vessel to Aednat's lips. Pleased she was able to get some fluids into her, Astrid struggled not to give Faolán any attention.

"D-do ye know what ye w-will do now that h-he has r-returned?"

Astrid debated feigning ignorance. Mayhap even questioning him about what he thought he'd seen. But why give him the satisfaction?

"Celebrating anyone's homecoming will have to wait until Aednat is returned to good health."

"Y-ye believe he w-will take y-ye to w-wife?"

She wasn't quick enough to stop the gasp from escaping or her shocked gaze from turning to him. He stood there with a dark expression, his arms about his chest.

"Y-ye are not the first," he said. "A-and ye'll not b-be the last."

"How ye overstep yerself!" Astrid stood on trembling legs. "Ye know nothing!"

"I-I care for y-ye."

"Then leave! I want ye gone." She pointed at the door but he didn't budge. "Now!"

Her screeching voice echoed against the stone walls and tears filled her eyes.

Faolán finally dropped his arms, his shoulders relaxing. "Whether y-ye believe me o-or not, I-I have o-only ever a-acted i-in yer best i-interest. R-remember that."

When he turned and finally left, Astrid was overcome with a sense of doom. Something in Faolán's features. Determination? Resignation? He of all people should understand how close she'd come to having a man force himself on her. He of all people should realize it was better for her to give herself to a man who loved her than to be taken by one who did not.

Astrid hated the woman she became when she lost control, so like her mother. Her voice growing louder and louder. Deep down she knew it came from her sense of having no control over anything.

"I am sorry for yelling, sister." Astrid took Aednat's hand again. "We have much to discuss. Plans to make. Celebrations."

She glanced around the empty room before kneeling beside the bed, her face close to Aednat's.

Her voice a whisper. "I have found the love of my life."

Even saying the words thrilled her and she smiled. It would not be long now before everyone knew.

"A better man does not exist. Well, ye may believe there does since ye are married to my brother, and he is indeed a good man. But no. Not like this man."

Their decision to wait until Aednat was better made their time together seem more like a dream than reality. She felt a powerful need to speak about it. Approaching Diarmuid with the news was the first step toward making it true. As king of their clan, he had the right to deny the joining, but she could not believe he would do such a thing.

"A wonderful man. Very brave. And handsome!" She looked at Aednat. "I should not tease ye. I have not even told ye his name." Astrid glanced around again. She was being more than silly. "'Tis Marcán."

Having said the word outside of her head was refreshing. She settled against the wall, bending her knees up to support her arms. "I did not even know how much I cared for him. He always seemed more of a nuisance, but…" Memories flashed through her mind like the lights dancing across the sky in winter. "…I see now how much he has always loved me. I realize he is the only man for me."

She lowered her forehead to her knees and felt again the heat of his hands sliding along her skin, the twinkle in his eyes when he smiled down at her, the gentle touch of his lips against hers.

"Astrid?"

Startled, Astrid dropped her arms. She must have fallen asleep. Diarmuid stood there in his mail, covered with mud and spattered with blood. He reached a hand toward her. Marcán stood behind him, his expression expectant.

"Ye have returned!" She sounded out of breath as she stood to greet them. Hugging first her brother and then Marcán, who held her tight. "Praise God."

"How is she?" The first words out of Diarmuid's mouth were not a surprise, his eyes staying on Aednat.

"There is no change," Astrid said, her tone more wistful than she'd intended.

"Did something happen?"

"I believe there may be a change now that ye have returned. She loves ye," she said. Marcán held Astrid's hand in his tight grip, hiding it behind her back. "She would not leave ye alone like this."

Her brother turned to her with a surprised expression, no doubt at her sentiment, but she averted her gaze, afraid he would see the new love spilling out of her.

Instead, Diarmuid smiled, glancing between the two of them. "I agree." Settling beside his wife, he brushed an imaginary strand of hair from her face, his loving gaze taking in every aspect of her. "And how is my sweet Aednat?"

His voice dropped to an intimate level, and Astrid's heart tightened with pain for her brother. She was suddenly awash with guilt at her own happiness.

"But certainly she is healing on the inside," she said. She wanted to encourage him. "Eating both broth and wine, she will return to health soon."

Marcán squeezed her hand, but she did not turn to him. His breath was loud in her ear, her entire body attuned to him. When Diarmuid sighed in resignation, she became overwhelmed with shame and moved away from Marcán, forcing him to release her hand.

"I am sorry, Diarmuid. Certainly her recovery will come to pass very soon," she said.

His breathing deepened. "Call for Maeve." He bellowed the words. "I will have answers!"

Astrid cringed as each of his words grew louder than the last. He was letting loose his anger, and she couldn't jump to do his bidding fast enough. "I will send her to ye."

"I will return as well," Marcán added, seemingly unaffected by the look Diarmuid turned on him.

Astrid's guilt was too much. She should have come to Diarmuid first. As soon as she and Marcán had awoken from their night of passion, they should have come right to see him. Even now, they would be betrothed.

Once outside, Marcán called after her when she kept going. "Astrid! Wait!"

She finally stopped, nibbling at her lower lip.

Closing the distance between them, he took her in his arms and kissed her. His lips so warm and sweet, the heady feelings returned to assault her senses. The stench of battle hit her and she couldn't stop herself from turning away, the back of her hand shielding her nose.

Releasing her, he offered a sheepish smile. "Forgiveness, I beg. I needed to feel ye in my arms again."

"Ye need a bath!"

"And would ye be seeing to it?"

She tried to smile and glanced around to see who was nearby. There was no one.

Marcán frowned. "Is aught a miss?"

"There is naught. I—"

"Then let us go to him now!" His eyes widening

in excitement, he took her arm, pulling her with him. "Come, we will ask Diarmuid's blessing on our union and be apart no longer."

"He is near broken. Can ye not see that? I could *never* seek my own happiness while he pines away beside his wife."

Marcán's expression shifted, a frown marring his brow.

"Astrid," Marcán said, his finger caressing her palm, where he held her hand in his own. "I have been beside yer brother all this time. I have seen his pain, and it truly runs deep... but would he not want us to have our happiness? I believe it could comfort him to see ye content."

A rustling from the trail ahead had Astrid jerking away from Marcán. Met by his steady gaze, she could guess her reaction disappointed him. Mayhap he even believed she had forgotten his earlier words. She had not, but her courage had left her. The decision to wait demanded they keep their relationship a secret, and she did not like secrets. Faolán's cryptic words had only increased her trepidation.

Maeve halted when she spotted them on the path, turning to one and then the other. "Astrid. Oh, Marcán! Yer men are looking for ye. There is some trouble with the hostages."

"My thanks."

Marcán paused, his fierce demeanor back in place. Always ready for battle. In command of all about him. But he showed no sign of leaving.

"Maeve," Astrid turned to the woman, "Diarmuid requires yer presence. Please go to him, but be forewarned, he is beside himself with grief."

"He'll be venting his anger at me?"

"I fear that is so, but do not take it to heart."

"If I had an answer for the man, I would give it to him." Her basket hanging from her wrist, the healer quickly continued to the longhouse. Neither moved as they watched her go inside.

"I should return to them," Astrid said.

When Marcán turned his suddenly warm gaze back to her, the breath in her entire body stilled. She read his desire there and her body responded.

"Are ye certain, *grádh*?"

With a tightness in her chest, she said, "I will not keep ye from yer duties. See to the hostages. We will speak later."

His eyes darkened. "I want to do more than speak."

He took her hand again in a light hold, his eyes never releasing hers, and kissed her palm. Her wrist. The bend of her fingers. "I wait on ye to decide when to speak to yer brother, but I will not wait forever."

Dipping his head, Marcán rushed past her toward the roundhouse.

Astrid felt better since having heard Maeve tell Diarmuid that Aednat's body was sound, and there was no reason she should not awaken soon. Where Astrid had found relief, Diarmuid had found more reasons to rail against the healer. She and Astrid had quickly made their exit, leaving Diarmuid alone once again with his unresponsive wife.

"If I knew what ailed his bride, I would heal it." Maeve's concern for her *ri* came through in her tone. "To my mind, she is merely restoring herself from the entire ordeal."

"And ye shared that with him?" Astrid asked.

Maeve snorted, "Yer brother hears only what he wants to hear. Since I could not say *why* she remains asleep, he preferred to get angry and dismiss me from his very presence."

Concerned for the old woman's feelings, Astrid was relieved when she grinned and added, "I know yer brother well enough to know when he blusters. I may fear his wrath as I do God's wrath, but I know his heart is kind."

When the two of them arrived at the roundhouse, people were still milling around to greet the warriors. Some of the men had been wounded in the fighting. A few moaned as they were carried past to follow Maeve.

Astrid stopped one of the men. "Was the battle that fierce?"

"More than we had expected."

The sight of Pádraig alongside her mother, standing outside the open door, had Astrid backing away, but she was too late. Pádraig spotted her and left Beibhinn to cross to her, fighting the crowd headed toward the wounded men.

"Astrid! Where have ye been hiding all day?"

"She's been in prayer for the warriors!" Merewyn came out from behind him, continuing toward Astrid with those swaying hips.

That Pádraig stopped to enjoy the view did not surprise Astrid. Nor did the sight of him pressing down the front of his *léine* as his body reacted to the blatant invitation. He was like an animal always looking to rut.

"Pádraig! What are ye here?" Astrid used her sternest tone. Merewyn came to stand alongside her in a show of support.

"Ah, sweet Astrid!" His eyes rounded as if her biting words had wounded him. "The very reason I came here today was to spend time with ye so that we may get to know each other better."

She knew exactly what he meant by getting to know each other. How would he feel when he realized she'd given herself to another man? A better man? And quite willingly?

"Astrid has much to see to now that the warriors have returned." Merewyn's words were an admirable attempt to protect her. Reminded of her earlier claims, Astrid had to agree that the girl was indeed helpful.

Pádraig did not see it that way. His lips flattened into a thin line. He took a step closer, his gaze settling somewhere near Merewyn's breasts. "*Ye* do not speak to *me* unless I give ye leave to do so. Ye may nod if ye understand."

Astrid's gut clenched, and she interceded before her proud slave was belittled further. "If I have any need of ye, Merewyn, I will find ye. Now go."

Merewyn turned to her, placing a hand on her arm. "Forgiveness, please. I had mistaken him for a nobleman who would understand the demands on the king's sister. I am set right."

His eyes narrowed, his jaw grinding, but he said no more, merely watching as Merewyn stomped back to the longhouse. Catching sight of Marcán, Astrid's heart soared. She lowered her gaze, but Pádraig had not missed her expression. He frowned and searched behind him before turning back to her with a knowing look.

"Diarmuid's lackey? Is that where yer interest lies now?"

Astrid's breath quivered in her chest, but she pushed against her fear.

"What are ye here? The truth, if ye please. We know each other as well as we need to."

He wrapped his arms about his chest and frowned. "Ye believe this is so?"

"I am certain of it." Her clipped words could leave no question about her true feelings.

"Then ye are ready to sign the contracts?"

Confusion gripped her, and she shook her head, not sure how to respond.

"Ah, ye have not spoken to yer mother then?"

"My mother? What does she have to do with anything?"

The last of the crowd pushed against them in their eagerness to get to the warriors.

Pádraig glanced down and took a big breath, almost as if composing himself before delivering some important message. When he looked up, she cowered at his fierce expression. Without warning, he moved in close, obstructing the view of the others with his large body. She caught his sly smile just before he clutched his hands around her throat. He pulled her back behind the building, and though she grabbed at the hands squeezing her throat, she was powerless to stop him. Finally, he released her neck and shoved her against the house. She sucked in air at the release, outrage coiling in her gut.

"Yer mother has everything to do with this! Ye thought ye could do better than me with Marcán? 'Tis of no account to me who yer wandering eye has settled on now, as ye are by now betrothed to me."

"I am not!" Her tears came through in her voice. "I would never marry ye!"

"Yer mother and I are in agreement."

"My mother oversteps her bounds if she has made an agreement with ye."

"Ye. Are. Not. Hearing. Me."

When he stepped closer, Astrid trembled.

"Heed me well! Beibhinn and I understand each other, and she assures me there will be no other."

Astrid's jaw was clamped so tight, it ached. He gripped her arm to drag her toward the outbuildings. Short of digging in her heels and screaming for help, she had no escape, and doing so would cause the same problems now as it would have when Faolán had first interrupted him. When he angled them toward the storage building, her heart sank.

No! Not where she'd made love with Marcán.

Servants moved about, but they were readying themselves to join the celebration, small as it would be, of the warriors' return and paid them no attention. No doubt they saw nothing unusual with Astrid speaking with Pádraig. And he seemed content to tarry with her in the shadow of the little building now, biding his time until the others left.

Once alone, Pádraig released her arm. She rubbed the burning skin but refused to face him.

"Not so interested in me now, little one?"

She sneered at him. He slid his hot hand down her throat, continuing over her breast, and she grabbed his wrist with both hands to stop him.

He smirked, pressing his length against her. "Are ye showing me disrespect, even while I hold yer life in my hands?"

Lost to her fear of what he might do, she couldn't respond.

"Release my arm," he said.

Astrid dropped her hands in defeat. His hand continued its assault, fondling her even as he lowered his voice to a seductive tone. "Just who do ye think ye are, little one? Ye think to deny my father's request that ye come to him? Even after my sister travels to ye in the rain?"

Struggling with her fear, she could barely squeeze the words out. "Yer father knows me. It was a ruse to again get me alone!"

"Hah! Listen to the timid little mouse speaking her mind and yet... look?" The arrogant dog turned to the left, then the right, before moving his face in closer. "Ye *are* alone with me. *Very* alone."

"Not if I scream." Astrid felt the stirrings of courage in her gut. She envisioned a number of people stepping up to intervene if she did just that.

"And yet I know ye won't." He whispered into her ear like a lover. "I wonder... if I'd had my way with ye that night? Would I even want ye now?"

A sob escaped, and he pulled back to search her face, but she refused to look away, even as hot tears of frustration slid down her cheeks. If that was all he wanted, why would he agree to a union between them? A high price, indeed, to pay just to possess her. Was it taking her virginity that he sought? A bit too late for that. Would his learning that be enough to turn him away?

"I would never mistreat Daimhin," he said, his stilted words revealing his irritation with her, "sending her out into the rain for my own selfish pleasure. 'Twas my father's wish that ye come to him. He liked the idea of our joining. He remembers yer mother as well."

"Then ye are jeopardizing much by treating me

this way. If ye are caught, they will kill ye."

"I jeopardize nothing." He raised both his brows. "I want to feel ye again, Astrid." He gripped her breasts with both hands, pressing his palms into her, snuggling his face against her neck when she turned away.

Her stomach tightened. She was going to be sick. When he pressed his stiffened prick against her, she feared she would not be able to stop him.

"I would take ye now. Here. But for the promise I made to yer mother."

A crowd of warriors came around the house just a stone's throw away, laughing and talking, and Pádraig stepped back. His hands were at his sides, but his gaze searched her face. He raised his brows as if to question her. Her nostrils flared.

"Is this why Marcán kept ye in his sights? Ye are too timid to seek help if it puts someone else in danger." Pádraig's expression was intent on her. When he quirked a brow and his lips began to curl up, her irritation shifted into a black rage, sitting like a snake in the pit of her stomach, rearing its head and demanding to be heard. Courage raced through her veins.

"Do not." His lips barely moved as he delivered her orders.

"Gréagóir!" Astrid called to the warrior closest and had the satisfaction of seeing Pádraig not only jump, but his eyes widening in surprise.

One of Diarmuid's warriors stopped a few feet from them. Five or six more warriors continued past. All she needed to do was order Pádraig be taken and the warrior would obey her without another word. Suffice to say their king's sister had respect from all of

Diarmuid's warriors.

"Is aught amiss?" Gréagóir came in close, the jagged scar above his brow intimidating to most. She knew he was a kind and thoughtful man despite his stern expression. When he extended a hand to pull her away from the house and into the light, she grabbed it.

"Why are ye hiding in the shadows?" Gréagóir asked. "Come! We have much to celebrate, do we not?"

Pádraig was left to follow behind, and Astrid blew a relieved breath. She would not make the mistake again of getting within reaching distance of that dirty swine.

"We have much to celebrate indeed," she said.

Chapter Thirteen

Astrid was escorted to the lead table, where she sat without comment beside her mother. Beibhinn was settled in the center of the bench, the same position she'd held while Astrid's father was alive, even surveying those before her as if she were still wife to the *rí túaithe.* Astrid wanted to rip the woman's pleased expression from her face.

Pádraig had wandered off before they'd even reached the roundhouse, no doubt to follow after the pretty lass who'd kept her eye on him as he'd passed. The woman was from Black Oengus's tribe, and her husband had been killed in the fighting. If she was willing to give Pádraig what her obvious interest implied, Astrid expected him back no time soon. The longer he stayed away, the better.

"Glad I am ye found time to speak with Pádraig. He came to be with ye so ye would not be afeared on yer wedding night."

Beibhinn's words halted Astrid's movements. She could not have heard her mother correctly. "Wedding night?"

"Do not look so shocked, Astrid! This is what we had hoped for."

The woman moved with slow, controlled movements, tipping her head to signal that the food and drink be served.

"That one is a handsome warrior. Ye are lucky to find a man like that interested in *ye.*" Beibhinn kept her eyes on those who sat opposite the head table. "Ye need not thank me. I am yer mother, and I only want what is best for ye."

Gasping in too much air at once, Astrid bent over and coughed in convulsions she couldn't control. Everyone in the room turned to watch her, some standing, some half sitting. Niall brought her his mug of water, setting it before her on the table. She quickly drank it and the spasms eased.

"My thanks, Niall," Astrid said right before clearing her throat yet again.

The lad smiled sheepishly, ducking his head. "The least I could do for ye."

Beibhinn scoffed beside her before turning away. Niall reddened, a look of confusion on his face, and returned to his seat.

"Ye seek attention from every man ye see! Do ye not realize what type of trouble ye can get yerself into?"

Astrid searched her mother's face. Trouble? She had merely said a kind word to Niall. Her mother had encouraged her, nay pressured her, into following Pádraig into the night while they were staying with the Meic Murchadha. More proof that her mother was concerned for her own well-being and not that of her daughter.

Astrid had never quite understood her mother's insistence that going back to the clan of her birth would make her life better. Who was even left of her family? Certainly when Astrid was brave enough to share with her mother what had actually happened, Beibhinn would admit Pádraig was not the man they had believed him to be. She would give up this notion of returning to the Meic Murchadha.

"*Mamaídh*," Astrid's stomach churned. "I do not want t—"

Beibhinn's eyes widened and her face tightened. "Of course ye do! A better match could not be made."

"But there is anoth—"

"There is another man interested in ye? That has this much power? That is this well connected?"

"Well, no, I do not—"

"Come. Come. Ye cannot be that fickle, Astrid. We've discussed this at great length. We need only get Diarmuid's approval and 'twill be done."

"He is not—"

"He is not what?" Beibhinn's eyes widened in obvious irritation. Astrid could actually feel her stomach tightening into one huge knot.

"I do not wish to marry him."

"Ye do not have a say."

"Why would I not?"

"Because ye have expressed yer interest. Ye've approached him with the idea. He has decided to accept ye as his wife."

Her world seemed to be spinning out of control. Beibhinn made it sound as if it were a signed agreement.

"But Diarmuid has not—"

"Yer brother is of little use to anyone." She shook her head in a display of sheer exasperation. "He is preoccupied with that woman, but—"

"His *wife*!" Astrid spat the words at her.

Already Beibhinn was speaking ill of the woman who required Diarmuid's time. Astrid feared how her mother would react upon learning Diarmuid's wife was a healer.

When Beibhinn turned her censuring eyes on her, Astrid refused to back down.

"Aednat. Is. His. Wife!" The need to defend the woman became overwhelming. "Did ye not just spend time with her? She's a lovely woman."

"She did not even know I was there, and I do not like this show of disrespect."

"He is not…" Astrid stopped talking when she noticed her mother's suddenly shocked expression. The woman stood, her eyes wide and fixed on a man who'd just entered the roundhouse. He wore dark brown trews and a tunic as green as moss. The gold chain around his waist spoke of great wealth, as did the layers of cloth covering him.

"Fintan?" Beibhinn's lips curled into a huge smile, and she gestured to the fair-haired man. "Fintan, come! Sit beside me. What brings ye here?"

It was not anyone Astrid recognized, but clearly her mother knew him quite well, even hugging his arm when he sat beside her. Her mother was not very demonstrative and to see her behavior now was surprising in the extreme, sending all other concerns from Astrid's mind.

167

"Beibhinn, it has been too long. I came to rectify that." Their hands were clasped as if they were close friends.

"It *has* been far too long." The woman nodded, that slow, sad, agreeable nod that always came right before she moved into her lamenting. "Wherever have ye been, my friend?"

Astrid had no patience for her mother's usual discontent. She smiled around the woman. "Fintan, is it? I am called Astrid."

"Ah, Astrid, I remember ye well." The man's face creased with his broad smile. "Not yet a woman when last I saw ye at yer mother's side."

Her mother also laughed. "And so she still remains with me. A good daughter."

Astrid flinched at her mother's assessment. "Would that be when my father still lived?"

Fintan lowered his eyes. "Ah, yer father. Kane was a great man indeed."

Astrid's chest tightened at the sentiment.

Fintan nodded before lifting his gaze to her. "D'ye know he was named for the son-in-law of our *árd rí*? A mighty warrior! He was aptly named."

Astrid flushed with pride. "Thank ye for sharing that with me. I did not know."

"Enough!" Beibhinn shifted forward, blocking Astrid's view of the man, and raised a hand to those waiting to serve the meal. "Names are seldom prophetic."

Fintan leaned forward just a bit and winked at Astrid before settling back. Astrid turned away to smile. She would need to speak to this man if given the chance. Her mother had such a poor opinion of her father, Astrid sometimes wondered if her own memories of him were true. He had always seemed bigger than life to her, and she still missed him more than she could say.

"Astrid?"

Beibhinn's irritated tone yanked Astrid out of her musings. And now her mother raised her eyebrows, not hiding her annoyance.

"Well? Do ye agree or not?"

"I did not hear—"

"Daydreaming again? I swear, Astrid, ye are going to be the death of me—"

Astrid stopped listening to the tirade she was so familiar with. As was her habit, Beibhinn was no longer speaking *to* Astrid but *about* her. Fintan was the polite listener this time, and she had compassion for him. It was no doubt an awkward situation for the man.

The pain that usually settled in her chest when her mother started in on her, the feelings of inadequacy, were surprisingly absent. Astrid swallowed hard, expecting the usual lump to show itself, but it was not there. Instead, the look of love on Marcán's face flashed through her mind. His compliments. His sweet words. All these things filled her mind as she struggled to take a deep breath through the tears stinging her eyes. *He* found her acceptable. More than acceptable. He desired her, and no one else, for his wife. She had successfully crossed the chasm between belittling and adoration, and her heart soared.

And yet her mother intended to take all that away from her. Well, she wouldn't let it happen! Surely there would be a way around this... this thing Beibhinn had set in motion. Watching Beibhinn's mouth flapping, the lines around her lips tight in her complaints, Astrid wondered why she had ever sought the woman's approval for anything. It had been obvious, even as a little girl, she would never receive it. That sudden revelation was like the sun bursting through on a cloudy day, and Astrid nearly sighed with relief. The woman found *everything* about Astrid wanting. Her looks. Her manners. Her embroidery. Her voice. As if the goal of a mother was not to encourage her children but to keep ripping them apart and discouraging them from ever believing in themselves… or ever having lives of their own.

Astrid hoped only to shower her children with love and acceptance. Life was brutal, and so many children died before they had a chance to grow. Just as her younger brother, Fergus, had died so young. Did her mother have any regrets about him? One of the last times Astrid had seen her father was when he'd learned of his youngest son's death. He had been devastated, but that had not stopped Beibhinn from laying him low with her mouth, placing all the blame at his feet.

The meal was finishing, and Astrid counted herself lucky on two counts. Her mother had not sought her involvement in their conversation again, and Pádraig had still not arrived. Mayhap he had even returned home. That would be a blessing as far as Astrid was concerned.

As it turned out, Fintan was a *fili,* a member of an elite class of highly trained and sought-after poets. He traveled from place to place, entertaining his audience with his poems of great conquests and the warriors that fought in them. Once the food was removed, he regaled them with his poems and songs, much like the stories Marcán was so good at sharing. Fintan even used a small stringed instrument to bring some of his words to music. A lovely voice.

The songs Fintan sang were of battles and lost loves. Poignant stories that stirred Astrid's heart and made her wish Marcán would show himself. She would feel more at peace if she could just see him now. Even if he had to keep his distance. He was Diarmuid's second, expected to sit at the head table. Not so when Beibhinn commanded the room. She made no secret of her dislike of him.

The room erupted with clapping when Fintan finished, all those present deeply affected by his words. Though the final song was about unrequited love, Astrid found herself imagining her own Marcán with his long, black hair. Hearing her mother sniffle beside her, Astrid looked more closely and was surprised to see she was indeed crying, as if also touched by the sentimentality of the lovers. These were real tears, which Astrid had long since learned to distinguish from her mother's fake ones.

Fintan bowed low to each side of the room with great ceremony before returning to Beibhinn's side.

"Ah, Fintan!" Beibhinn wiped at her face. "I have missed the sound of yer voice."

He took a long draught from his horn, which was quickly refilled by the many willing attendants surrounding him. Fintan smiled his thanks to them, acknowledging each in turn before they drifted away.

"Glad I am ye enjoyed that, Beibhinn. I sang the last one for ye."

The sight of Beibhinn dropping her face into her hands nearly had Astrid gasping. She tried to remember what it was the man had sung about to cause this depth of emotion.

A handsome warrior with hair dark as night

His bright green eyes twinkling with pleasure at the maiden's sighs.

Astrid looked askance at her mother. Her father's eyes had been dark brown, his hair the blond of his Norse father. Not Kane then. No doubt the song was about the man Beibhinn would have preferred to marry.

"My thanks," Beibhinn said, then her voice became so quiet that Astrid had to shift closer to hear her. "I remember him that way still. Just as ye sang of him."

"Ye speak of him as if he had died in his youth."

"He might as well have."

Fintan sighed, patting her mother's clasped hands. "What happened was for the best. He lived a long, happy life."

Her mother's painful sigh sent chills along Astrid's spine. As did the raspy whisper that followed. "He could have been happier with me! He should have been mine."

Fintan's hand stilled atop her mother's. "Ye found no comfort in his happiness? Would ye have wanted him alone with no family of his own?"

"I wanted him with *me*."

Sneaking a peek around Beibhinn's head, Astrid searched the man's face. It had darkened and his eyes, directed at her mother, were mere slits of narrowed indignation.

His lips tight over his teeth when he spoke, he said, "Yet he chose another. Ye would have done better to make yer peace with that than to harden yer heart so."

Fintan turned away with such finality, Astrid

expected him to rise from the table. Instead, he emptied his horn and asked for another—a request his many enthralled attendees were eager to fulfill.

"Do ye have news from the north?" one young lass asked as she poured the mead into his horn.

Fintan's expression had relaxed with the increased amount of drink, his hand resting on the table in front of him. "I have many tales to tell from both near and far!"

The lass giggled and her friends crowded around, eager to hear something new or exotic.

Astrid smiled, recognizing herself in their enraptured expressions. Ignoring her mother, who now sulked beside her, she addressed the man. "Any news at all would be welcome, of that I am certain."

Her mother flashed her usual disapproving expression, but Astrid merely sighed. Fintan leaned forward now, keeping Astrid within his sight.

"Ah, I have a gruesome tale, if ye're of a mind to hear it."

The young girls glanced at each other, nodding as if they'd been offered something quite delectable.

"That would be very entertaining." It was the first girl who answered him, her eyes wide in anticipation.

Fintan took another long pull from his horn before beginning. "A few villages away, there was a burning. A burning at the stake."

Astrid's stomach tightened.

The girl's giggles died off, but their attention never wavered, their expressions shifting to fear as he continued.

"'Twas the woman that lived the farthest away from the rest, on the land she'd gained from her father as a dowry, though she'd never married. She had been warned before by their *ri* to keep to her work at the loom and stop dealing in the dark arts. She had been called out as a witch."

"A witch," the first girl repeated, her voice awed.

"She was well known among the villagers, but they kept their distance, of course. The priest himself had warned her about her dealings with the devil, though she had vehemently denied any such wrongdoing." He divided his attention between his avid listeners, pausing for effect.

"On the full moon last, she had told the woodman to be weary of the coming rains, that his wood should be moved lest the flooding send it all downstream." Fintan searched the faces intent on him for a long, quiet moment before speaking again. "There had been no sign of rain that day."

The first girl turned to her friends. "Do ye remember? There was such a dry spell? Right before Diarmuid and his men went off in search of his wife?"

"A terrible rain."

Fintan smiled when they turned their attention back to him. "They said the rain came without warning. That only a Seer in league with the devil could have known it would come."

Astrid gulped, her hand on her silver goblet, unable to bring the drink closer to her mouth. Unable to move at all.

"They burned her at the stake like a witch." The man turned his gaze from one to the next of those sitting closest to him. Astrid had been so intent on his story, she had not noticed the crowd that had gathered around them, four and five deep. "And like a witch, a Seer cannot be allowed to live."

"Did ye watch the entire thing? Her flesh bursting

into flames? Her screams?" It was the first girl again, but it became obvious she was asking what they all wanted to know with their wagging heads and wild, staring eyes.

Fintan shrugged, sipping from his horn again, feigning a disinterest that Astrid questioned the sincerity of. Surely a man with such a heart for these tender stories would feel the pain of so horrendous a death.

"I have seen many burned alive," Fintan said. "'Tis not pleasant."

"A terrible punishment!" Astrid said.

"Well-deserved!" Beibhinn chimed in, her voice ringing with indignation. "And the scriptures clearly state we cannot suffer a witch to live."

"I believe the scriptures also say any *sinner* is no better than a witch." Astrid said, turning her wide, blue eyes on the man. Compelled to speak despite the strong sense of foreboding filling her, she ignored her mother's censuring glare. "…and certainly we are all of us sinners."

"True. We are all sinners," Fintan replied.

"Do we all deserve to be burned alive?" Astrid asked.

"Ah, Astrid, yer father often spoke of yer kind heart," Fintan said. "Always caring for the downtrodden."

"As we are *all* called to do." She had to force the words out, but the man's expression was gentle. Not at all like he had taken offense.

"And so we are." Fintan leaned back, rubbing his neck, his expression weary. "The punishment was not objected to by any of the villagers."

The lasses had their bit of gossip and wondered off, chattering among themselves, until Joan dispersed them to see to their duties. The celebration, subdued as it was, would continue for many hours yet.

"Mother, shall I see Fintan settled?" She turned to him. "Ye may return to the festivities if ye desire."

Beibhinn seemed far away, and it took a moment for her eyes to focus on her daughter. "A fine thing for ye to see to, Astrid."

Astrid stood along with Fintan.

"I need very little. A pallet would suffice." He followed her through the door but stopped to look up at the star-filled skies. "A lovely night."

Glancing up, she nodded. "A night sky without a single cloud is very good indeed."

"Ye sound as if ye're pronouncing an omen."

She scoffed. "I do not believe in such things."

He glanced back at the roundhouse. "And if I remember yer mother, 'tis a good thing ye do not. Is she still so bent on ferreting out wrongdoers?"

"She believes she alone is capable of it, and if the priest concurs? So be it. But if he does not, he too may receive an earful."

Astrid led the way to a small roundhouse opposite the large one, seldom used and hidden among the overgrown trees. A place of honor for visiting *fili*. A king's reputation could be made or broken by the words of a man such as this. And those words would be repeated far and wide. His opinion mattered, so he was always well treated.

When Fintan reached the closed door, he turned toward Astrid. "I do not mean any disrespect to yer mother, but ye do realize her views are quite contrary?"

His eyes were intent, their brightness reflecting the moon hanging just behind her.

Astrid shrugged. "It matters not what others believe as long as we cater to what *she* believes."

"It cannot be an easy thing to sit beside her, and ye with such a tender nature. Have ye never considered speaking to her about her baleful behavior?"

Astrid would have laughed at such an outrageous question but for the pang it caused in her heart. "She has little respect for me or my opinion. Diarmuid has managed to keep her from doing too much harm."

"Yer father always considered ye his brightest child."

Her chest tightened. "He did?"

Fintan cupped her cheek, staring at her with a gentle expression. "He thought the world of ye and only wanted the best for his only lass."

"Would that he had seen to a betrothal for me when last he was here, I would no longer be under Beibhinn's thumb."

"He tried. Repeatedly. Yer mother refused her consent, and even though he could have forced his will, as was his right, he was tired of the constant bickering. Like ye, he preferred peace in his own home."

Fintan averted his gaze, but Astrid knew he wanted to say more. She had a prick of a memory of him as a younger man, his hair less gray. Her father had been there, and the two men had been speaking so seriously that Astrid had felt the need to break the tension and approached them with her freshly collected wildflowers.

"I will miss seeing this one most of all."

Astrid closed her eyes against the painful memory. Certainly, she must be remembering it incorrectly… When she opened her eyes, Fintan's sad, expressive gaze was on her.

"Ye remember his leaving, don't ye?" he asked.

Tears rolled down her cheeks and she nodded.

"He did not want to leave ye here, but he could not remain and be subjected to her nastiness."

She sniffled, wiping the dampness from her cheeks before speaking. "I remember my father as a wonderful man. Why was she so unhappy with him?"

Fintan shook his head, his expression shifting to anger. "Yer mother believed she was meant for another, and she would never let it go."

"A-Astrid?"

So intent on their conversation, they were startled to be interrupted by Faolán, who stopped a few feet away.

"Y-yer mother i-is not feeling w-well. She w-wants ye beside h-her."

Fintan's brows arched as if in disbelief, but he said nothing.

"Is there anything else ye need?" Astrid asked the *fili*.

He glanced over at Faolán, who had kept his distance, before taking her hand and moving in close. "Beware, Astrid. Remember yer father's kind thoughts on ye. He was a wise man and knew of what he spoke."

Astrid swallowed, withdrew her hand, and forced a smile for Faolán's benefit. "I enjoyed our talk. I will see ye on the morrow."

Moving away from the man without a backward glance was a hard thing to do, but she did not wish for Faolán to know of her interest in the *fili*. She had so many questions for Fintan. He seemed to know all the secrets of her parents' lives, and there was so much she wanted to understand.

"A-as I-I said, ye are a-a good daughter." Faolán walked abreast of her, but Astrid refused to turn toward him and instead picked up her pace.

"Certainly I am." It was not as if she had a choice.

"There i-is o-one thing, I-I w-wish to w-warn ye a-abo—"

Astrid stopped dead in the doorway of the roundhouse. Her mother was flanked by Pádraig, who stood to her left, and Daimhin, who stood on her right. Beibhinn had never looked happier.

"Pádraig i-is w-with yer mother," Faolán's voice was very quiet.

Tight-lipped, she turned to confront him. "It would have been a kindness to give me some warning."

"I-I-I tried."

Her nostrils flared. "Not hard enough!"

"There ye are." Her mother called to her. "Astrid, come! See who is here to entertain us with more stories."

Grinding her teeth, Astrid searched her mind for a way to escape, but there was no help for it. Unless she was willing to confront the man in front of half the clan, she could not leave. And confronting him now would no doubt make some wonder why she had waited so long to speak up. Faolán's intent expression reminded her that all eyes were on her, waiting for the good daughter to return to her mother's side. Her shoulders rounded, Astrid struggled against a defeated sigh that threatened to escape and walked toward the head table. It felt as if she were headed to a death sentence.

Pádraig's leering gaze made her want to scream. Daimhin's genuine smile of encouragement, however, surprised her. Could the other woman know what inner turmoil this visit was causing her? When Astrid looked to her mother, she felt like she'd been punched in the gut. Beibhinn's look of triumph, her nose in the air, was an arrow firing right through her heart.

While Diarmuid remained in seclusion with Aednat, all were subject to their mother's inclinations. If Beibhinn invited Pádraig and his sister to stay, there was nothing Astrid could do about it.

Pádraig turned his attention to Beibhinn, and that was fine with Astrid.

"'Tis good to see ye," Daimhin said to Astrid.

"Have ye only just arrived?" Astrid asked.

"I came with Pádraig. He said he wished to spend time with ye."

Astrid could think of nothing to say in return, so she did not respond, which didn't seem to bother Daimhin.

"My father was very pleased with the idea of ye joining with my brother." Daimhin's eyes roved the many people before her as she spoke. "He said it would be a wonderful match."

Swallowing a retort, Astrid waited until Daimhin looked at her again before responding. "I am not so inclined. Mayhap there is another yer father would prefer to me?"

"Oh no!" Daimhin laughed in an awkward way, as if Astrid had mentioned something totally unheard of. "There will be no dropping the issue with him now. He is bent on having *ye* in our clan, and the sooner the better. And yer mother, of course."

Well, the Meic Murchadha was about to become very disappointed. The dark-haired lass turned away again, her eyes still intent on the crowd.

"Is there someone in particular ye seek?"

"I thought I might see Marcán. Is he about?"

The memory of this woman straddling Marcán's lap came back in full force. Now Astrid could see it was an attempt at seducing him. She'd probably whispered a promise of it in his ear. Astrid wished she'd thought to question him.

Daimhin's breasts—she could hear Marcán's voice describing how they hung "like heavy fruit"—were crowned with a thick gold chain. It was suddenly difficult to string two thoughts together, but Astrid managed to pry her jaw loose. "I do not believe he has much idle time."

Daimhin merely glanced at Astrid. Beibhinn, however, hadn't missed Astrid's flat tone. Turning to her, she asked, "Is aught amiss?"

Astrid was not about to even try to respond, her hands clenching into fists on her lap.

Daimhin smiled at Beibhinn. "I had just asked on Marcán. Is he about?"

"Oh, yes, Daimhin! Do go and locate the man." Pádraig said, his wide, innocent eyes barely pausing on Astrid before continuing to his sister, but Astrid did not miss it. He was being intentionally cruel. "Sure I am that the man will be more than pleased to tarry with *ye*."

Daimhin stood. "I wish to rekindle our friendship."

He laughed. A loud, attention-getting bark. Like a seal. Astrid tightened her jaw, the image of ripping her nails down the man's face, drawing blood, relieving some of her ire.

"Rekindle what ye like," he said. "Ye've yet to find a suitable man. Mayhap he is the one."

It took every ounce of Astrid's control to not jump up and shove the woman as hard as she could, knocking her flat on her arse. But taking her ire out on Daimhin would not satisfy her—if she relented to the violent wish, she would then want to throw herself at

Pádraig with fists flailing.

"Mayhap." Daimhin nodded and went off through the throng of people, a sweet smile for everyone she passed.

Astrid counted to five before she stood herself.

"Where are ye off to?" Beibhinn asked.

"Ye seem fine. I will make sure Fintan is set for the night."

Pádraig started to stand, but Astrid impaled him with her look. "Do not!"

Her mother frowned.

Astrid adjusted her tone. "Ye can stay and enjoy yerself here. I will be back anon."

With a yank of her *léine* from beneath the table, Astrid strode across the hall toward the door, looking neither left nor right. There was not a chance she would be returning. Everyone in her path parted once they saw the expression on her face, but she did not care what they thought of her. There was no way Daimhin was going to get *close* to Marcán. Not if Astrid had anything to say about it.

Chapter Fourteen

Marcán had been on his way to find Diarmuid when Gréagóir intercepted him. The hostages were acting up and refused to settle down, which only added to the bad feeling he'd had in his gut since his return. Not being able to spend much time with Astrid had left him with a sense of disquiet.

"It may have been nothing, but Astrid gripped my hand as if I was saving her life."

Marcán's gut churned at the ominous words. "And it was Pádraig she was speaking with?"

Gréagóir looked uncomfortable, averting his gaze. "I would not say they were speaking." When he finally looked back at Marcán, his stern expression had returned. "They seemed a bit too close, no disrespect intended."

"None taken. Diarmuid may see the man as harmless, but I'm finding more reasons to think it may not be so. Had I the chance to share my concerns, I am certain our *rí túaithe* would agree with me. We must keep a close eye on that man."

"And I've sent young Nechtan to do just that." Gréagóir smiled. "I can pass it on to some of the others, as well. Pádraig will be kept under tight scrutiny. Astrid may be a handful, but she's our handful. We'll not see another taking advantage of her."

Marcán smiled, unable to take offense at such an honest assessment. Gréagóir looked on Astrid as his own sister, or daughter, but never in an unkind way.

"So be it." With time, Marcán hoped he could help Astrid move away from the lessons her mother had taught her. She would no longer be considered a handful. But Pádraig was more than a problem. He needed his own teaching—and Marcán would be more than happy to be the one to show him the error of his ways.

"I need to get inside before all the best meat is gone." The man patted Marcán's shoulder. "I'll sit beside Ian and be sure we are of the same mind. Don't worry yerself on it. She will be watched over."

Blowing a heavy breath, Marcán watched the man until he disappeared down the path. Diarmuid was beside himself with concern for his wife. Marcán understood Astrid's wish to give her brother time to heal, but things were getting out of hand. Pádraig was coming and going as he chose. That needed to stop, but unless the man was caught doing something offensive, Marcán could not overstep his power by ordering him out of the *túath*. What was needed was for Diarmuid to return to his duty as their king.

Marcán continued down the small path leading through the woods that led to the longhouse of the *ri*. He was the only one who could have this conversation with Diarmuid. It wouldn't be a pleasant discussion, but the man had ignored his duties long enough.

"Marcán?"

He halted at the small voice, waiting for the caller to emerge from the trees. The sight of Daimhin in all her glorious regalia and gold chains immediately set him on guard. He was in no mood to see her or her brother.

"Daimhin."

She smiled, lowering her eyes before glancing up at him again. "I've been seeking ye out."

A provocative statement, or did he simply not trust her? Although he knew the answer, he would play along. He crossed his arms about his chest before answering. "And why would that be?"

The way her slow gaze swept over him might have been effective in the past, but there was no response in his body this time. He finally had Astrid. He had no need for another, although this sudden change in her behavior did raise his alertness. Daimhin had straddled his lap, pressed her breasts against him, and whispered how handsome she found him, but that had been in full view of all her clan. Now she was seeking him out in the dark? Alone? Not a good sign.

"I missed ye the last time I was here," she said. "I did not want to miss ye again."

"I've much to see to this night. Ye need to return to the others."

Despite her hot gazes, she didn't seem at ease as

she moved in closer. "I'm... I'm uncertain how to return."

The path from Diarmuid's home to the rest of the village was intentionally hidden. The man preferred his solitary ways. And yet... Daimhin had managed to make it here just fine. Dare he point that out?

"Come!"

He passed her, leading the way back to the roundhouse.

"Wait!" Daimhin had to run to catch up with him, but he did not slow his pace. If she was still here, then her brother was still here. He needed to speak with Diarmuid as soon as possible so the *ri* would kick the man out on his arse.

Marcán turned on her, his head tipped in open annoyance. "Is aught amiss? Are ye not returning to the others?"

When the lass put her palm flat against his chest, he narrowed his eyes.

"And what are ye about? Touching me?" He lowered his gaze to her hand until she removed it. "If that is what ye're seeking, ye best return home."

"Seeking? I thought we might spend some time together." She moved in closer, as close as she could be without actually touching him. "That ye might like to kiss me."

She offered up her lips to him, closing her eyes, but he remained where he stood, his hands at his hips. "Ye were wrong."

Her eyes flew open, full of shock. "Ye do not wish to kiss me now? Was it that very long ago that ye had yer hands all over me?"

"We were children. I didn't mind groping what ye offered me. Why are ye behaving so?"

She heaved a sigh. "I like the look of ye, Marcán. I won't deny it. Diarmuid was the one I'd set my sights on, but now he's married." She shrugged. "I've heard yer kisses could make an angel sigh."

"An angel?" Marcán was aware of the rumors, but he was not interested in demonstrating. "Go back to yer brother and keep yerself for yer husband. Yer father will kick ye out of the clan if ye keep up like this."

"He cares very little how willing the women are in our clan."

"He'll care about *ye*."

"Not if 'tis *ye* that takes me."

He glared down at her, all but snuggling against his chest. "And why would that be so?"

"Because of who yer father was."

Grabbing both her arms just above the elbow, he set her away from him. "Ye mistook the man. My father had naught to do with yers."

"But Colmán is the very reason my father wants Pádraig to take Astrid to wife." She offered him a dubious look. "Ye've never heard the story?"

His father had seldom spoken of his youth, but that was not surprising. He had become a great warrior, so all the stories he'd told were of his prowess in battle. The past had mattered little. Marcán merely shrugged.

She burst into a huge grin. "Ah! Ye have not!"

"Yer excitement may not be long-lived."

"Ye believe my story is not true?"

"If I remember correctly—and I do—my father thought very little of yers."

"Ah, now that was after their falling out. Our fathers were quite close before that."

187

"My father *never* spoke of yers in a kind way."

"My father was older and wouldn't have been included in the tales of battle told of yer father, but he helped in the training of many of the young warriors in this area, including Colmán."

The two clans had always tried to stay close even after they had been divided generations before. However, they were too different to be peaceful for very long. Like any good storyteller, Daimhin paused for effect, assessing his interest before continuing. "They had a falling out… over a woman."

Unprepared, Marcán was not quick enough to hide his shock, and the woman's eyes narrowed, like those of a cat enjoying its cream. Marcán inclined his head, awaiting further details.

"She was a young lass from our clan. A beautiful woman all the warriors fought over, but she only had eyes for one man. My father encouraged her interest, believing yer father was the best match."

This could only be a lie. Marcán's mother was not a Meic Murchadha. She had been visiting from the Ua Neill clan, and his father had fallen in love with her upon their very first meeting. The point of this story was apparently to keep Marcán from getting back to his duties. He'd had enough of it.

"Astrid will not be marrying yer brother."

Daimhin studied him a moment, and Marcán feared what she might see. "Are ye still out to protect the lass?"

"Always."

"Pádraig told my father he'd had at her."

The lie filled Marcán with outrage, and his lungs expanded with the urge to proclaim it as such, but he had no proof he could share with her. Not yet. Not until he'd settled things with Diarmuid.

"Ye're saying I failed as her protector?" Marcán wrapped his arms about his chest to keep his rage in check. "Astrid would never have lain with yer brother."

Daimhin shrugged again. "I did not say she was willing."

Marcán shook his head at her, scowling to reveal his disgust. "Ye think nothing of yer brother claiming he raped an innocent lass? And ye believe he should take her to wife? Ye've a hard heart, Daimhin."

Beside himself with emotions stirred up by the gruesome battle still fresh in his mind, Astrid's strange behavior toward him, and his fear that Pádraig did indeed have his mind set on the rape of his beloved, Marcán closed his eyes and struggled for a steadying breath.

Daimhin came in closer, wrapping her arms about his waist. It was obvious she had misinterpreted his inner struggle. "There is no need to hold yerself back from me. I want ye. Pleased I am to give myself to ye!"

"Marcán?"

Astrid's questioning voice filled his ears at the very moment he opened his eyes to pull Daimhin's arms off him.

"Astrid! Did ye follow me?" Daimhin stepped back, pressing down her hair, and looking suddenly bemused. "Sorry I am ye had to witness that."

The dark-haired woman was putting on quite a show, even nibbling at her lower lip and turning a passion-inflamed expression toward him. The lass was definitely schooled in her behavior. Would she next be claiming they'd been intimate?

Marcán opened his mouth to speak his defense, but Astrid held her hand up to halt him. She wouldn't even look at him. He was filled with guilt at being caught in this position. Nothing was happening, but no doubt it appeared otherwise, just as Daimhin had hoped.

"Daimhin." Astrid's voice went up at the end as if speaking to a child. "I told ye this warrior had duties."

Astrid's cool demeanor had his total attention. The raise of one slender brow. The hand fisted at her jutted hip. The slight tilt of her head. He was captivated by her.

Daimhin had the nerve to scoff at her. "And he has needs. Be a good daughter now, Astrid, and return to yer mother. *I'll* see to him."

Astrid's eyes widened. Silence hung in the air for a moment, and that intimidating pause, along with his beloved's stoic yet stern expression, caused his breath to hitch.

"And *ye* overstep yerself," Astrid finally said. "Certainly. Ye are a guest here only. Now I ask ye again, return to the others, and do it now."

The command could not be denied, nor could Marcán's pride at Astrid's unmovable stance. She was glorious to watch. Daimhin recognized that she had no choice and tossed him a sad glance. "Mayhap another time."

"I do not believe so." Marcán was quick to set her straight.

The spread of redness across Daimhin's cheeks matched the speed with which she stomped away. He wanted to applaud his beloved but for the expression she now turned on him. His body tensed.

"Certainly ye know I had no interest in the lass."

"Certainly." Astrid's expression never wavered.

"Then what are ye waiting for?" He opened his arms to her. She paused only a moment before accepting the invitation, filling him with relief such as he had never known. "My sweet love. Ye are a commanding woman when yer ire is pricked." He resisted her attempt to move away. "I have no desire to release ye yet."

With her face flat against his chest, it was a challenge to make out her words. "I did not like finding another's arms about ye."

"Nor did I like having another's arms about me." He kissed the top of her head. "'Tis ye alone that I want here. Ye alone belong in my arms."

Rubbing his cheek against her hair, he rocked her in his arms until she finally relaxed and hugged him back. He sighed. "I was sore afeared ye would be foolish enough to believe the show she put on."

Astrid pulled her head back to glare up at him. "I will tell ye again I did not like it. And that is for certain. I also know there is no man in this world that I trust more than ye."

The words touched him deeply and it took a moment for him to speak past the lump in his throat. "And I will live the rest of my life deserving that trust, *a ghráidh.*"

Standing there, holding her against him, he knew a peace that had been a long time coming. His parents had shared a love like this, with absolute trust binding them together. He'd never imagined he could have the same, and yet here she was, within his arms. Nothing could jeopardize their connection—and that knowledge gave him the courage to voice his concerns.

"Has Pádraig been bothering ye?"

"How did ye—" She shifted in his arms. "Gréagóir?"

Astrid's astuteness never ceased to surprise him. "He mentioned it to me."

"I was foolish to allow him to get me alone."

Marcán pulled back, fear tightening his chest. "Tell me."

"There was naught. He… he made rough with me."

Marcán's chest expanded. He was incensed, and only the sight of the other man's blood would calm him. "I shall kill the man!"

She pulled on his arms when he tried to release her. "Please, no bloodshed. Nothing worse happened. Gréagóir interrupted whatever the vile man had in mind."

With his arms locked once again around her, he peered into her face. "Yet ye came here alone, giving him another chance to assault ye. Do not do so again."

"I left the man with my mother. I believe she is enamored with him."

"And she can have him!" Marcán said before blowing out a breath. "I will see ye back to where ye will be safe."

Her eyes rounded. "I am not happy to be such a burden to ye."

"A burden? Never. I wish it to be no other way."

He lowered his lips to hers, bestowing gentle kisses not meant to enflame her desire but to indicate his deep regard for her. There was nothing he would not do for her. Hand in hand, he walked her back to the village, ducking for cover whenever someone passed by like it was a game. Each time stealing a kiss.

"I will sleep out here." She indicated the small building where they'd made love.

It was not well protected, but few would expect to find the sister of the *ri* sleeping in such an uncomfortable place. "Are ye certain?"

"I consider it my place of refuge." Her eyes glistened. "Even more so since our night of passion."

Marcán kissed her again, deeper this time, wanting nothing more than to lay with her again. He forced himself to break the kiss. She looked up at him with a puzzled expression before replacing the look with a tight smile.

"I have much to see to this night," he said. "If I can come to ye, I will."

"If ye are able."

He cupped her cheek. "I look forward to the time when I can take ye in my arms every night."

"As do I."

A final kiss and she entered the dark room. Marcán could not very well leave her there unprotected. Light spilled out from the roundhouse behind him when the door was opened and someone came out. Farther behind the roundhouse was the hideaway where the hostages slept, a guard watching over them in case they continued their troublesome ways. He took the few steps to the hideaway, keeping Astrid's refuge in his sight, and approached Peter, who had been left on watch.

"Marcán. Is aught amiss?"

"I wish the storage shed to be guarded as well. From a distance."

Peter glanced toward the building. It had only the one door and it stood in plain sight. The man nodded. "I've a man coming to relieve me shortly. I can add someone here if that would make ye rest easy."

"It would." Marcán had trusted the man would not question his orders. He was a warrior and did as he was told. "The guards alone need to know of this. Understood?"

Peter nodded. Marcán glanced toward the roundhouse and could imagine Pádraig making himself at ease beside Beibhinn. The man needed to be seen to by Diarmuid, and soon. Marcán headed back down the path to see that done.

Word of Aednat's sudden awakening was cause for days of celebration and revelry, not to mention free-flowing mead and ale. The clan had been in a state of concern and distress for too long. Knowing the wife of the *ri* would soon be joining them—and be properly introduced—made everyone sigh in relief.

There was dancing among all, even the servants, and much storytelling. The *fili* told his new tale of Diarmuid's prowess in battle, which brought great pride to the clan, for the story would soon be repeated wherever the storyteller went. Fintan's sweet song of love between Diarmuid and Aednat would be shared with the couple once she had recovered enough to partake of festivities with the clan.

As the days passed, the sight of Aednat resting in the roundhouse brought a smile to Astrid's face. The woman was still very weak and though Astrid worried for her recovery, she hoped for the best.

Word of a visit from Aednat's cousin and the clan's *ri túath,* Sean, caused even more chaos. It was probably the reason both Pádraig and Daimhin finally returned home. The Meic Murchadha, their father, would no doubt be wanting to see Sean, who was also their overking. An overking had no direct power over the kings under him, but earning the title was a great accomplishment and tribute to a warrior's prowess. It was a distinction most *ri túaithe* sought to attain.

The hostages, a constant source of upset, had kept Marcán busy and away from Astrid. And the ongoing festivities had drained her both physically and mentally. Exhausted again this night, and with no sign of Marcán, she slipped off to her place of solitude with no one the wiser. She had begun to fear their one night of passion was all she would ever have. Though she tried to take comfort from those sweet memories, they blurred in the recesses of her mind as she dropped off to sleep.

"*A ghráidh?*" Marcán's quiet voice drifted into her dreams. The press of his warm body brought her fully awake. "I had hoped to find ye here."

Marcán embraced her and she sighed against his chest. "I have missed ye."

"Not as I have missed ye."

Tipping her head up, she kissed him, and he set her heart to racing with his passionate response.

"And who has been seeing to yer bath?" Her breath unsteady, she tamped down the need he ignited in her.

"I saw to my own bath, and the memory of yer hands on me made it near impossible to finish." Marcán's whispered words sent waves of excitement across her skin. His hand slipping along her length, tracing every curve, made it hard to take a deep breath. "And now that I have ye in my arms, I find I am quite overwhelmed."

"Do ye not fear discovery?" She licked her lips, desiring his kisses more than that elusive breath. The thought that Faolán had indeed discovered them was shoved to the side. This was still *her* place, *her* refuge.

But Marcán halted and propped himself on an elbow to peer down at her. "Did I not tell ye my love for ye should be no secret?"

His gaze followed along her length and she knew his need. Her chest tight, she could not respond.

"I told no one how I desired ye for my wife, because ye showed me no interest, not because it was a secret." His hot gaze met her eyes. "I have wanted nothing more than to shout to the world of my love for ye." He kissed her without restraint, his hands making free over her body. "Make me wait no longer. Let us go to Diarmuid this night. Aednat has awakened. Certainly we can have his blessing now?"

Marcán did not wait for her answer but lowered his head to her breast, tonguing her nipple through the cloth of her shift until it tightened into a sensitive nub. He stilled upon hearing her moan, dipping his head to his chest, his labored breathing the only other sound.

"I have never experienced such little control over my own body, I fear I am unable to hold back when I am with ye." His voice was strained, the tension on his face apparent. "I never want to take ye for my own pleasure alone. Not ever."

"I will have pleasure—"

He made a strangled sound before answering. "Ye will have little pleasure, as I will not last long."

She reached toward him, but he grabbed her hand before she could touch him.

"Do not. Allow me a moment."

He lay on his back, his breathing as ragged as if

196

he'd run a very long distance. Astrid wasn't sure what she should do, so she lay still beside him, cold covering her where the pleasant warmth of his body had been. He had been quiet for so long, she wondered if he had fallen asleep. With all that he had seen to these last days, he must be exhausted. If she snuggled against him, would she awaken him?

The sound of his voice startled her. "The hostages are too much on us. Diarmuid has never taken so long to decide what to do with the men we've conquered. It's his concern for Aednat's feelings and his own wrath that is making this such a hardship for him.

"I am left not knowing whether I am coming or going. The hostages are disgruntled. Demanding. Well-trained and bent on escaping. The entire clan was made up of trained warriors, and they were merciless in battle." His stark words startled her. "They were fighting for their lives. They knew we would give no quarter, and why should we? They had taken the wife of our king."

Astrid didn't dare speak. Didn't dare touch him, lest it silence him. She'd never heard any warrior speak of such things. Not even her brother.

"I feared for my life."

The revelation shocked her and she sat up to watch him, fighting against the fear that lay like a rock in the pit of her stomach. She wanted him to take her in his arms. She wanted him to tell her all would be well. She wanted him to tell her he would always be here, and she would never have to live her life without him, but his revelations required her silence.

"All the things I had longed for, but never had, came to my mind. It seems I have waited a lifetime to take ye to wife." He looked at her with eyes full of raw emotion. "Make me wait no longer, Astrid."

She gulped, tears making it difficult to swallow, but she nodded. "Wait no longer."

Marcán jumped up, shifting from one foot to the other, as if not sure which way to go. His partially shadowed face revealed his excitement. "Ye have made me a happy man."

He moved toward the door, only to immediately turn back and drop to his knees before her. A hand on either side of her face, he drew her close and kissed her. A tender kiss that spoke of the depth of his love. Tears slid down her cheeks.

Pulling back, his expression was somber, and he scanned her face as if seeing her for the first time. "I love ye with all my heart. Trust in my words, and I will see ye well cared for, heavy with child, and cradled safely in my arms every night."

"I will trust in ye. Always."

Marcán's nod sped up and a huge smile spread across his face. "I will go to Diarmuid now."

"This very minute," she agreed.

He stood, wrapped the mantle around himself, and headed out into the night, closing the door behind him.

Astrid lay back down, heaving a great sigh. She would need to wait no longer. Diarmuid would give his blessing and all would be well.

Chapter Fifteen

Astrid scanned the area around her for Marcán, as had become her habit these last days. Between overseeing the hostages and taking on some of Diarmuid's other responsibilities so he could be available to the *ri túath*, he had been constantly occupied and she had seen little of him since his late-night visit to the hut. That he had not yet approached Diarmuid about his desire to take her to wife seemed apparent since no congratulations had come her way. A devastating disappointment.

True, there had been many distractions to fill her own days. Aednat was up and about, which felt like a blessing to everyone in their clan, and their overking, Sean, had arrived for a visit. Astrid's eyes had teared up upon witnessing the reunion between Sean and

Aednat. The cousins were extremely close. Even so, she had not been able to stop thinking about Marcán. What had kept him from speaking with her brother the other night?

Astrid knew there would be an explanation, but it was hard to remain patient. She'd seen Pádraig outside the roundhouse just a few minutes ago with his warband, telling Sean his father had passed the night before, which had made her trepidation increase threefold. He'd even mentioned to Sean *and* Diarmuid that he hoped to take *her* to wife!

"Aednat does not seem very happy here." Joan's observation brought her out of her meanderings.

They were preparing the meal, the meats well underway. Joan stirred a mix intended for the hearth with skilled speed as she spoke, balancing the wooden bowl on her hip, while Astrid chopped the vegetables.

"She's just recovering from a long illness. Give her a chance to get the color back in her cheeks."

No longer able to sit still, Astrid was setting the iron cooking tools aside when Marcán ran in from the direction of the hostages, his face a mask of anger. She moved out of his path, unnoticed.

Joan set her bowl down. "There is aught amiss now!"

Merewyn, who had been shucking peas by the fire with the other slaves, came to stand beside Astrid. The remaining women headed out the door, eager not to miss any of the excitement. Even Joan left.

"Is Marcán hurt?" Merewyn asked.

Astrid's heart leapt into her throat. "He didn't seem to be hurt."

Yelling could be heard outside, and crowds ran past the open door toward the hostages. Her sense of dread only increased. Merewyn took her hand and smiled at her, a reassuring smile. "I am certain he would have shared that with ye if it were so."

Nodding, Astrid tried to smile back, but feared it came out as more of a grimace. What she really wanted to do was to stay inside. She preferred to hide from whatever catastrophe was unfolding and definitely did not wish to witness whatever was causing the commotion with the hostages.

"I believe it was Gréagóir who was guarding them." Merewyn said, as if reading her troubled thoughts. "He is a good man."

Merewyn settled on the bench, urging Astrid to sit beside her, but she sensed the other woman's tension. The roundhouse was empty now except for the two of them. In the silence, the shouting got louder. Astrid found herself straining to hear. Had that been Marcán's voice? She turned to her slave. Suddenly it seemed worse not to know what was happening.

Astrid stood. "I must see what is amiss."

Merewyn stood, her smile tight. "The winds of change."

Astrid glanced around to be sure her mother wasn't nearby. Merewyn might be trying to lighten Astrid's fear, but like as not, Beibhinn would take Merewyn's words as a premonition.

Hesitating but a moment, Astrid asked, "Are the winds changing for me?"

"I was speaking of myself." Merewyn's smile quickly dropped into a very somber expression. She lowered her voice. "But yer fear of yer mother is wise indeed. She cares not how *ye* feel about anyone. Not even Marcán."

The piercing green eyes sent a ripple of fear over

Astrid's skin like the warm breeze just before a summer storm. "I do not understand."

"She will stop at nothing to get what she wants, even if it destroys the man ye love."

Diarmuid's angry voice carried to them. "Ye are headstrong."

Was he speaking to Aednat? As one, she and Merewyn ran toward the crowds gathered out back, behind the roundhouse. They worked their way to the front, Astrid leading the way. There was a dead man on the ground, Marcán's sword in his back, which made her gasp, but the sight of her handsome love made all else around her fade away.

The fear and trepidation that had been steadily working their way up her spine left her, and in their wake she felt a heady sense of relief. The raw need to touch him, to know for certain he was unharmed, caused an ache of longing deep in the recesses of her heart. His anger was undeniable, but it didn't frighten her. Instead, she longed to go to him. Were they betrothed, it would be an acceptable gesture, even expected at times of upheaval, as this gave all the signs of being.

Astrid turned her attention to the scene before her, trying to make sense of the chaos. People yelling. Diarmuid standing beside Aednat, his expression fierce. She appeared quite pale. Thomasina was with them, as well as Sean and Marcán. Astrid gave up the struggle and turned her eyes back to Marcán. So distressed. He didn't see her, too intent on whatever was happening.

"She lies!" Merewyn called out, startling Astrid. When the lass's green eyes turned toward her in a silent question, Astrid had no idea what she was asking but saw her desperation. That was something Astrid understood quite well and she nodded her consent. The girl moved toward Sean, but it was Marcán who again caught Astrid's eye.

From the crowd, she heard murmurings about the hostages' attempted escape. Had Marcán been attacked then? Astrid shifted her gaze back to Marcán, who seemed unharmed and solid as a rock. These hostages were an ongoing problem, and she would be happy when they were gone. When he finally noticed her watching him, his brows dipped low as if in annoyance, and her sigh of relief shifted to concern.

Someone latched onto her elbow a moment later, and Astrid turned to see Pádraig's smiling face. "Ah, ye are a little late for the entertainment."

"Release my arm!" Astrid's breathing sped up at the sight of him despite her show of bravery.

The man merely smiled. A slow, conniving smile meant to intimidate, and it certainly did that.

"Do as she ordered." Marcán's voice held no room for refusal and the sight of him set her heart to soaring. He stopped an arm's distance from them with narrowed eyes and a menacing glare. "If ye've a mind to keep that arm sound, let her go *now*."

Pádraig released her arm, even taking a step away from her. "Well, aren't ye the hero this day?"

"My thanks, Marcán." Her sigh of relief was cut short when Pádraig turned to her, his immense anger obvious.

"Ye have yer protector still, Astrid? And when will ye be explaining to him the change in my status to ye?"

"Yer status to *me?* There is no status, hence there is no change!" Astrid's tone was more than firm.

"Ye prefer I tell him? Or mayhap yer mother?" Pádraig turned to Marcán. "Are ye interested in the news?"

Astrid's breath was trapped in her chest.

Marcán crossed his arms in a show of patience, but the height of his brow indicated something different, as did his tone. "The only news that interests me is why ye don't appear as a man mourning the death of his father."

"Pádraig?" a short, red-headed man, one of his warband, called from behind them. Ian was with him as well. "Yer sister has sent word. She needs ye to return posthaste."

Ian moved in closer to Pádraig, barely glancing at Marcán. "They question ye becoming *ri túaithe*, brother," she overheard. "I am afeared for our safety."

Pádraig snorted, looking back the way the men had come. Ian glanced at Marcán then, trying to catch his gaze, but Marcán's eyes were intent on *her*. She wished to be anywhere but here.

"Astrid." Pádraig turned his gaze to her, his face surprisingly relaxed for one with such turmoil needing his attention. "I wish ye to visit with Beibhinn and listen well. I will be back anon, and we will speak then."

The words themselves were unremarkable and his tone was calm, but Astrid wanted to scream at him. To tell him to leave her alone and never come back. To tell him it didn't matter what her mother had to say, Astrid would not be marrying him. Ever. But she had no words for him.

Tipping his head, Pádraig acknowledged Marcán and left with the red-headed man.

Marcán was beside her in two strides, a single finger sliding against her cheek, his gaze intently searching her. "What was he about? Did he cause ye trouble? Diarmuid has been as elusive as smoke. Please—"

"Marcán?" It was Ian. He stood a few feet away. "May I have a word with ye?"

The boy's cowering manner sent off alarms in Astrid. His paleness indicated the situation was much worse than Pádraig had said. The lad glanced around nervously when Marcán didn't immediately consent.

"I am fine," Astrid said.

"Are ye certain?" Marcán continued in the same intimate tone.

Ian coughed before he spoke again. "A moment of yer time. I beg of ye."

"Wait for me here, Astrid." Marcán's eyes remained on her, but the concern he'd been hiding came through in his expression. She nodded and then watched as the two stepped away, leaving with the dispersing crowd.

"A-Astrid?" Faolán had come upon her so silently she wasn't prepared for him. Her eyes must have shown her blatant fear of him, because he immediately lowered his gaze. "I-I do not like to see such u-upset i-in those eyes w-when ye look o-on me."

She considered telling him he was wrong but decided against it. "What is amiss?"

"Yer mother w-wishes to see ye."

Astrid glanced again toward Marcán. He and Ian stood off to the side, deep in conversation. She gritted her teeth and turned back to Faolán. "And where shall I find her?"

"C-come this w-way."

Instead of leading her back to the roundhouse, Faolán guided her down the path toward Diarmuid's house. What was he thinking? Her brother was with the group they were quickly leaving behind.

Astrid's chest tightened as she followed Faolán onto an offshoot from the path. Marcán's warning not to go anywhere alone rang in her ears. Was she no longer safe with Faolán? She didn't know for certain, but when they came to a clearing, her mother sat there on a rock as if she'd been awaiting her. Astrid had the feeling she had walked into a trap.

Beibhinn's expression was blank even when she spoke to Faolán. "My thanks."

"Are ye not well?" Astrid asked.

Beibhinn slumped slightly, a sigh escaping her lips. "I am weary to my very bones, daughter."

Astrid moved in closer, placing an arm around her shoulders. "Do ye need help getting back? Faolán can hel—"

"No." Beibhinn's eyes bore into her, but Astrid could not sense if she was vexed or sad. "I need to talk to ye."

Astrid glanced at Faolán. The way he avoided her gaze gave her a sick feeling in the pit of her stomach.

Beibhinn continued. "Faolán has brought me some news that I find quite upsetting."

"Oh has he?" Astrid's jaw tightened.

"He has. He believes ye may have been taken in by a man ye should not trust."

Astrid glared at him, but he squared his shoulders, his nose tipped up.

Beside herself with fury, Astrid barked back a reply without even thinking. "And would that be Pádraig?"

The man's pallor was the only change she saw.

Beibhinn gasped. "There is nothing wrong with Pádraig."

"There is much wrong with that man." Astrid shifted toward Faolán. "Tell my dear mother what ye know of him."

"I know nothing for certain about Pádraig, but my eyes do not deceive me, Astrid."

Heat stole over her face when she remembered the sound of the door. She would not dirty that special moment by discussing it now. "Then surely ye shared how ye came upon Pádraig accosting me."

Beibhinn was only momentarily distracted. She quickly reclaimed control of the situation with her loud, overbearing voice. "Enough, daughter. Do not attack the messenger. I trust his word that he heard ye speak of Marcán to Aednat."

Astrid hesitated. Relief, however brief, washed over her.

"Ye may leave us, Faolán," Beibhinn said, taking advantage of Astrid's distraction. "Sit, Astrid. Hear me."

Astrid did as she bid but refused to acknowledge Faolán's departure, fighting down the unease that churned in her gut.

"I have cared for my children the best way I knew how. Mayhap I have not always done the right thing, but 'twas never for want of trying." She glanced at Astrid, who nodded on cue. "I've loved ye all, and when Fergus died I... I felt as if my heart had been ripped from my chest."

As Beibhinn wiped at the copious tears that seemed so genuine, Astrid's own eyes began to water. She missed her little brother and wondered what kind of man he would have grown to become. Probably very much like Diarmuid. But Beibhinn's voice called Astrid back from her wistful thoughts.

"That was when I knew I would never belong here. Not ever. If I'd had my wish, I'd have remained with my clan and never come to this God-forsaken place. Especially now…"

Astrid knew how much her mother disliked their clan, but she could never agree with her assessment. Her mother's animosity was very hard to understand.

"…when yer brother has married himself a healer."

Astrid had noticed her mother's clipped attitude with Diarmuid's wife. All her talk of Aednat's powerful connections had fallen away. "Aednat is a good woman—"

Beibhinn halted her with her hand. "I cannot abide by such devil worship in my own home. I am happy to say I've found a way back to the clan of my youth, but I need yer help."

The gray eyes that met Astrid's were wide with accusation, and she shriveled up inside at the thought of the confrontation that was finally about to take place.

"Mother, I do not—"

"Ye've always been a good daughter to me. Always. And I know that."

Astrid dare not breathe, though she was certain her eyes were wide with fear.

"I cannot expect ye now to set aside yer own happiness for mine," Beibhinn said.

Astrid sighed, her shoulders rounding with relief. The thought that perhaps her mother did somewhat care for her was comforting.

Her mother continued, "I am an old woman and my life is near done now—"

Astrid fought against her trembling lip. Regardless of how her mother behaved, Astrid would miss her terribly when she passed.

"—Ye are still young with yer life ahead of ye. Certainly yer happiness means more to me than my own. I grant ye that…"

Beibhinn's voice trailed off, and Astrid waited for her to resume. Her confusion had to be apparent on her face, but Beibhinn gave no indication of noticing.

"So I will stay," Beibhinn said, "spending my remaining days here among these people. I will learn to make do."

Astrid's guard slipped, her vulnerability open. "I love ye, *mamaídh*. I will see that ye are well cared for always."

Beibhinn nodded in a thoughtful way, and Astrid became aware of the guilt growing in her. Guilt for ever having questioned her mother's motives. Guilt for believing her mother would choose her own happiness over that of her daughter. Guilt for a hundred times that she'd wished her mother would leave her alone.

"But I find I cannot stay and be quiet any longer."

And like that, Astrid's need to escape shot high into the air like an arrow seeking a target.

"There is darkness around us."

Astrid became mindful of the air passing into her lungs through parted lips, her jaw slack from disbelief.

"I'm needful of seeing it cast out."

Facing Astrid, her mother's eyes were like twin dark holes piercing into her, their depths unfathomable. "I've called for the priest."

Her breath was trapped in her chest, squeezing her lungs, but Astrid forced the words out. "What are ye saying?"

Beibhinn tipped her head as if speaking to a child. "I cannot stay *here* among the healers… and the Seers… any longer. They must be punished for their evil works, and if I am the one who must stand by and watch? Then I will see them taken down."

The birds chirped overhead, and the voices of the others in the yard carried to them while Astrid considered her mother's words. It was an ultimatum, no question about that. The exact threat, however, was more vague. Not just Aednat then? But—

A painful gasp ripped from Astrid's throat. "Why are ye so hateful?"

Her mother's eyes narrowed and her lips flattened. "My concern is for the clan I am a part of and none other."

"Who would stop ye from returning to the Meic Murchadha, mother? Who would tell ye no if ye wanted to return to them?"

Beibhinn tipped her nose up. "I left the clan with no standing to come back. My father told me as much."

"Yer father is dead! Certainly ye would be welcomed back into—"

"They will not have me!" Beibhinn screeched the words.

Astrid stood, for the first time in her life afraid of her own mother. "What did ye do?"

The gray-haired woman shook her head. A final answer.

"It must have been bad indeed if they will not accept ye back," Astrid said.

"I have a way back in… but 'tis not acceptable to

ye." Her mother's eyes swelled with tears, fat drops sliding down her cheeks. "I will not force my daughter to do what is reprehensible to her."

"Do ye know what kind of man Pádraig is? He tried to force himself on me, *mamaídh*. Do ye not even care how he treated yer only daughter? Certainly ye cannot be saying I should marry him after that?"

"If ye are one of the lucky ones, ye will not see him often. Ye will not be forced to take him into yer bed but to get with child."

Astrid's jaw went slack, her mouth again hanging open, unable to believe what her mother was saying and unable to respond.

"I would not ask ye to do what I would not do myself."

"What are ye saying?" Surely she must be misunderstanding the implication, but her mother's stoic expression pushed her to be certain. "My father would *never* have forced himself on ye. Not ever!"

Beibhinn closed her eyes, as if guarding herself against an overpoweringly painful memory. "He was not who I wanted in my bed."

Astrid covered her ears, shaking her head. This could not be true. Her father had been gentle and kind. Pelting hail on her head would have hurt less than this assault of words. Long ago, she had believed her parents had been truly in love, but all her innocence was gone now.

"Is aught amiss?" Diarmuid's voice startled both women.

Astrid jumped, angling away from him to wipe the dampness from her face before turning back. Her mother, silently watching her, made no move to answer her son's question. Astrid's blood ran cold. The woman was leaving it to her to answer him.

Diarmuid turned to her as well. "Astrid?"

The world spun around her, and Astrid struggled with all she had just learned. Her mother didn't care if Pádraig mistreated her daughter. She didn't care if Diarmuid's wife was burned as a witch like that woman in the *fili*'s story. Beibhinn didn't care who she hurt as long as she got what she wanted.

But Astrid *did* care. She cared about Diarmuid and Aednat's happiness. Her love for Marcán could never allow her to do anything that would cause him harm. The fear she'd felt earlier came back to swamp her, and she realized she'd rather die herself than allow anyone to hurt him. If she had to give him up to know that he was safe, she would do so. She would give her mother what she wanted, rather than have Marcán *and* Aednat subjected to such an outrage.

Astrid shoved her shoulders back and took a deep breath before responding.

"Mother and I were discussing my betrothal to Pádraig."

Chapter Sixteen

Marcán didn't like leaving Astrid, but Ian's behavior was a bit disconcerting. If the lad hadn't mentioned his worries about his brother taking over as *ri túaithe*, Marcán wouldn't have been quite so willing to abandon her. It felt an eternity since they had last met in the shed, and Pádraig's allusion to some sort of announcement was just what he did not want to hear.

Even with Pádraig gone, Marcán had a bad feeling about the situation. Every attempt he'd made to discuss a betrothal with Diarmuid had been interrupted. Short of holding his friend still and forcing him to listen, Marcán could find no way to speak alone with him. He realized now that was exactly what he should have done.

These hostages were certainly more than a handful

for everyone involved, and after their attempted escape, Marcán was almost ready to help with their execution just to be done with them. Almost. They worked well together, which made them an asset to any clan, and a threat to anyone trying to hold them.

Ian paused a good distance from the others but still searched around to be sure they were alone, his eyes rounded with concern. Finally, he turned to Marcán, his face tight. "I am afeared my father did not die unassisted."

Not at all what Marcán had believed the lad was going to say. It took a moment for him to recover enough to respond. Murder was a serious offense. Murdering a *ri túaithe* even more so, as it would render the clan more vulnerable to attack. Normally a *tánaiste* would quickly take over, but Ian's clan had no one. And to make such an accusation? Ian was young, but the repercussions for making claims such as these could alter his entire life.

"Ye *think* he was murdered?"

"I *know* he was murdered."

"Ye *know*?" Marcán studied the lad. "I know the loss of yer father must be a great blow to ye—"

"I am not wrong!"

"Did ye see it happen?"

"No—"

"Then ye don't *know*."

Ian spoke through clenched teeth. "It was made to appear that he died in his sleep."

"And were ye in the bed with him?"

"No."

"In the room with him?"

"No, but—"

"Then. Ye. Do. Not. *Know*."

Ian's face crumpled, and the lad clearly struggled with his emotions. Marcán refused to back down. Such accusations would not go unpunished if they were proven wrong. He liked the lad. He didn't want to see his future ruined.

"Short of a firsthand account, and even better a second witness, ye need to keep yer thoughts to yerself."

"I knew my father, Marcán. I knew his habits."

When Ian gripped his arm, his trembling fury surprised Marcán.

"He had a bit of chamomile tea each night before he lay down. Every night."

"And he had not?"

"Oh the cup was there, but 'twas not only chamomile flowers I found in it."

Ian pulled his closed fist out of the sack hanging from his belt and opened his hand. The telltale white flowers of a poisonous plant sat crushed in his palm.

"Ye found hemlock in his cup?"

Ian nodded, his eyes brimming with unshed tears.

"Then he was indeed murdered," Marcán said.

"Thank ye." The lad's voice cracked, but he struggled for composure.

"And who would want to see him dead?"

Ian's frown pushed the tears down his cheeks. When he raised his brows, Marcán realized the lad didn't need to say the name. Pádraig.

"Is yer brother that heartless?"

"They'd had an argument, a bitter argument that neither would back down from. I tried to block it out. They said such vile things."

"And what was the argument about?"

"Daimhin." Ian wiped his face with an impatient

gesture, his face reddening with his anger. "When Daimhin came back without Astrid—"

"Astrid?"

"My father had sent her to bring Astrid to him. Daimhin refused at first. She did not want to go, but my father... compelled her to do his bidding."

Marcán's own blood was beginning to boil. "He beat her?"

Ian nodded. "When she returned with Astrid's refusal, he beat her again. He said she hadn't tried hard enough to persuade her. When Pádraig found out about the beating, he was beside himself."

Marcán could not actually imagine that man coming to the defense of any woman. He was a user of women, not a defender of them. "So they had an argument about yer father's treatment of Daimhin?"

"Pádraig and Daimhin are very close. Closer than most siblings."

Marcán sensed there was something Ian was not saying, and he was nearing the end of his patience. "Ye asked to speak to me, Ian. Either do so, or allow me to return to my duties."

Ian shifted, averting his eyes. "Do ye know how our clans are connected? How the land was once owned as one *túath*? A great and powerful clan?"

Ready to rip the boy's face off for dragging out the story, Marcán merely nodded. "Two brothers had a falling out and the land was divided."

A terrible waste. Once the clan was divided, they became of little importance, their glory days behind them.

"That is correct. My father wanted to be the one to unite the clans again, to bring our people back to their previous prominence. He was a very ambitious man."

216

"Through battle?" Marcán asked.

"Not his first choice. He had hoped to do it peaceably, though marriage, and his eyes were on yer father—"

"*My* father? How so?"

"If Colmán were to take a woman from our clan to wife, my father could have someone he knew and trusted at his side. He believed he could convince Colmán to be his second and unite the tribes."

"There was one woman he believed could win Colmán—a most beautiful woman, much sought after. He encouraged her to spend time with yer father, woo him into marriage. Yer father was interested at first, but then he met yer mother."

Daimhin had begun to tell him this story the other day, he realized, only he had not let her finish. Up until now, Marcán had never heard of his father's interest in any woman other than his own mother. "And who was this woman?"

"I do not know her name. Daimhin marrying Diarmuid or Pádraig marrying Astrid would accomplish the same thing. My father would have settled for either. When Diarmuid married, that left only Astrid."

Of course, it didn't leave Astrid at all, and the sooner everyone knew she was taken, the better. "I have had much to contend with here, Ian—"

"I believe Pádraig murdered our father."

The words hung in the air like a bad smell. "He did not want to be forced to marry Astrid?"

"Oh he was fine with marrying her. Seeks her hand even now, playing up to Beibhinn."

Marcán gritted his teeth but remained focused. "But ye do not know for certain if 'twas Pádraig?"

Ian's look of betrayal hit Marcán in the gut. "I

have spoken to ye of this. He has reason! He wants to be king."

Certainly Marcán believed the man was capable of murdering someone, but his own father?

There were many fathers who treated their children thus—men who had a taste for cruelty didn't always care to protect their own families from their wrath. His own father and mother had been kind, choosing to be patient with him rather than using their fists.

Marcán hesitated but a moment before asking the question on his lips. "And why was it different for ye?"

Ian seemed taken aback.

"Ye never spoke of yerself when ye mentioned yer father's behavior. Was it only Pádraig and Daimhin who felt his wrath?"

The lad nodded. "I am from the second wife my father took, a younger woman he loved very deeply. I assumed he did not love their mother. From the stories I have heard, there seemed to be constant strife between them. She would be locked in her room for days, also receiving beatings at his hand."

A cruel man then, although Marcán had never sensed it himself. "Ye're saying Pádraig murdered his father so that he could take over as king?"

"And he does not have the support of our clan."

"Then the *derb fine* will not be behind him. He will have acted for nothing."

"They will support him, because they have no choice. That is why we are without a *tánaiste.*"

"There is no one but yer brother?"

"The *tánaiste* died suddenly last fall. Many believe he was killed. No one has named my brother.

218

Not yet."

Marcán sighed. "Ye fear for yer clan. I understand, but what would ye have me do?"

"I am uncertain what ye can do." Ian shrugged, his shoulders rounded in defeat.

Marcán struggled for words to encourage the lad. "Ian, the *derb fine* are nobility. A *fine line* of nobility. They are powerful men. Trust the ones that will serve on this council to do what is best for yer clan. Ye yerself are descended from kings and may someday serve on this council. Would *ye* accept a bribe to give support to someone who cannot even defend his own clan?"

"I do not trust them. I cannot trust them, not when I know many are indebted to Pádraig!"

"The *derb fine* are above such things. How are they indebted?"

"I do not know for certain." Ian's glance shifted, as if searching for an answer that refused to come. He finally looked at Marcán. "But *ye* are a man I trust. If ye would come and be near when they meet, I would be grateful."

Marcán was from the line of kings, so he could be part of the council and had done so when needed. But he was a man of action, preferring to be at Diarmuid's side to sitting around discussing how things should go.

"I will do what I can for ye, Ian. I will remain close at hand to them, and if I can speak any truth to them, I will."

"My thanks." Ian grasped his wrist in a show of respect, and Marcán returned the gesture. "They meet in a few days' time, and until then our clan is vulnerable. Please speak to no one of my concerns. I do not wish to be found dead as well."

Searching his face for any sign that he was but jesting, Marcán instead recognized his resoluteness. "Nor do I. I will speak of this to no one."

By the time Marcán returned, Astrid was nowhere in sight. He searched the faces of those in the roundhouse, but again there was no sign of her. Astrid was not there, and his exhaustion was quickly overtaking him. Gréagóir had been given the duty of seeing to the hostages, no doubt as a show of support from Diarmuid, which suited Marcán fine.

Joan approached with a trencher. "The goings-on outside have ye missing the repast."

"Not by choice." He accepted the food, leaning against the wall to partake. "And has Astrid been about?"

He had done his best to sound merely curious, but Joan's eagle eyes were on him, her lips curling slightly. "She is attending her mother."

"Her mother?"

The cook shrugged and returned to her own food. "Faolán said they sent word for the meal to begin without them."

Faolán and her mother. Not the best combination. The two could easily light a fire under his sweet Astrid by their mere presence. He hoped she'd be strong against them, knowing now that she had nothing to fear, not with him supporting her.

Marcán dallied in hope of Astrid's return, but after finishing the food and a second horn of mead, he had to admit she was not returning. He sought the refuge of the little building he now thought of as theirs. Mayhap he could get some rest with the memory of their lovemaking foremost in his mind.

A moonless night, the room was so black that he

could not see his hand in front of his face. He closed the door behind him and felt along the walls, touching the stacked wooden barrels as he sought the spot that he'd cleared for them.

"*Oomph.*"

Marcán had hit someone with his foot. "Who is there?"

"Who do ye wish it to be?"

Astrid's sweet voice was like a balm to his tired body, and he dropped to his knees beside her. The memories coming back, bombarding his senses.

"I searched ye out," he said, his words breathy with desire.

"And ye didn't find me." She sounded to be sitting up now, a smile in her voice.

"Had I known ye were here, I would have come at once."

"And that would have given me great pleasure," Astrid said.

He reached for her.

"And what trouble is yer mother getting into now?" Marcán asked. An audible gasp. "I was but teasing. Certainly ye know she is no longer a problem for ye? Ye have *my* protection."

Astrid flattened her cold hand to his cheek. "And *ye* have mine."

He smiled at the odd statement before turning her hand and pressing a kiss to her palm. "Ah, my lovely Astrid."

Her deep sigh spoke of contentment. "Happy I am that ye are here with me now."

"As am I."

With a hand flat against his chest, she urged him to the ground. "I have missed ye."

221

Astrid rested her head against his shoulder and Marcán wrapped his arms tightly around his love.

"And this is where ye shall remain," he said.

Her body tightened, but she kept quiet.

"Do ye fear discovery still?" he asked.

She nodded her head against him, the scent of lavender drifting to him.

"Ye have nothing to fear. Discovery will make everything fall into place."

Her moist cheek brushed his hand when she leaned up to kiss him. He pulled her closer as if to devour her sweetness and she returned his kisses just as passionately. Breaking away, he stroked her damp skin.

"Why do ye cry?"

There was a long pause before she answered. "Because I am where I belong."

"Ye are indeed. Now let me love ye."

Astrid closed her eyes, determined to take in every detail of his lips on hers.

Despite her mother's insistence, Diarmuid had neither agreed to give his consent nor to discuss Astrid's betrothal to Pádraig. In this way, he had given her hope. He'd watched her closely while their mother had gone on and on about the rightness of the joining and how well Pádraig would take care of Astrid. As if he could see into her soul and knew this was not the way it should be. Mayhap for the first time, Astrid had truly felt the depth of her brother's deep love for her as well as his wisdom. Wisdom all of the kings were said to possess.

The forceful way he'd told Beibhinn to set it aside for now had made Astrid breathe a sigh of relief. And the way that he'd asked *Astrid's permission* for Merewyn to return to her own people? That had gone a long way toward showing Astrid that her brother was seeing her differently. She would miss Merewyn, but trusted Diarmuid when he said it was what the lass wanted. And no one could deny that it would be safer for someone with Merewyn's healing ability and low status to keep well away from Beibhinn.

No sooner had Diarmuid walked away than Beibhinn had repeated her threat. She'd narrowed her eyes shrewdly and said, "When the priest comes, all things will be settled. Do ye not agree?"

Astrid, clinging to the slender strands of hope her brother had given her, had replied, "All things will indeed be settled in due course… for all of us."

And now here she was with her love. After saying a farewell to Merewyn, Astrid had snuck away unseen to lie in wait, praying for Marcán to come to her. Her prayers had been answered.

Desperate to remember everything, Astrid could not get enough of him. His sweet murmurs of love, the arousing touch of his hands on her bare skin, and the gentleness of his mouth setting her aflame were all etched in her mind. Just when she was certain she was satiated, the tears returned and she again sought his ministrations.

"Ye are like an unquenchable need in my soul," he said, as if it were him seeking to remember her rather than the other way around.

Repeatedly she told him she loved him, and she would only ever love him. When he held her close, their bodies spent, he kissed the top of her head and her eyes drifted closed. This could well be the last time she would be held in his arms, intimately entwined in

both body and soul, and the thought crushed her.
She was in no hurry to see the night end.

Chapter Seventeen

The sun was just cresting the horizon as the party accompanying the *ri túath* began to gather near the *ráth*. The group included Diarmuid since Sean sought his support at a meeting with several other *rig túath*. Aednat's reprehensible treatment at the hands of Black Oengus needed to be addressed. With a rogue noble stooping to such behavior, a long-standing agreement had been breached, and a new level of understanding was required. Sean had even considered going so far as to put it into writing, which gave it the same importance as the word of God. His hope was that with Diarmuid present, the others might be persuaded to take this monumental step.

Brighit, Sean's daughter, seemed particularly

interested in getting the trip started. Her reins were so tightly held, the animal was having a hard time staying still. The others who'd gathered for the journey east to the Drogheda Clan seemed less anxious. The lass's parents had not even joined her yet.

Marcán, who'd come early to wait for Diarmuid, gripped the lead of his friend's prized horse and approached him as soon as he arrived. "I had hoped we could speak."

"Brighit, please settle yer horse," Diarmuid called to the girl before turning his attention back to Marcán. "Sean has his hands full with that one."

"More so her betrothed, I believe." Marcán dropped his smile. "I have been trying without success to approach ye w—"

"Let loose the reins, lass." Diarmuid's voice carried across the group.

"I am trying!" An angry blush spread across her face as her mount continued its skittish movements.

"Have ye never ridden before?"

Marcán turned away to hide his smile at Diarmuid's teasing.

She was a proud lass and her response was not surprising.

"If ye think ye can do a better job, Diarmuid, ye're welcome to try!"

A quick look at Diarmuid's face betrayed his irritation. His concern for his wife, and reluctance to leave her at such a time were obvious to Marcán.

"More than a handful," Diarmuid mumbled.

"And ye said the same about yer sister," Marcán replied in the same hushed tone.

Diarmuid's eyes widened at Marcán, who simply

226

smiled and asked, "So now do I have yer attention?"

Brighit's horse's antics made the rest of the horses restless and caused general disgruntled comments. Silently, Marcán and Diarmuid watched until she finally got the beast to settle down.

"Will ye see to things here?" Diarmuid pulled on his riding gloves with irritating precision.

"I will see to all things," Marcán said. "Do not fash yerself. Astrid will keep yer wife company until yer return."

Diarmuid's sharp glance gave Marcán pause, as if he'd heard something in his tone. Was his affection for Astrid so obvious that even saying her name revealed his true feelings?

"And what did ye wish to speak to me about?" Diarmuid asked, his eyes narrowing.

Something in Diarmuid's expression caused an uneasiness to creep into Marcán's chest. He searched his friend's face. Was Marcán being overly suspicious, or was the man playing with him?

He decided to tread lightly. "We have not had much time for discussion, try as I might to speak with ye…"

Thomasina and Sean joined the group and the horses shifted around them.

Diarmuid's gaze did not wander. "I am listening *now.*"

"Marcán." Sean acknowledged him with a nod. Then he mounted his horse in a single leap and reached down to pull Thomasina up in front of him.

Thomasina's quiet laughter carried to them. "Do ye fear I will leave ye if I am given my own mount?" she asked.

"I will not take the chance," Sean replied.

"Diarmuid," Thomasina said, "is Aednat not joining us?"

Diarmuid finally turned to the overking and his wife. "A long ride for one still recovering, but I will return straightaway."

Sean adjusted the reins, his horse shifting farther away from Brighit's antsy mount.

"I sense an urgency among our group. *Reidh*?"

Keen disappointment ripped through Marcán, but he stepped back, ready to see them off. He could not risk upsetting the overking. Certainly when Diarmuid returned, there would be a great celebration to go along with his betrothal to Astrid.

Diarmuid, however, remained unmoving. He glanced at Sean. "Give us a moment."

Sean tipped his head, turning his horse about to exchange pleasantries with the others in the group.

Diarmuid took hold of Marcán's arm in a surprisingly strong grip, leading him a few feet away before releasing him. "If there's something ye need to speak to me about, best ye say it. Waiting at this point can come to no good."

The man knew! Anger tightened Marcán's face and he crossed his arms. "Would I be telling ye anything ye didn't know by now?"

Diarmuid raised his brows, not even trying to hide his annoyance. "I said waiting at this point can come to no good."

"If ye know I am in love with yer sister, why would ye make me wait and ask ye when ye know how difficult 'tis been to speak with ye? Just let me take her to wife and put me out of my misery."

Diarmuid's eyes narrowed. "I'm thinking there's not been *too* much misery. Something else entirely,

228

something much more pleasant."

Heat spread across Marcán's face. Diarmuid's attempt at embarrassing him was quite effective. "Never without a promise to be joined in truth. I will have the church's—and yer—blessing."

"Ye've had my blessing from the beginning."

"The beginning?"

Diarmuid snorted a laugh. "Even when I had no idea what ye saw in Astrid, or if she'd ever come to her own realization about ye."

"With yer mother scheming against me for her own purposes, what was I to think?"

Tipping his head, Diarmuid replied, "And was I to make it so very easy on ye? What sort of man would ye be if I needed to fight yer battles?"

"I'd lost hope she'd ever come around." It felt as if a great weight had been lifted from his shoulders, and his sigh of relief was long and deep. "I've wanted her forever."

Seeing the warning in his friend's eyes, Marcán realized how lustful he'd sounded and spoke more quickly. "She's the only woman I've ever wanted to take to wife."

Diarmuid watched him a moment more before nodding his head, a tightness around his mouth. "Heed my warning. There's some sort of trouble about that ye'll need to see to… and I give ye leave to deal with it however ye decide."

"Would that be yer mother's scheming?" Marcán spat out the words.

"I trust ye with my sister, but tread lightly until I can announce it myself."

Marcán gritted his teeth, his patience at an end. Diarmuid's agreement was all he'd ever sought. It was all that had held him back from outwardly seeing her as his own. The thought of waiting even longer did not sit well with him. "Why the delay? Diar—"

Diarmuid raised a gloved hand to halt his word. "It seems my sister is quite different from our mother after all and chooses not to be the cyclone causing havoc. If there is trouble between our clan and the Meic Murchadha over yer betrothal, I prefer it be on my head and not yers. I need to see to this matter with Sean. Do what ye need to in my absence, but be certain to protect her from any that would harm her... as if she were yer own, even now."

"My thanks." Marcán clasped his wrist, pulling him closer for a hug and a slap on the back. "My thanks!"

"Do we have more cause for celebration?" Thomasina asked, Sean shifting their horse around so they were openly watching them.

Diarmuid leapt onto his horse before answering. "Indeed, but an event such as this requires time, which I will not have until my return. Let us be off so my return will be sooner."

Marcán watched them long after they were out of his sight, thinking over Diarmuid's warning... and his consent to allow Marcán to see to the matter as he saw fit. He would do just that. With determined steps he entered the roundhouse, his eyes seeking and finding Astrid easily among the bustling crowd cleaning up the room and preparing it for their daily duties. He stopped to watch her, contentment settling in his gut with the knowledge of Diarmuid's blessing. Dare he share that with her? Would she be as excited as he was? She'd been quiet in the shed, too quickly running off even as Marcán had been inclined to make love yet again. Her kiss goodbye had been sweet—

He stood straighter as he remembered her kiss and parting words.

Know that I carry yer love in my heart always.

The finality of those words struck him now. With a deeply furrowed brow, she appeared upset even from this distance. When her mother came to stand beside her, that worried look only deepened, and Beibhinn's words caused her to gawk at the woman. Before Marcán could get his feet to move closer, they both turned to him, almost as if the old woman's words had been about him. The look of satisfaction on Beibhinn's face only increased his trepidation, but Astrid's expression of horror had him quickly closing the distance. Beibhinn drifted away.

"What is amiss?" Suddenly aware of the others in the room, he stopped himself from reaching out to her. "Is it washing day?"

She dropped her gaze to the material in her hand. "My mother prefers I keep to my embroidery and allow the others to see to such things."

Her voice was tight, and Marcán's sense of disquiet deepened. To hell with anyone watching. He touched her hand, and she looked up at him with wide eyes.

"What has ye so upset? Is yer mother causing problems still?"

Astrid's obvious attempt at composure made him even more worried. Fear rippling through his gut, he moved in closer still. "Tell me what she has said to make ye so upset."

"Marcán!" Beibhinn called to him with a stern tone.

He did not look away from Astrid but lowered his voice. "I can give aid only if ye tell me what is amiss."

231

"Leave my daughter alone."

The woman had the audacity to come right up to him, even pulling on his arm until he finally turned his anger on her. "Remove yer hand from me, woman."

The sudden quiet assured him they had the attention of all in the room, but Beibhinn refused to listen.

"Do not be upsetting Astrid." Beibhinn spat the words at him.

"*Ye* are the only one upsetting anyone here." Marcán's soft words were for her ears alone, then he met the eyes of those taking in the scene, raising his voice to them. "Move along with yer work."

They immediately dispersed, which eased Marcán's rapidly rising ire. Slightly. He got a quick glimpse of Astrid—her trembling lips, the huge tears slipping down her cheeks—but he kept his attention on Beibhinn. "Obey me or bear the consequences, woman!"

The old woman dropped his arm as if she'd been touching something quite repulsive and took a step back. An expression of satisfaction moved across her face and she smiled. "And ye would do well to do the same."

When Astrid pulled her hand out of his grip, he finally looked at her. Her face was controlled now, her fingers clasped so tight they were colorless. Marcán had seen Astrid be pushed around by her mother for years. Pathetically desperate for her mother's approval, Astrid had always struggled against Beibhinn's dominant ways but avoided direct confrontation.

"She does not appreciate such familiarity," Beibhinn said.

Astrid's expression remained unchanged but for her gently flaring nostrils. Marcán recognized the anger sitting just below the surface.

While Diarmuid had once dismissed his sister as being too much like his mother—and their mother certainly believed she had bullied Astrid into obeying—Marcán had watched the fire in Astrid's eyes for years. He knew her deep need to break away from her mother's side. Her mother may have believed she'd cowed Astrid into approaching Pádraig about their joining, but she'd only done Beibhinn's bidding as a last attempt to escape her clutches.

"And neither will her betrothed," Beibhinn added.

The words felt like a fist into his gut and Marcán turned wide eyes to Beibhinn. "Betrothed?"

"Oh, did ye not hear of her betrothal to Pádraig?"

Blood pounded in his ears, and Marcán gritted his teeth before speaking. Diarmuid's order to hold back on making the announcement until he returned tied Marcán's hands.

"I did hear of *yer* desire for such a joining, but I did not hear Diarmuid announce any such thing."

"There was not enough time for the announcement before he left."

The woman lied. Marcán exhaled slowly, struggling against the desire to allow his ire to erupt. He would know satisfaction in the end, no matter what Beibhinn was plotting.

"Ye are claiming there is a betrothal between Astrid and Pádraig?"

"His father and I discussed it even before he passed." Beibhinn shrugged. "And it was her father's wish as well. Kane would be quite pleased."

Marcán couldn't help turning his astonished gaze

233

to Astrid. She had spoken of her father but never mentioned any such agreement. On the contrary, she'd said her father had left her without prospects. Beibhinn's lies had grown bolder.

"'Tis an agreement between us, as he is soon to be *ri túaithe* for his clan. Ye would do well to keep yer distance from her henceforth."

And that fact was no doubt what was making Beibhinn so giddy at the prospect of Astrid wedding Pádraig. Astrid's sudden paleness was making it difficult for Marcán to take a breath. He wished she would find the courage *now* to reject her mother's words and stand up to these lies. Surely she realized he would support her.

Despite the near panic crawling across his body like a thousand spiders, Marcán crossed his arms about his chest and gave Beibhinn a speculative look. "Have ye no care for yer daughter? That man is a most vile creature."

"Yer opinions will matter very little to either of us once we are happily reunited with my clan."

"Ye mean once *ye* are reunited. 'Twould not be reuniting for Astrid, as she is not a Meic Murchadha."

"Not yet!" Beibhinn countered.

"Not ever!" Marcán's temper flared and his words came out louder than intended. Astrid's small hand on his arm brought his gaze back to her. When she shook her head in silent resignation, he felt the floor shift beneath him.

"Ye are agreeing to this?" He regretted the question as soon as he spoke it.

It gave power to Beibhinn's words and put Astrid on the defensive. That her chin trembled against her tears confirmed his worst fears. She would allow her mother to continue to bully her. When he moved toward her, intent on comforting her and giving her the strength she needed, Beibhinn got between them.

"See to yer duties," Beibhinn said. "*I* will see to my daughter."

He had more to say. Much more. If this woman cared for her daughter at all, it was a well-hidden affection. The look of fear on Astrid's face made him hold his tongue. Stiffly, he gave them his back, keeping his eyes focused on the door to the outside. Forcing one foot in front of the other, Marcán made it out of the roundhouse, but his mind was in a fog, uncertainty nipping at his heals like an irritating mutt.

"Marcán."

Someone called his name and he turned toward the sound without thinking. His mind awhirl with events and sights, he struggled to decide how best to proceed. Two men had come up alongside him, but Marcán's mind refused to recognize them. He was certain he could no longer feel his own breath in his body.

"Murdoch?" It was Ian who spoke, he realized, and through the haze in his mind, the lad's concerned expression struck a nerve.

When Ian turned toward the older man at his side, Marcán tightened his resolve to focus.

"I have spoken to ye of Marcán, son of Colmán," Ian said.

Both sets of eyes turned toward Marcán, but he was again feeling the touch of Astrid's hand on his arm, seeing the defeated look in her eyes when she had shaken her head and told him no.

"Ah, yes, Marcán. My name is Murdoch, son of Alastar. Happy I am to see ye again. I remember yer father well, Marcán," said the older man with snowy white hair and a matching beard. "A fine man indeed, and I hear the same of ye."

Marcán made no response, and the man glanced toward Ian, a questioning expression. The men serving on the council changed depending on who was available, and this was not a man Marcán recognized. His thoughts drifted. Why would Astrid agree to a betrothal to Pádraig?

"We do not wish to impose on ye, but were wondering if ye could offer yer assistance," Murdoch said. "With Diarmuid away and my brother ill, the council is short. We're in a bind and there are pressing matters that cannot await his return."

Marcán's thoughts turned to his father. He had served on the council for many years, wearing his long, fur-lined robes, the gold circle brooch prominently displayed. The symbol of their council. He'd worn the mantle with pride, and his mother's delight in him had been undeniable.

"Ye are truly needed, Marcán." Ian's voice was stern, more stern than Marcán had ever heard the boy, and that fact pressed through his disturbed meanderings. "The final decision of who will lead our clan comes before them."

The choice of the Meic Murchadha's *ri* was the pressing matter? Marcán's eyes focused on Ian, the boy's eyes widening with meaning and his body taut as a bow. The older man was saying more, but Marcán had stopped listening as his brain churned over the implications of participating in this meeting of the *derb fine* at this particular time—just as the great Pádraig Meic Murchadha was about to come before them for their blessing.

The flat line of Marcán's lips loosened just a bit. Ian watched him, his eyes narrowing as if attempting to puzzle out his thoughts. Marcán let the smile lighten his face and acknowledged the answering relief on Ian's face with a pat on the lad's back.

"Ah, Murdoch," Marcán said, "'twould give me great pleasure indeed to assist on the council at this time."

Murdoch's frown lifted and he smiled. "I believe ye will bring great wisdom to our table. My thanks."

"And I shall serve as diligently as my father before me. None shall be taking advantage of *this* council."

The man nodded, his gray eyes piercing Marcán. He'd swear he caught a sigh of relief. Was this one of the men Ian had insisted was indebted to Pádraig, or had Murdoch heard the same rumors as the lad? Regardless, Marcán would make sure, one way or another, that Pádraig would not be taking over as *ri túaithe* of Clan Meic Murchadha, not if he had a breath left in his body.

Chapter Eighteen

Days flew by in a blur, followed by sleepless nights, leaving Marcán's insides raw and his temper short. Beibhinn had been surprisingly effective in finding ways to keep him from speaking with Astrid. And although each night he went to their place of refuge and waited for her, she never came to him again.

Clonmacnoise, the same spot where Diarmuid Uí Cerbaill, the first *Christian* High King of Éire had been crowned, was where the council would meet. The glen was marked on four sides by massive boulders where animal sacrifices had been performed during pagan times, a reminder of the many sacred ceremonies that had taken place there, including the anointing of many a *ri*. The council would attend in all their finery, with much celebration to follow.

"The council is waiting on ye." The black circles under Ian's eyes indicated he shared the same malady as Marcán but for different reasons. The lack of sleep made the boy look much older.

"Are ye not well?" Marcán asked.

Ian lowered his gaze. "I have been unable to keep any food down. 'Twas the same for my father before he passed."

Marcán gripped the lad's shoulder and met his frightened gaze. "Ye fear ye are being poisoned?"

The simple nod spoke of the lad's feelings of defeat. Marcán handed him his cup of mead. It certainly was not poisoned. "Drink this to keep up yer strength. I am ready for this. Do not fash yerself."

Ian nodded and finished the drink.

"Come. Let us see this done," Marcán said.

Despite Marcán's words of assurance, he could think of only one way to give the aid Ian had requested, and he wasn't certain it was something he could do. There had been secret meetings with the others in the *derb fine,* but no clear decision had yet been made. That was telling in itself, since there was no competition and anyone who met the requirements should have been granted approval. Not this time. Instead, it was being left up to Pádraig to state his case, showing his worthiness to be named *ri túaithe.*

There was a great deal of satisfaction to be had in the knowledge that these men were not falling over themselves to pay homage to Pádraig. The man was a vile creature, and not just in his treatment of women. Their clan had fallen far from acceptable practices, even if they did not directly break their laws. If any of the *derb fine* were now willing to overlook that behavior, it would send a sure signal that would drop all higher expectations. No longer would there be a standard of behavior.

They were meeting as agreed at the place of anointment. A king would be decided today either way. Many were gathered in anticipation of the ceremony and the feasting that would follow. The workers lay about on their blankets with the children jumping around and making mischief. And why not? It was a bright, sunny day. Very unusual for this time of year, which many saw as a good sign—not that they believed in such things.

"Murdoch!" Pádraig was clasping the older man's hand, his eyes squinting at the corners in a show of sheer happiness, when Marcán took his seat at the long table. The quickness with which Pádraig's affable countenance dropped was almost humorous. "Marcán?"

His recovery was not quick enough to hide his annoyance. Marcán could not have ordered a better response, for it revealed the man's true nature.

"Pádraig." Marcán's low, steady tone was met by the man's confused glare. There was never any advance notice given of who would be at a meeting, who would be providing their counsel. If Ian was correct about Pádraig's influence, his ally was not someone informed of the latest developments. Otherwise, he'd have heard of the new addition to their numbers, wouldn't he? Marcán glanced to the farthest man to his right. The red-headed father of the twins, Eric and Eoghan. The man had arrived only this day, traveling from some trouble farther to the south. He was the reason the anointing had been postponed.

Pádraig's bright blue eyes turned on Murdoch.

"What is amiss? Why is Marcán at table?"

His accusatory tone was met with a stoic expression by their leader. "Pádraig, if ye've a mind to approach us with yer desire to become king, ye'll need to show us proper respect."

"I am not required to receive yer approval, though it would be beneficial." Pádraig's eyes shifted to Marcán repeatedly as he spoke. "Even knowing that, I am mindful that the man has no great regard for me. I am concerned at how fair he can be in considering me so that I may receive yer acceptance as king."

Murdoch did not move. Neither his body nor his direct gaze, which now held the man as if by an unseen force. "This council is a body of men outside the petty fighting between clans, and well ye know it. Ye insult each of us by voicing concerns over the motives of any one of us."

Marcán kept his eyes locked on Pádraig, as he would any contemptible creature that intended to do harm. Murdoch's response had shut Pádraig's mouth, and now he was angry. More than angry, *livid*. The clenching fists. The flaring nostrils. The way his eyes flashed when they finally settled on Marcán.

All these things gave Marcán great satisfaction, and he met Pádraig's glare with a smile. A quiet smile. A smile meant to raise his hackles even more. A smile meant to unnerve the man, causing him to slip up in this pretense of solemnity and respect for a group he'd had the audacity to try to bribe. A smile meant to stir him into action that would reveal his true nature. Even if the *derb fine*'s approval was not required, a king would have a hard time garnering support from more warriors if the council expressed disapproval.

"And what of Diarmuid, Marcán? Have ye heard

from him?" Murdoch asked.

"He has returned and is seeing to his wife." Marcán addressed Murdoch but kept his eye on Pádraig.

"But ye'll stay on with us, will ye not?"

Marcán did not miss the spark of hope that flickered in Pádraig's eyes. A spark he was happy to extinguish. "Without a doubt. I would not want to be missing such an *important* decision as this."

Murdoch nodded. "True enough. True enough. The *túath* covered by this new king is strategic. We need someone of great influence and power to keep our coasts protected." He turned to Pádraig. "What say ye? Do ye have what it takes to defend this land? Yer father was *rí túaithe* for a considerable number of years."

So the questioning began. Pádraig shifted to a more amicable stance and accepted the seat that had been brought to him. He nodded, but before he could respond, Marcán interjected. "And I heard he kept ye under his thumb rather than have ye share in the oversight."

Mumbles rippled beside him as the others at the heavy, wooden table considered his words. The redhead remained apart, his eyes darting between the other men and Pádraig. Marcán was confident he had indeed located the compromised member.

The narrowing of Pádraig's eyes was the only indication that Marcán's comment had hit its mark.

"Ye are in error, Marcán. My father took me with him always; in battle, to the villages, even having me sit beside him when complaints were brought forth. I have vast experience in caring for our clan lands." He turned to include the others before continuing. "And have done him quite proud in how quickly I've learned."

The mumbles shifted to a more accommodating tone.

"And yet he is not among us to say so." Marcán paused, feeling the eyes of the others upon him. "Was it in battle then that I heard ye were found lacking?"

A quiet hush fell across the men as well as those gathered around, their eyes wide with wonder at the accusation. And by the look on Pádraig's face, he was seething. Marcán's chest filled with anticipation at the opportunity to finally knock this man on his arse. When Pádraig stood to drop the sack from his side and the mantle from his shoulders, Marcán did the same, his eager fists clenching at his sides.

But Murdoch quickly rose to stop them. With his hands patting the air in a conciliatory gesture, he said, "Gentlemen, please. Settle yerselves as we address this matter peaceably." His light eyes, shaded with a thick gray brow, shifted from Pádraig to settle on Marcán. "Once peace has been *proved* ineffective, we will certainly see the matter dealt with in this manner. Are ye agreed?"

Marcán inclined his head in acceptance, settling again on the bench. He could certainly wait for his chance to kick Pádraig's arse.

"I have never heard such a thing, Marcán." The redhead leaned forward to make eye contact with him. "Pádraig made his father quite proud in all he accomplished."

"My thanks," Pádraig said. "I see both yer sons quickly following in my tracks."

And thus the means by which Pádraig had acquired his support was revealed. No doubt Eric or Eoghan would be named *tánaiste*. Murdoch continued with the questions, others at the table joining in, and

243

Marcán bided his time.

Before too long, a break was called, and Marcán could not get away soon enough. Although he had noticed Astrid in the crowd, she'd avoided looking directly at him. But he could *not* avoid her. She was like the moon in a cloudless night, calling his eyes to her, beckoning him not to look away. From the graceful manner with which she'd settled on the blanket beside her mother—whose tongue never stopped flapping—to the way she kept gazing off into the distance, toward the unseen ocean, her shoulders straight and proud, he couldn't focus on anything but her. And he moved toward her at his first opportunity.

"Astrid?" Marcán's voice was quiet, his eyes on Beibhinn, who had just left.

Astrid's bright blue eyes widened at the sight of him and her lowering lashes did not hide a look of excitement.

"I have missed ye."

Astrid shook her head. "Ye should not say such things."

With the slightest brush of his fingers across her cheek, he savored the feel of her before dropping his hand and looking around to see that no one observed him. "'Tis how I feel… and ye as well."

"I do not."

If not for the tightness in her voice, Marcán might have actually believed her. Beibhinn had managed yet again to twist Astrid to her will. Should he tell them both of Diarmuid's blessing? Mayhap not. Astrid clearly believed that he, Marcán, would give up on her. He needed to show her that there were no lengths to which he would not go for her.

"Ye forget how well I know ye."

Others were busy around them as food and drink were brought to a side table set up for that purpose. He took the opportunity to move in closer, again glimpsing over his shoulder.

"Look at me, my love." His voice was quiet, but the finger that tipped her head up to his was insistent.

Her eyes were filled with tears. "Do not."

"I will." He thumbed the single tear slipping down her cheek. "Ye will not cry on account of me."

"I have no choice."

"Ye do." With his palm flat against her cheek, he lowered his lips to hers for the gentlest of kisses. The taste was sweeter than he remembered, the softness of her lips a boon to his shredded nerves. Despite his desire to ignore all around them, he heard the surprised sounds of the crowd, followed by quiet murmurings about this public display. He pulled back enough that he could look into her eyes. "Ye are not alone, my love. I am here with ye. I will stand beside ye against any that look to hurt ye even when 'tis yer own flesh and blood. I vow this to ye. Always."

Her eyes rounded. "I love ye and will love ye until I have breathed my last."

The unexpected declaration caused a sudden tightness in his chest, and an aching began deep down inside him. "I have waited so very long for ye. Do not push me away now that we have found each other."

"If I had a choice, I would not..." She swallowed, fighting for her composure. "I would not see ye hurt because of me. I would prefer ye live a long, happy life."

Marcán was so close, his breath brushed her face. How she longed to move into his embrace and accept his kisses. That was where she belonged and she knew it. Her knees weakened with the desire to take his strength upon herself.

"Clearly someone has threatened me and ye wish to protect me," Marcán said.

Her jaw dropped at his astuteness, but she quickly recovered. "Suffice to say I would die before I saw ye harmed."

"I would be the same as dead if I could not take ye to wife."

He did not realize that if she rejected her mother's desire that she marry Pádraig, Beibhinn would proclaim him a Seer and have him burned at the stake. Astrid could never allow that. She would rather subject herself to marrying a cruel, depraved man than see one hair on Marcán's head harmed. "But ye will have life."

"Astrid!" Beibhinn's shrill cry carried above the din, quieting those around them. "I leave ye for a moment and ye throw yerself into this man's arms?"

Others were following this interplay, including Pádraig. Marcán's face tightened and he turned, ready to face her mother.

"Do not!" Astrid whispered her plea, but he showed no sign of hearing her.

"Will ye take yerself away from her!" Beibhinn yanked Astrid's arm, pulling her closer and turning her so they were facing each other. "Why must ye throw yerself at every man?"

Marcán latched onto Beibhinn's arm. "Do not speak to her so."

His voice was much quieter and those around moved in closer, desperate to not miss a word of the drama playing out before them. Astrid cringed.

"How dare ye tell me what I may do with my own daughter."

"Ye will not speak to her so." Marcán lowered his face to Beibhinn's, looking into her eyes. "If ye persist in behaving thus, I will gladly see ye punished as one who demonstrates no restraint on their mouth."

"Do not threaten me. I am—"

"Ye are what? Who is it ye believe ye are to belittle yer daughter? To humiliate her so?"

"Enough, Marcán." Pádraig stepped to the front of the crowds gathered close around them. "Ye overstep yerself."

A knowing smile worked its way across Marcán's face as he stood to his full height then turned to the man. "Do ye speak to *me*?"

"I do."

"By what right?"

"As the lass's betrothed."

A gasp rose from the crowd, followed by instant chatter as if a signal had been given for each person to begin talking at once. Marcán raised his hand, and the group fell silent. He glanced at Astrid, but she couldn't meet his gaze.

"Now how is that possible? I believe she has been spoken for. When our *ri* sees fit to make the announcement of whom she will wed"—Marcán moved to stand toe to toe with Pádraig—"*ye* are not the one he will name."

"The words of the Seer are a lie." Beibhinn's voice rang out as clear as a bell and all those gathered around took a great step back, their eyes wide with fear. "And ye are an abomination!"

"*Mamaídh*!" Astrid hissed the words, shock gripping her gut. "Do not."

247

Pádraig smiled, a huge smile, and said, "As I am the one who deflowered her, I am willing to take her to wife."

The man never saw the punch coming. Astrid screamed and jumped back while Marcán's fists flew, catching Pádraig's face, his sides, and the flat of his stomach. The man appeared too dumbfounded to even move, finally responding by protecting himself with both arms. One or two misplaced punches were all the liar could manage. The crowd cheered, quickly choosing Marcán's side over Pádraig's, despite Beibhinn's declarations.

Pádraig's face was bloody and he doubled over in pain before the combined efforts of Murdoch, Faolán, and Ian successfully hauled Marcán back from his assault. Marcán was winded but clearly still ready for more, while Pádraig was dragged to a bench to recover.

Gripping his chin, Marcán shifted his jaw back and forth before impatiently wiping the blood from the side of his mouth. His chest heaving, he did not look directly at Astrid, but she sensed he knew she stood but a few feet behind him. Even now, he was ready to continue defending her virtue while she merely stood there, awed by his courage. The wrongness of that suddenly struck her.

Beibhinn straightened beside her, preparing to open her mouth, but Astrid yanked her mother's arm before she could put herself at the center and declare her damnation of the man Astrid loved. There was no way to know how the crowd would shift. Would they join her mother's demand for punishment? Or would they stop and think and realize Marcán was a good man and a brave warrior?

"Do not." Astrid used her firmest tone, her gaze locking onto her mother's eyes, which widened in surprise or outrage. Astrid couldn't be certain which, and cared even less.

Beibhinn's face tightened. "I will! Do not defy me in this, daughter."

"To what purpose?" she asked, clipping each word. The need to defend Marcán rather than cower to the side blossomed in Astrid's chest and refused to be denied.

"I will not have ye marrying that man. He is in league with the devil."

If her mother didn't have her own motives for wanting to prevent the union, Astrid might have been convinced of her mother's concern. As it was, she knew the truth, and there was no reason a good man should be left in the wake of her mother's all-consuming selfishness. "I tell ye he is not."

Beibhinn moved in close. "Ye are taken in by his fine manners and bravery, but I tell ye he is in league with the devil and needs to be taken down. His mother was the very same."

The words caught Astrid off guard and she paused. All she knew of Marcán's parents was what he'd shared over the years. They had been very deeply in love. She could remember no instance when her mother had *ever* spoken to either of them.

"His mother?" Astrid had a sudden acuteness of hearing and sight. Her mind became fixed on this woman before her, as if seeing her for the first time. The deep lines at her mouth from years of scowling and unhappiness, the dullness of her skin, and the perpetual look of upset. Outrage and disbelief filled every corner of Astrid's body and she let her tone say as much. "Ye did not like his *mother*?"

"A bad seed, that one."

A handsome warrior with hair dark as night.

Like Marcán!

I remember him still...

Yet he chose another.

Astrid took a deep breath, trying to quell her indignation enough to speak. "And what of his father?"

Beibhinn blushed and glanced away. "He was taken in by her wicked ways."

Astrid staggered back as if she'd received a blow to the head. "Ye did not like Marcán's mother, so ye do not want me to care for her son? A wonderful, loving man? Ye would prefer I marry a defiler of women?" Her voice was getting louder, but she didn't care who heard. "I cannot be with Marcán because ye were in love with his father?"

Her mother's look of warning only brought a smile to Astrid's face. A smile of relief. A smile of release from any guilt. A smile of sweet satisfaction.

"His father chose another over ye, so ye wish to punish the son?" Astrid asked. "Ye do not care for anyone but yerself!" Astrid stabbed her finger at Beibhinn. "*Ye* are a horrid woman! I denounce ye as my mother. No creature as baleful as ye deserves a daughter as loving as me."

Confusion covered her mother's face, but Astrid turned away, refusing to say more. She walked toward Marcán, whose expression was unreadable, and took his hand and stood beside him. He never took his eyes off her. There were people gathered around them, whispering, but she paid them no mind.

"Again, I say ye are not a woman to be crossed."

Marcán's quiet words brought the flash of a smile.

"And well ye know it," she said, her head still shaking in disbelief. "This is all about yer father, Marcán. Is her behavior not a terrible disgrace for any mother?"

"I am sorry, my love." He lifted their joined hands and kissed hers. "But glad I am that ye stood up to her."

"She wants to see ye burned as a Seer."

Marcán scoffed. "I am not afeared of what she can do. Rest easy, *a ghráidh*."

It took but a moment for Beibhinn to recover, her face tightening into an angry mask. "Seer!" She delivered the words in a loud, clear voice, but no one moved. "That man is a Seer! He should be burned alive!"

Those gathered around her shook their heads, unsure how to proceed.

"Call for the priest," Beibhinn demanded in a shrill voice.

Chapter Nineteen

The crowd that had gathered around took several steps back, away from Beibhinn, too afeared of her to stand up to her declaration naming Marcán a Seer. Astrid felt a tug of sympathy for the pathetic woman who instilled fear by her very presence because of her many wild accusations.

"The priest is here."

It was Fintan who stepped forward, closing the distance to the woman. A man with a long brown robe followed him. A bit older than Diarmuid, he was a handsome man with broad shoulders. But for the small shaved spot on the back of his head, he could easily be a warrior. Even his ready stance made him appear able and well-trained.

"I have brought ye the priest, Beibhinn, just as ye

asked. This is Father Thomas."

"Oh, Fintan, my dear friend." Beibhinn crossed to the man, hugging him tightly before facing the priest. Her expression serious. "We have dire concerns here, Father. Seers... and healers, all practicing the dark arts."

The man in the brown robe nodded his head, as if considering Beibhinn's words. Astrid felt the world tilt beneath her, and she squeezed Marcán's hand. They needed to escape before the priest could hurt him, but Marcán didn't seem inclined to move. The look of love and confidence he bestowed on her warmed her heart. He kissed her on the lips, a gentle kiss. "Be easy."

"Beibhinn," the priest spoke. "It has been many years since last I saw ye. Do ye not remember me?"

Immediately perplexed, Beibhinn's expression turned to one of confusion, and she shook her head. The priest's eyes held hers a moment before the man nodded to Fintan. Astrid couldn't be certain what that meant.

Wearing a stoic expression now, the priest strolled within the little circle as if contemplating the best way to continue. He looked from face to face, acknowledging a few by name. Then he came to Marcán and stopped.

"Is this the man ye accuse?"

"The same. That is Marcán, son of Colmán."

Astrid cringed at the way the priest searched Marcán's face. She hugged his arm against her breast. No one could entice her to release him.

"And yer concerns, Beibhinn?"

"This man," she pointed directly at Marcán, "is a Seer."

"And is yer evidence against the man well-founded?"

"Very well-founded. Do ye not see his eyes? Two different colors. The mark of the devil."

Thomas tilted his head. "Hmm, I do not believe I have ever heard such a thing as that. What of ye, Marcán?"

Beibhinn blanched. "Why are ye asking him? He will not admit it!"

The priest held up his hand to silence her. Raising his brows in question at Marcán, he awaited a response to his question.

"I have only heard of such things from her... several times, and from others who have also heard it from her."

"And why do ye suppose she believes a Seer needs to have two different-colored eyes?" Thomas asked.

"Accusations are usually made against those who are different, are they not?" Marcán heaved a great sigh before speaking. "*I* have two different-colored eyes."

"I agree." The priest turned to her again. "Is that yer only proof?"

Beibhinn dropped her gaze as if searching for an answer. "Well, he... he sometimes knows... when it will rain!" The triumphant expression returned. "Quite often I have heard him declare as much."

With lowered brows, Thomas responded, "The ability to tell from the clouds and the direction of the wind that it will rain does not make one a Seer, it makes one observant. Admittedly, he is more observant than most and always has been. How fare ye, Marcán?"

Gasping as the two men clasped hands, Beibhinn said nothing, but Astrid's heart soared. This priest knew Marcán!

"Thomas. How was yer trip?"

The priest tipped his head and shrugged his shoulders. "The same as it always is this time of year. Cold nights and dreary days."

Fintan moved closer to Beibhinn, whose head was violently shaking, and wrapped an arm around her shoulders. "Why would ye wish the man to be punished as a Seer?" His voice was soothing, and she accepted his comforting embrace but remained quiet. "Marcán is a good man, Beibhinn. Kane thought so as well."

Astrid held her breath. She had few memories of her father with Marcán, although they must have spent much time together. Marcán had been chosen as *tánaiste* for Diarmuid because her brother believed it would have pleased their father. Her father must have thought quite a lot of Marcán. Tears gathered in her eyes as this realization sank in.

"And ye know that is what ye fought about the most," Fintan said.

Astrid stiffened, ignoring the light squeeze of Marcán's hand. She was intent on Fintan, the man who had known her father so well, who could tell her how he'd truly felt.

"I remember well it was ye who did not like the thought of yer daughter marrying Colmán's son."

"Because of who his mother was!"

"Colmán and Kane had been the best of friends, Beibhinn. *Ye* forced Kane to turn from Colmán because of yer own viciousness, but he would not turn from the son."

Beibhinn's imploring expression nearly choked Astrid with tears. "Colmán was mine. Doran said 'twas so and then he allowed that witch to marry *my* betrothed."

Fintan took Beibhinn into his arms while she cried. When his eyes met Astrid's, he nodded and offered her a reassuring smile. She had not heard wrong and her heart soared. Her father had wanted her to be betrothed to Marcán.

Astrid wiped at the tears slipping down her cheeks, but Marcán tipped her face up, bestowing a gentle kiss on her lips.

"It seems yer father did choose for ye, Astrid. He chose me."

"As do I."

Thomas came alongside them, glanced down at Astrid and then smiled. "And is this the woman ye never spoke of by name, Marcán? The reason ye would not join us?"

Astrid frowned and looked up at Marcán. "*Ye* considered becoming a priest?"

Marcán gave her a beaming smile. "Never seriously."

The expression on Thomas's face indicated he definitely had a different opinion on the matter.

Thomas's eyes shifted to Astrid. "Do ye know he reads and writes Latin better than most priests?"

Astrid shook her head and they both turned toward Marcán, who replied, "I enjoy the learning."

"Ye *were* considering the priesthood." The priest's tone left no room for doubt.

"But for the fact he'd no penchant for abstinence." Diarmuid's voice cut through the assembly, causing every head to turn toward him. He was quite a sight, riding into the throng of onlookers, who gave him a wide path to enter.

Thomas replied, "Ah, but abstinence is not required everywhere. Not yet."

"'Tis only a matter of time." Diarmuid jumped from his horse, handing the reins to the lad who'd come to assist. "My apologies for the late arrival, Murdoch. I needed to… reacquaint myself with my bride."

"Welcome, Diarmuid." Murdoch said from his position at the table, where he'd remained with the others. "I have heard of yer Aednat. How fares she?"

"She is well."

"I look forward to meeting her."

"And so ye shall." Diarmuid nodded, then turned to the crowd, pulling off his riding gloves. "And what is amiss here? I see we have the good Father in our presence. Are we disproving my mother's tales of devil worship at last?"

Thomas inclined his head but offered no further explanation. Diarmuid's gaze went to his mother, who withdrew from Fintan's arms.

"Ye should heed me, son, not make light of my warnings."

"And is that what ye went to tell Doran when ye visited the Meic Murchadha, pretending 'twas to collect our sheep? While ye sent Astrid off to flirt with Pádraig?"

"I didn't speak to Dor—"

Diarmuid halted her with a raise of his hand. "Others saw ye coming from his room, mother. I have spoken to them myself."

Beibhinn's lips flashed a smile. "Oh, I had forgotten. Ye are correct. I went to speak to him about uniting our two clans through the joining of Pádraig and Astrid. He was very ple—"

"He had refused to see ye." Diarmuid's firm tone matched his expression.

Beibhinn quickly shook her head, but Diarmuid would have none of it.

"They said he became upset with ye for forcing yer way into his room." He pulled the sack from his belt, opened it, and withdrew a square, jeweled box. "And that ye had sent *this* to him in apology for upsetting him."

Beibhinn's face went white, her eyes wide. "I... I do not recall."

"Ah, Beibhinn, what have ye done?" Fintan's sad question went unanswered.

Diarmuid kept the item closed and flat on his open palm. "Doran has always been well protected and surrounded by his men. Even if *ye* forgot, *they* did not. They said ye begged him to forgive ye, to allow ye to return to the clan of yer youth."

Beibhinn closed her lips flat, her face becoming stoic, and said no more.

"Ye should speak in yer defense." Fintan's eyes remained on her. "Do ye wish to tell *me*?"

Her eyes darted from him to Diarmuid and then back again as if she were a trapped animal looking to escape. Or a crazed woman. She did not move.

"Doran told his men ye were never to be allowed back." Diarmuid glanced at Pádraig, who slowly approached, an expression of dread on his face. "He also told them ye were not to be trusted."

"I've seen that box." Pádraig's distress was apparent. "It sat beside my father's bed when we found him. I don't remember seeing it before that time."

"Beibhinn, do ye wish to explain about the box?"

258

Diarmuid asked.

It was as if she did not hear the question.

Diarmuid lifted the lid to reveal the dark leaves of the chamomile bush, dried and brittle. He pinched it a bit, rubbing it between his fingers, before dropping it back into the pile. Beibhinn looked on with wide eyes, her breathing labored, as he reached in again. When he pressed his finger deeper into the box, Beibhinn could hold back no longer.

"Cease!"

Diarmuid's hand stilled, the leaves no longer touching his fingers. "Is aught amiss, dear mother?"

"Do not touch the leaves… they are… poisoned."

A gasp went up from those around them, Pádraig's being the loudest. "What say ye? Ye gave my father poison?"

Beibhinn gulped, her eyes wide as she spoke. "Doran promised me if I were to win over Colmán, I would be married to an even more powerful king when the two clans were united. He promised he would step down and Colmán would rule alone. I had only to woo him into offering for my hand and all would be seen to.

"But that witch from the islands came and"— Beibhinn snapped her fingers—"Colmán fell in love with her. He couldn't set me, or his ambitious dreams, aside fast enough. I was in love with him, but Doran refused to enforce the agreement we had reached. I was given to Kane instead."

"*Ye* killed my father?" Ian's words were quiet against her loud, harsh explanation. He came to stand beside his brother and they exchanged glances.

"Did ye believe 'twas me, little brother?" Pádraig asked.

"It had occurred to me," Ian said haltingly. "Ye were both so angry."

Pádraig lowered his gaze. "I loved him, but not his fists… and not his fists on our sister."

"I am sorry, Pádraig," Ian said.

Searching Ian's face, Pádraig seemed to be looking for something. "I see yer mother in ye. She was obedient and thoughtful, which pleased our father greatly. *My* mother was willful and defiant, and he wished to break her. He saw *her* behavior in everything Daimhin and I ever attempted. We could not escape his wrath."

"God rest his soul," Thomas said, watching Fintan lead Beibhinn to settle on the bench a short distance away. "She is not right in the mind. For so long, she has let her thoughts be poisoned with anger and resentment."

"As ye know, Diarmuid," Murdoch's voice carried to them, the crowd moving aside so the older man and the *ri* could face each other again. "The punishment for murder is the honour price, and the *enach* required of a king is considerable."

"And if I haven't the fee to pay?"

"She'll be put to death."

Astrid's next breath stilled in her chest. She did not want her mother to die no matter what kind of horrible person she was.

Her throat tight with tears, she said, "Diarmuid! Do not let—"

"Certainly ye see she is not in her right mind," Thomas interrupted her. "Mercy, I beg ye."

"Leniency could be considered, but murdering in secret?" Murdoch paused, shifting his gaze between the three of them. "*That* is more reprehensible than murdering even in a rage."

Diarmuid thoughtfully stroked his chin. "I do not wish to see my own mother put to death."

The tension was thick, but Beibhinn appeared not to notice despite Fintan listening intently.

"If I am able, I will pay the fee." He sighed, his concern still apparent.

Astrid had no thought of how high the fee could be, but it seemed obvious it might actually be too steep.

Diarmuid turned to offer a hand to Ian. "I am saddened for yer loss, even more so that 'twas at the hands of my mother."

"My thanks. Though I am saddened to hear of yer mother's betrayal, 'tis better than the belief that one of our own is poisoning us." Ian's grief was plain to see, unlike his brother's. Pádraig, a haughty expression on his face, received no such sympathy.

"I have women who can care for her if ye wish to see her gone," Thomas said.

Diarmuid exhaled slowly, as if he'd come to the end of a great journey. "'Twould be best for all. She cannot stay here and continue to cause havoc."

"If she is allowed to live, I will see her well cared for," Thomas said. "And we will pray for the softening of her heart of stone."

Diarmuid looked to the man, a small smile on his lips. "And is this the Godly man ye spoke of so often, Marcán?"

"The very same." Marcán's face brightened considerably. "Thomas? This is Diarmuid."

"I believe my second is one of the greatest warriors I've had the honor of fighting beside," Diarmuid said. "To learn he also has a head for things of a spiritual nature—and Latin besides—is quite impressive. I would never think twice about allowing him to take my sister to wife. And I must say that now"—Diarmuid took Astrid's hand in his, kissing it lightly on the knuckles—"I would never think twice about my sister being the wife to my dearest friend."

Astrid glowed at the well-deserved compliment, kissing her brother's cheek. "Many thanks."

Like a net being cast onto the ocean, excited murmuring spread across the assembly.

"Wait!" Pádraig exclaimed.

"Pádraig. And what are ye about today?" Diarmuid glanced back toward Murdoch and the others at the table. "Ye hope to be given yer father's kingship? While ye behave as a man with no restraint?"

When Pádraig made a move toward Diarmuid, Marcán happily shoved him back, gritting his teeth to contain his rage.

"If there will be a battle here today, Pádraig, rest assured 'twill be between *ye* and *me*. I will happily dole out what ye so richly deserve."

Diarmuid hid his smirk, dipping his head, before addressing Pádraig. "Did yer father ever wish yer clan to be in union with ours? For if so, he never spoke of it to me."

"When he was young, he had such aspirations," Pádraig said, struggling with a rage so deep his face was red.

"'Tis the truth. I heard him speak of it when I was younger but not now," Ian said. "Before his death, he spoke more of the men he'd trained in his youth, of Colmán and Kane." The boy glanced between Diarmuid and Marcán. "He said the *fili* spoke the truth of their abilities. They were warriors without compare."

Pádraig glanced away and took a deep breath.

"Have ye nothing to add?" Marcán had no reason not to goad the man.

Ignoring him, Pádraig faced Diarmuid. "I believe my father would have been happy to have ye marry Daimhin. And as a second choice, for me to marry Astrid."

"And that will not come to pass in *yer* lifetime," Marcán declared.

"If the two *túath* are joined, 'twill be under Diarmuid." Astrid's voice surprised everyone. "For as Marcán has said, I am certainly not going to wed ye, and as Diarmuid is happily married, I do not see how that could ever come to pass."

Pádraig narrowed his eyes at her but looked away when he noticed Marcán's glare.

"Yer betrothed is well versed in our law, Marcán." Murdoch cleared his throat and addressed Pádraig. "We have questions about yer ability as king."

Pádraig's anger rose with each word. "I have all that is required to become *ri.* Ye have nothing against me that allows ye to withdraw me from consideration."

"How about the way ye behave? Far from a kingly presence." Astrid could not hold back the comment.

"Do ye have something to bring before the council?" Murdoch's question immediately sent Astrid into a panic. She could not share what had transpired and she hoped to never have to.

"I-I do!" Faolán's eyes leveled on her as he approached the table. "A-and I-I w-will bear w-witness on my testimony a-alone."

"Have ye news that would change our minds?"

Pádraig's face reddened.

"I-I do. This man i-is a-a defiler of w-women. I-I have seen so w-with my own e-eyes."

"He lies!" Pádraig's words ripped through the assembly. "He has a fondness for—"

"Do not say it." Marcán's voice was low and threatening, respectful of Astrid's obvious reluctance to recount her experience.

Pádraig was wise in clamming his mouth shut, but he shook his head, his gaze turning toward the trees in the distance.

"I also bear witness."

Pádraig's head circled quickly back to stare at the red-haired man at the table.

"He has approached me with promises for my sons. I am… I am ashamed to admit I considered his bribe. Forgiveness, please."

Ian placed a hand on his brother's back. "Mayhap we need time to meet together to decide what is right for our clan."

"*I* am what is right for my own clan!"

"Brother, they rise against ye even now."

A look over the crowds gathered around showed the disgruntled faces of Pádraig's own clan.

"They do not know what is best for them." His condescending tone was unmistakable.

"They do not believe 'tis ye," Marcán said.

"I will show them!" Pádraig grabbed at his sidearm, a long, solid sword, and withdrew it from its scabbard in one swift movement. "Step forth, Marcán.

Ye believe ye are the better man? Let me show ye the error in yer thinking."

With a slicing motion, Pádraig caught Marcán's sleeve before he was able to withdraw his own blade.

"Not fair!" Astrid yelled, aggressively stepping toward the man as blood soaked Marcán's sleeve.

Ignoring the minor sting, Marcán set Astrid behind him with a smile. Then he was in Pádraig's face, their swords crossing as they pressed wrist to wrist.

Astrid continued to shout from the sidelines. "Is that the way of it, then? Ye must catch a man off guard and a woman unprotected to get whatever ye want?"

Pádraig bared his teeth in a snarling grimace. "Yer whore is speaking to ye."

With a hard thrust, Marcán shoved the man back so forcefully he stumbled to keep his footing.

"What, Marcán? Ye can't bear the truth?"

Disbelief flooded Marcán—the fool was so intent on taunting him, he wasn't paying attention to his sword. He pressed forward, ducking beneath Pádraig's flailing sword, and shoved the hilt of his own weapon into his enemy's belly. Pádraig doubled over in pain. Marcán did not hesitate to thrust the sword end against the bend of the man's shoulders, sending him plummeting the rest of the way to the ground.

Cheers went up, but Marcán remained focused on his vile opponent, his chest heaving. Pádraig fell to his side, rolling out of harm's way. Marcán kept on him. Blood trickled from the downed man's face, but he wiped at it, shifting to his knees.

"Ye think ye can best me with a few thrusts?" Pádraig jumped to his feet, shaking his head, no doubt to clear it. "I am made of firmer stuff."

"What ye are made of remains to be seen, but I've a mind to take a look." With a hacking motion, Marcán brought his sword down, aiming for Pádraig's unprotected side, but the man twisted out of harm's way and the tip of the blade just caught his *léine*, ripping it.

"Making mending for my wife, are ye?"

Anger flooded Marcán's brain, pushing out any reasonable thoughts, the noises of those around them, and his immediate surroundings. His eyes focused on Pádraig, keeping him in his sights. The man's mouth moved again, but Marcán did not hear him this time. As he pushed him back, one of the large rocks came into view, and Marcán steered the man backward toward it. High enough to sit upon, it would send the man tumbling.

Pádraig's eyes were red-rimmed and his mouth continued to flap. Just shy of the target, Pádraig's sudden halt and thrust forward caught Marcán off guard. The man charged him with the impetus of a mad bull, then locked swords with him. The clash of steel rang through the trees. They'd turned about, so the boulder was at Marcán's back when Pádraig came swinging for his head, a wide arc of the blade. Marcán dropped down, the point of his own sword piercing Pádraig's leg, causing him to stumble against the obstacle. Too late for Pádraig to stop the momentum that slammed his head against the rock. His body dropped dead beside it, his hand releasing the sword upon contact.

Epilogue

No one objected when Diarmuid united the two clans under his kingship. Ian, in particular, appreciated the change of leadership as he matured. His new king was more than willing to train him, where his father had not been. By day they battled, attacking nearby clans, and by night they spoke of the Greeks and Christ, sparking the lad's imagination as well as building his confidence in his own abilities.

Astrid believed Diarmuid's friendship with the lad was helping Diarmuid heal from the great loss of their brother, Fergus. She certainly did not miss the fact that Ian and her younger brother would have been of a similar age had Fergus not died. No doubt they would have been very good friends.

Tucked tightly in bed between the wall and

Marcán's warm body, Astrid could not be happier. They lay belly to belly, and she was hoping for the baby to resume the violent motion that had awakened her, the little elbow or knee even visible as it rubbed along the inside of her womb.

"There! Did ye feel it?" Astrid asked.

"No." Marcán's disappointment tugged at her heart. She adjusted herself a little more, pressing her belly flat against him again.

They waited.

"There! That time?"

Marcán beamed. "A strong child." He cupped her cheek. "And a beautiful wife. I am a blessed man, indeed."

The snow continued falling outside as it had for two days now. The supplies in their little longhouse dwindling, this would be the last day they'd be able to stay within. The thought of leaving their intimate cocoon, where no one mattered but the three of them, made Astrid sad.

"Do ye believe 'tis a boy?" Marcán asked, his palm reaching beneath her *léine* to slide over the bare skin of her stretched abdomen.

Astrid's eyes closed at the pleasant sensation, the baby again moving about.

"I felt him," Marcán offered without being asked.

She smiled. "'Tis a girl."

"Ye sound quite certain."

Her eyes flew open, a look of fear there, but he stroked her cheek.

"Do not fret. No one questions yer source. Ye are a good guesser."

"Or God makes these things known to me."

"Does He?"

Astrid frowned. "I do not know where else I would get the knowledge from."

Marcán kissed the tip of her nose. "As I said, ye are a good guesser."

"I am a good guesser, and I am always correct."

He narrowed his eyes at her. "Always?"

She gasped and slapped his chest. "Aednat had twins! And I was still correct."

Shrugging, he pulled her close against him, urging her head against his shoulder. "Ye were not correct, or ye would have known 'twas *both* a boy and a girl, but Diarmuid and Aednat did not mind."

When she tried to escape his hold, he pressed his lower body closer to hers, leaving no question of what he desired, and she stopped resisting.

"I am so large, how can ye still desire me?"

Such an expression of disbelief spread across his face, Astrid had to stop herself from laughing. "Yer size matters not. 'Tis *my* child growing inside ye. How could I not desire ye even more now?"

Marcán covered her mouth with his own, his tongue seeking hers out, and she was again drawn into his pleasurable lovemaking. This was not what she had imagined marriage to be like, this closeness between them. His concern for her, in all things. Whether he was holding her hair back while she threw up each morning—and that had gone on for many weeks—or rubbing her swelling feet that ached, or holding her in his arms throughout the long nights, she now knew what it was to feel safe and loved. The love they shared was more than physical. It met a need deep inside her. A need to belong. A need to be accepted. A need to be cared for.

While she and Marcán spoke more of her father,

the times she had shared with him, she remembered many instances where Kane had tried to tear down Beibhinn's defenses. Teasing her sweetly, bringing her flowers, and providing her with more lovely trinkets than any woman in their clan had ever received. Mayhap his desire had been to bring her around to loving their family as he had. Astrid even believed deep down that he'd loved her. At least in the beginning. But the woman had refused to let go of her anger and resentment. Their marriage had never stood a chance at happiness.

Fintan and Thomas had accompanied Beibhinn to the priory and, no doubt, got an earful as the location was the very island Laoise had come from. Laoise. That was Marcán's mother's name, and it was the name Astrid had decided on for their daughter. Since he refused to consider the possibility that his first child might not be a boy, she'd wait until the birth to share her decision with him. It was a beautiful name. She was certain he'd be pleased.

Fintan had decided to remain at the priory as well. Always a good friend of Kane's, he had chosen to watch over his widow and, if possible, give her some peace as she became more and more confused. He wrote to them, telling them how Thomas was trying to help Beibhinn let go of her anger and her fixation on the past. The priest believed this would give her room to build new memories. Happy memories. That was Astrid's hope for her mother.

Astrid's hope for herself was that she could accept her mother as she was rather than continue to wish she could change. Beibhinn had to live with the choices she'd made for herself, but Astrid did not have to live in the shadow of those choices.

She snuggled against Marcán. "Glad I am to be yer wife."

"*A ghráidh.*" He kissed the top of her head, pulling her tighter against his length. "If not for ye, I would be living the celibate life of a priest."

"Ye said ye were never serious!" She tipped her head back to look at him. "Besides, Thomas said that not all priests remain unmarried."

"How could I settle for anyone else when all I wanted was ye? If I'd had to watch ye marry another, knowing ye were lost to me, I would have taken those vows, abstinence and all."

"And what a waste that would have been!" She stroked his plump bottom lip. "I've heard yer kisses could make an angel sigh. Is that true?"

Easily flipping her beneath him, he hovered over her now. His strong arm surrounding her, arching her against him. "I cannot speak for the angels, but I do hear quite a bit of moaning from my passionate wife."

Raising an eyebrow, she gave him her most dubious expression.

"Do ye doubt me?" His disbelief seemed genuine.

She shrugged. "I may require proof."

His lips covered hers, silencing her teasing, and she was lost again in his embrace, moaning in passion just as he had said.

THE END

GLOSSARY

Kingship in Ireland:

ri means "king" (plural is ***rig***) and the second word below refers to the number of people and the amount of land that each *ri* is king of:

>*ri túaithe* – The king of a *túath* (small territory)
>*ri túath* – The overking of several *túatha* (several small territories)
>*ri rúirech* – The king of a *rúirech* (lordship, a huge territory)
>*ri cóiced* – The king of a *cóiced* (province)
>*árd rí* – The high king

Definitions:

>*a ghráidh* – sweetling
>*enach* – honour price
>*grádh* – darling
>*lough* – lake
>*mamaídh* – mama
>*mo mhíle stór* – my love
>*mo chroí go deo thú* – my heart to you forever
>*ráth* – stone circle, ring fort
>*tánaiste* – selected as successor at the king's inauguration

Pronunciation of Names:

>Marcán – Mork-an

Astrid – As-trid
Diarmuid – Deer-mid
Aednat – Ain-it
Beibhinn – Beh-vin
Faolán – Fway-lon

To hear many of the names pronounced by the late, great Frank McCourt, please visit this website: http://www.babynamesofireland.com

ABOUT THE AUTHOR

Aside from two years spent in the wilds of the Colorado mountains, Ashley York is a proud life-long New Englander and a hardcore romantic. She has an MA in History which brings with it, through many years of research, a love for primary documents and the smell of musty old libraries. With her author's imagination, she likes to write about people who could have lived alongside those well-known giants from the past.

Connect with her online at:

Website: www.ashleyyorkauthor.com
Email: ashleyyork1066@gmail.com
Twitter: @ashleyyork1066

The Warrior Kings Series continues with *Daughter of the Overking*, Brighit and Darragh's story.

"York expertly combines her historical knowledge with romance and intrigue..."
—Publisher's Weekly

A mistaken identity.
A gruesome murder.
The uniting of two powerful clans.

Trained as a warrior...

Brighit of Clonascra is the only daughter of the fearsome overking, Sean, but despises the trappings and demands of womanhood. She's far more comfortable training for battle than preparing a meal. Long held alliances require she set aside selfish dreams and take Darragh as her husband. The union intended to promote peace between the clans is interrupted by the shocking murder of a neighboring king and she quickly discovers there are far worse things than being wed.

Trained to be king...

Darragh of Drogheda has no wish to follow in the path of his father, Tadhg, but he is an obedient son and supports his father's plans. His marriage to Brighit, however, will be no hardship at all since he finds her most intriguing especially when she fights him at every turn. A she-warrior indeed. Her persistent dismissal of him merely blows the fire aflame and sets him down the path to discovery of all her most tightly held secrets.

When she stands accused of the murder, can they finally come to an agreement that will give them each what they truly desire?

www.ingramcontent.com/pod-product-compliance
Lightning Source LLC
Chambersburg PA
CBHW031226120726
47905CB00002B/483